G000089330

CORRUPTION OF POWER

G W Eccles

PEACH PUBLISHING

About the Author

George Eccles, writing as G W Eccles, graduated from the London School of Economics with a law degree and subsequently became a partner in one of the major international financial advisory firms.

In 1994, George left London to move to Russia and Central Asia during the tumultuous period that followed the breakup of the Soviet Union. His work involved extensive travel throughout Russia, Kazakhstan, Uzbekistan and Turkmenistan – often to places with restricted access to foreigners. During his time there, he advised a number of real-life oligarchs how best to take advantage of the opportunities that became available as regulation crumbled and government became increasingly corrupt. Against this background, while his novels are fiction, many of the anecdotes and scenes are inspired by actual events.

His first thriller: The Oligarch, was awarded a Silver Medal both at the Global E-book Awards 2013 and at the Independent Publishers Book Awards 2013, as well as being selected as IPPY Book of the Day.

George is married and now lives with his wife in a hilltop village not far from Cannes in the South of France.

ISBN 978-1-78036-292-2

Published by
Peach Publishing

In memory of Letitia

*Glossary of Terms
and
Principal Characters*

Russia
Alex Leksin – Independent troubleshooter
Igor Karpev – President of the Russian Federation
Nikolai Koriakov – Deputy Minister at the Department of
Overseas Development

Chestny Kombinat – Major Russian consortium

The Usenko family:
Lev – Oligarch, founder of Chestny Kombinat, recently
deceased.
Vika – Lev's daughter, chair and CEO of Chestny Kombinat
Max – Vika's brother, director of Chestny Kombinat
Sergei – Lev's illegitimate son

Other Moscow characters:
Olga Chernikova – Lev's former mistress, mother of Sergei
Pasha – Max's boyfriend

Turkmenistan
Government officials:
Nassah Rashid – President of Turkmenistan
Minister of Energy – In charge of the lucrative oil and gas
sector
Ali Orazov – Well-connected public figure

Chestny Kombinat, Ashgabat:
Adam Smolinsky – General Director
Borzov – Head of Security

Other Turkmenistan characters:
Talgat – FSB country head
Batyr – Shepherd on the Garabil Plateau
Hassan – Desert Caravan elder

Uzbekistan
Nadia – Professional terrorist
Stas – Nadia's live-in colleague

National security services and terrorist organisation:
FSB – Federal security service (formerly KGB) based in Lubyanka
KNB – Committee for National Security in Turkmenistan
SBN – National Security Agency in Uzbekistan
IMU – Islamic Movement of Uzbekistan, centre of fundamentalism

The Caucasus and Central Asia

Prologue

Garabil Plateau, Turkmenistan -Twenty-four hours earlier

A helicopter crested the hill, flying high and fast. Spotting two figures hunched below, the young recruit drew them to the pilot's attention. The helicopter banked sharply and swooped across. Hooking a protective arm around Yana, his daughter, Batyr dragged her down and shielded her from the downward draught with his own body. The helicopter hovered above while the recruit inspected them. Apparently satisfied, he waved the pilot onward.

Batyr remained crouched until the helicopter reached the far side of the valley then, clambering to his feet, he brushed the grit off his daughter's faded tunic.

"We need to get a move on, Yana, your mother will be worried."

But she slipped his hands. Something had caught her attention, and his eyes shifted towards a herd of Saiga, long-nosed antelopes, grazing on the slope above them, the adults in a protective circle around the young. The startled animals pressed closer to one another, their bulging eyes combing for danger.

To their left, a caracel cat, laying low in the scant undergrowth, edged furtively forward. Its elongated, tufted black ears twitched as it bided its time for an unsuspecting youngster to stray from the herd. In a flash, the antelopes picked up its scent and raced off, huddled together as if glued by shared panic, leaving no straggler open to attack. As another helicopter clattered into view on the next loop in the meticulous circuit that had raked the Garabil Plateau all day, the cat veered off, abandoning its pursuit.

"What the hell's going on?" Batyr grumbled, grabbing his daughter's hand. The helicopters and patrols had been out since dawn, an unwelcome intrusion into this remote region's usual stillness. What were they looking for?

1

The path wound along the contours of the hill. Below them lay the fragmented rock-bed of a stream, dry now in the middle of summer. Its banks were covered with mandrakes, their tiny blue flowers framed by ragged teeth-like leaves. Beyond them, the Paropamisus Mountains loomed across the Afghan border, etched precisely in the late afternoon sun.

As they rounded the bend, they stumbled straight into a team of conscripts searching the hillside under the local commandant's stern, unforgiving glare. Batyr knew the man a little – sometimes they shared a bottle of bootleg vodka together – but he harboured no illusions about him. The commandant was an out-and-out bastard. As a young subaltern in the Afghan War, he'd learned his craft at the notorious interrogation centre at Tagtabazar where Afghan prisoners were questioned before they disappeared, and he never tired of boasting of the tortures he'd inflicted. Nonetheless, out here on the plateau, Batyr knew, it paid to keep on the right side of the military, so from time to time he bit his lip and raised a glass with the man.

One of the conscripts moved to block their path, but the commandant intervened.

"I know this man," he growled. "Move on, Batyr. Nothing for you here."

*

A bang at the door. Batyr threw a quick glance towards Tania, his wife, then shooed her and Yana to the back of the room. He waited until they were both out of sight before opening the door just a crack, his left foot rammed against the inner edge.

Outside a lean-framed man slumped against the stone wall, chest heaving as he struggled for breath, his bloodied shirt in shreds. He turned his head as the door opened and Batyr took in the angry scratches crisscrossing his haggard face.

"Let me in . . . Please . . . They're after me." He pleaded in Russian, his voice rasping like an athlete after a race.

Batyr drew back, in no doubt that this was the soldiers' quarry. As if to rub it in, search dogs lower down the valley picked up the scent and began to bark furiously. It was only a question of time before they closed in.

"Please, man, let me in . . . They'll kill me . . ."

Batyr glanced back at his wife. Her eyes stabbed his, hard and unrelenting. No, she mouthed, pointing at Yana, you can't. A moment of indecision, then he gave a resigned shrug.

"I'm sorry." He squeezed out the words, sounding as if he meant them. "My family . . ."

And heaving the door shut, he slammed the bolt across.

*

A shot echoed, followed by shouts of excitement, brutal in the heavy silence. Batyr's shaky hand poured another vodka, his fifth.

"We should have taken him in, woman."

His wife stared at the table, as if she hadn't heard.

"You know what'll happen," he continued.

Another shot, and this time a scream.

Batyr sprang up, his chair toppling behind him. "I'm going out," he grunted.

Outside he covered the ground nimbly, moving towards the sounds in the valley. Catching the glimmering of light from the soldiers' torches, he stalked them with a hunter's ease as they headed for the track that ran between the new factory and the village of Garkent. Two army jeeps were parked on the verge, and Batyr watched as they heaved the wounded man onto the back seat and set off towards their barracks. Pausing until they were out of sight, he crossed the track and took the shortcut over the hill.

By the time he caught up, the two jeeps had pulled up outside a low-lying building in the barracks thirty metres from the sleeping quarters. In the faint moonlight, he could just discern the outlines of the soldiers dragging the wounded man inside. They looked far too preoccupied with their prey to notice much else, and slipping under the wire, he darted towards the rear of the building. Cautiously, he peered at an angle through a window, slightly ajar.

Batyr watched as the soldiers tied the man to a chair, his head bowed, blood seeping dark on his shoulder. A moment later Batyr's muscles tensed as the commandant came into view and, grabbing the man's hair, jerked back his head.

"Who sent you?" the commandant asked, almost in a whisper.

No reply.

Placing his hand on the man's injured shoulder, he pressed down until the man convulsed in pain. Easing back, he repeated the question: "Who sent you?"

The man tried to twist away, his face taut but resolute.

"You will tell me," the commandant told him. His voice was soft but his eyes were hard. "Everyone breaks in the end."

The man stared back defiantly.

Almost in slow motion, the commandant removed his pistol from its holster and, with careless ease, put a bullet through the other shoulder. Stepping back, his eyes displayed the perverse pleasure he took in his handiwork.

Leaning against the wall, the commandant waited for the man to break. When he didn't, he muttered something that Batyr didn't catch, and one of the soldiers disappeared through the door and across the compound. The commandant waited in silence until he returned a minute or two later. Placing a petrol can just inside the room, the soldier handed over a white, plastic container. The commandant extracted a small canister, like a miniature fly spray, and held it out for his victim to see. His next words were softly spoken, like parents talking at night trying not to wake their children.

"Let me explain how this works. This can is filled with liquid nitrogen. Applied to your eyes, it will take twenty seconds to freeze the eyeball so that it blisters and cracks. Do you get the picture?" His lips curled into a sick smile.

The man shook his head violently and struggled to lean back. Two soldiers sprang forward to clamp down the chair.

"Fix his eyes," the commandant ordered, tossing over a roll of tape.

One of the soldiers prised open the man's eyelids while the other fastened them in place with the tape.

"Your last chance," the commandant warned.

PART ONE

Chapter One

Moscow, Russia

Alex Leksin stood at the far end of the vast room, his tall figure outlined by the soft evening light of the Moscow summer that streamed through the high windows behind him. No stranger to the Kremlin, he was unfazed by the splendour of his surroundings. They may have renamed it Pobeda (or Victory) Chamber, as his companion had just informed him, but in all other respects the room stood testimony to the corruption and double standards of the Soviet era. The long Hepplewhite table and chairs came from London, the spectacular crystal chandelier had been hand-crafted in Venice, and as Leksin surveyed the walls he attributed each of the paintings of ancient woodlands and shining steppe to leading Russian masters.

He looked around as the floodlights suddenly flicked on outside in Cathedral Square to find a line of well-groomed guests pouring through the checkpoints for the evening's high profile event.

Checking his watch, Leksin turned back and glanced questioningly at Nikolai Koriakov, Deputy Minister at the Department of Overseas Development. Nikolai shrugged back with the ease of a long friendship that stretched back to their student days in Cambridge. The son of an apparatchik, Nikolai had won a State scholarship to study abroad. Leksin, the product of English schools but the son of Russian émigrés, had immediately recognised another outsider. He'd empathised with Nikolai's predicament and admired his tactics in dealing with it, affecting a love of things English and swiftly adopting a tweedy dialect culled from public school acquaintances. It was part of a jovial routine, a trick developed to disarm others and not to be swallowed whole, as Leksin had soon realised. From the start the two men had taken to each other. Even now, though they'd both been Moscow-based for several years, they still spoke in English when they were alone.

The heavy double doors swung open, and the two men turned as Saidov entered. Bald head tilted forward by a distinct stoop, his dinner jacket accentuated the downward slope of his shoulders, and the lines on his face betrayed the stress of years at the top of Russian political life. He wore an easy, no-nonsense smile, but his almond eyes were a survivor's, steely and unwavering.

"Prime Minister, allow me to introduce – "

"Mr Leksin," Saidov interrupted, finishing Nikolai's sentence. He shook Leksin's hand a fraction too firmly. "I'm so pleased to meet you. Your reputation precedes you. I count myself very lucky you might be available to help us with our little problem." He took a seat at the head of the table, and one eyebrow stretched upwards as he added: "Forgive the get-up. President Karpev's hosting a birthday party for his swimmer this evening."

Leksin suppressed a smile. The President had recently ditched his wife of twenty-five years in favour of a member of Russia's synchronised swimming team half his age. It had been grist to the Moscow gossip-mill ever since.

"Nikolai's told you about the pipeline deal?" Saidov continued, getting down to business.

"Yes, I've got the fundamentals."

"Then I'm sure you understand the implications."

Leksin hesitated, sifting the issues, while he framed his response. The proposed oil pipeline would extend via Turkmenistan and Afghanistan down to the Indian subcontinent, for the first time giving Russia access to the markets of the Far East. It was a crucial link, he acknowledged. In today's world military might was no longer where power really lay. Energy was today's battleship – and Russia's vast oil and gas resources positioned her perfectly. Physical control over distribution – in particular, the pipeline supply network – was the key. Through the exercise of that control, Russia intended to bludgeon her way to domination. Georgia had been an early trial run for this strategy: a tourniquet around the country's energy sources had quickly cowed her government back to the negotiating table. More recently, when Russia advanced on Crimea, all attempts to form an effective, European response had been stymied by the continent's dependence on Russian gas. Even after Russian-backed separatists shot down a Malaysian airliner, its leaders had found it hard to agree on sanctions for fear of damaging their own self-interest. And still the trap tightened: Gazprom and other Russian giants continued to buy up Europe's own energy companies.

"Russia's been utilising her massive weight in the energy market for some while to rebuild her influence in Europe," Leksin replied at last. "Control over this new pipeline would enable her to extend this concept to the east."

"That's one consideration, yes," Saidov agreed. "But there's a much more important aspect, Mr Leksin. The attitude of Europe's leaders is changing. Their nightmare scenario is that, as a result of any action we might take, the lights go out all over the continent. Consequently, largely prompted by the row over Ukraine, they've started exploring ways of reducing reliance on Russian energy. It's a long process, they're not going to find alternatives overnight. But, of course, in the end they will, and as things currently stand, the effect would be to drastically shrink the market for our oil and gas. The resulting drop in revenue would plunge the country into a recession that would blow the economy apart. Karpev could never survive the fallout."

"So the new pipeline does much more than give Russia the chance to extend her influence eastwards," Leksin interrupted, seizing the point. "It reduces her own exposure to the whims of Western leaders."

"Exactly. As you'll have read, we've already started to take protective measures. We recently entered into a massive deal to supply gas to China. Within Europe itself, we're actively spreading disinformation about the dangers of fracking. We've also been exploring possibility of installing new pipelines that by-pass the former Soviet republics, but the costs look prohibitive and we'll still end up being exposed to Europe. No, neither of these solutions work long-term. To my mind, the real key is to open up new eastern markets for our oil, just as we're doing with our gas and, quite frankly, this proposed pipeline deal is a heaven-sent opportunity to do so. We can't afford to miss out." Saidov paused. "Did you explain, Nikolai, that the detailed planning's been handled by Chestny Kombinat?"

Nikolai flushed a little as he shook his head.

"They're putting up a sizeable chunk of the financing," Saidov continued, reverting to Leksin. "They're also responsible for bringing in other investors. You'll need to start there."

Leksin shifted uneasily in his chair, surprised that Nikolai hadn't mentioned this earlier. The conglomerate, Chestny Kombinat, had been the corporate vehicle of the late Lev Usenko, one of the most powerful oligarchs to emerge out of Yeltsin's ill-fated privatisation programme. And Leksin had once been engaged to Vika, his daughter, who was now at the helm of the business. Their breakup hadn't been easy, as Nikolai was aware.

"I've been helping the company with the project from the outset." Saidov's tone was imbued with heavy significance. "We're nearly there. Max Usenko's lined up for me to meet the oil company bosses shortly, then President Karpev's due to fly down to Turkmenistan in twelve days time to sign the contract with his opposite number."

"It sounds like a done deal," Leksin commented, his frown deepening at the mention of Vika's brother. "So where do I come in precisely?" Aware that time was short, he was keen to get to the heart of the matter. Time enough later to work out how to handle Vika and her brother.

Saidov glanced across at Nikolai, who returned the cue by pushing across the table the thin file that Saidov had earlier requested. Saidov skimmed through it. Cambridge . . . MBA at Harvard . . . Forensic financial unit . . . Freelance corporate troubleshooter . . . 1 million euro non-negotiable success fee . . . He gave Leksin a hard look. "Karpev tells me you did a good job for us with that mining business in the northern Siberia." He paused. "I want you to check the pipeline deal's above board, nothing there that's going to rebound on us later."

"But if you've been involved yourself since the start – "

"All of us have masters to satisfy," Saidov observed, forestalling the question without actually answering it. "Karpev should stick to he-man stunts or bullying punk rock groups." He shook his head disapprovingly before adding: "I want you to give the project a clean bill of health. The all-clear from a man of your reputation would help silence the doubters."

"Of whom President Karpev's one?" Leksin probed.

Saidov gave a meaningful shrug.

"There isn't much time," Leksin pointed out. Even if, as Saidov seemed to be hinting, he was just looking for a whitewash, it was tight.

Placing a hand on Leksin's arm, he looked him straight in the eyes. "That's why I've chosen you, Mr Leksin. I understand tight timetables are your speciality." He rose to his feet. "Now I must go or I'll miss roll-call for this evening's charade. It's a front really, though I suppose we all have to make an effort." He raised his eyebrows again. "Nikolai, you report direct to me on this one. Just me, understand?"

Nikolai's awkward grunt was not lost on Leksin. The two men stood up.

"I'll clear the lines in Turkmenistan," Saidov said as he strode towards the door. Pausing, struck by an afterthought, he turned around. "Mr Leksin, please be careful. Turkmenistan's a dangerous place for an outsider. Russians, in particular, are not currently flavour of the month there."

Leksin waited for the sound of Saidov's footsteps in the corridor to fade before looking across at Nikolai.

"Interesting, though I'm not at all sure what he's after," Leksin commented, slipping back into English now the two of them were alone. "Seems like a decent chap, though."

Nikolai looked surprised. "You haven't met him before? Oh

yes, he's very affable and charming. I could see you falling for his flattery," he joked. "But don't let that fool you. Underneath lies a real tough nut. There's a rumour from his days at Defence. Some accident at an underground chemical weapons plant in Krasnodar. As soon as Saidov learnt there'd been a leak, he ordered the whole plant permanently sealed. Over two thousand people interred and left to die. A few made it to the surface, but they were immediately shot and their bodies burnt. Saidov, apparently, didn't even break a sweat."

Leksin pursed his lips, a sign of admiration or disapproval, and asked: "So what's his power base?"

"Good question, old boy," Nikolai commented. "In practical terms, his main contribution is his close contacts in Central Asia. His mother was Kazakh, and he did much of his education in Almaty. Karpev, as you know, has always been paranoid about what he regards as Russia's soft southern underbelly – all the more so with the spread of ISIS – and he relies on Saidov to keep an eye on things down there." Nikolai paused, gave a little chuckle as he led the way into the corridor. "And of course he kept the seat warm for Karpev when he stood down temporarily. Karpev definitely owes him one for that."

Chapter Two

Moscow, Russia

"This way," Nikolai told Leksin as they came out of the lift on the ground floor. "I told my driver to meet us at the rear entrance."

Leksin followed Nikolai along a wide, discreetly-lit corridor that led away from Cathedral Square towards a central lobby. As they crossed the lobby, their footsteps on the marble floor echoed in the silence under the high ceiling. Continuing towards the exit, Nikolai suddenly slowed down and, without knocking, opened the door to one of the offices and ushered Leksin in.

"What's going – ?" Leksin stopped in mid-sentence as he recognised the tall, blond-haired figure in a dinner jacket who stood the far side of the large mahogany table that swamped the small room.

President Karpev pointed to a chair. "Sit down, Leksin. I've only got a few minutes."

Leksin sat down, concealing his surprise at a turn of events he hadn't anticipated. As his eyes lifted to the President's face, he caught the knowing look and barely perceptible nod that Karpev exchanged with Nikolai.

"So what's Saidov said?" Karpev demanded, pulling up a chair.

"About the pipeline?" Leksin questioned, testing the ground.

"No, about your role," Karpev corrected him. "I assume he told you to do fuck all, just go through the motions and give the project your blessing. Perhaps not in so many words, but . . ." – starting to mimic Saidov's voice – " . . . something to silence the doubters. Is that right?"

Leksin nodded, non-committally. The phrase was spot on, almost as if Karpev had been listening in.

"Well, let me make one thing quite clear," Karpev began, raising

14

his forefinger in warning. "That's exactly what I don't want, do you understand?"

Leksin threw a glance towards Nikolai, searching for guidance. Whatever was going on here, there was an undertone he didn't as yet fully comprehend. What exactly was the message Karpev wanted to convey? Did he have reservations about the pipeline? Was he looking for an excuse to abort the deal? It seemed to Leksin that he might have walked headlong into a turf war between the Russian President and his Prime Minister and, if so, this was neither a comfortable, nor a safe, place to be.

"Don't get me wrong," Karpev continued, aware of his predicament. "I'm every bit as keen as Saidov on expanding the market for our oil eastwards, and for all the same reasons. We have to reduce our reliance on the West, so that we can take the next step."

"Next step?" Leksin asked, seeking further clarification. Was this where the conversation was leading?

Karpev nodded and crisply outlined his agenda, his face hard with determination. "Ukraine was just the tip of the iceberg, Leksin. With that behind us, my focus is turning towards other former Soviet States, particularly those around the Baltic. If we're truly going to reassert ourselves as a world power – and dominate – then we have to re-establish our hold on these territories. But before I make my move, we have to find new markets for our energy, so that when the storm comes – and believe me, the storm will come – the West's in no position to hold us up to ransom."

"Which makes this pipeline deal a perfect fit," Leksin prompted.

"Exactly."

"But?" Leksin asked, figuring this was where he came in.

"*But* something smells." Karpev leant forwards, and his harsh voice lowered to a conspiratorial tone. "The three key movers in the pipeline deal are Max Usenko from Chestny Kombinat, the Turkmen and the Afghans. Personally I wouldn't deal with any of them if they were the last people on earth. They're all utter shits. The three of them combined ... well, God knows what we're

15

letting ourselves in for. The whole idea gives me nightmares."

"But Saidov himself has been involved from the outset," Leksin pointed out. "Surely you can take comfort from that?"

"Hell no!" Karpev retorted firmly. "If anything, that just adds to the problem. The man's staked his reputation on this pipeline deal, he's completely incapable of looking at it objectively." Standing up, Karpev started to pace the room. "Look, Leksin, let me be perfectly honest with you. I don't have to tell you, Russia's currently a pariah throughout the world. Crimea, Ukraine, the Malaysian jet, our support of Assad, you name it, we're damned for it. Under normal circumstances, of course, I couldn't give a shit for world opinion. You couldn't ask for a more gutless bunch of losers than the present rabble of Western leaders. They're all empty threats and chit-chat – " Karpev clicked his fingers repeatedly against his thumb " – and they can't agree a bloody thing. Look at the way they've dithered about Syria. No, it's not their sanctions that are hitting our economy, in themselves they're just a minor irritant. It's the sudden crash in oil prices that's screwing us."

"But these are not normal times?" Leksin prompted.

"Too damned right, they're not – or, more accurately, they soon won't be. We may not currently be in the middle of a new Cold War, despite Gorbachev's unhelpful claims to the contrary. But think about it. Once I make my move in the Baltic, we bloody well will be – there's going to be hell to pay. In the run-up to that, I can't afford to pick another fight, at any rate not until we're properly prepared. Do you get where I'm going, Leksin?"

Leksin nodded. "You need some space to minimise the inevitable fallout once you start to implement your planned expansion," he said, careful to keep any note of recrimination from his tone. Karpev's expansion was a dangerous, egotistical strategy, but Leksin's job depended on him remaining neutral in such situations. "In particular, the whole of Central Asia's a powder keg, and the last thing you need at present is a crisis down there that sets it off. The pipeline deal has to be completely above board."

"Too damned right it does. There can be nothing whatsoever

there that's going to come back and bite us in the arse." Karpev paused in front of Leksin and fixed him in his glare. "I'm relying on you to tell me whether it's safe to proceed. You're the backstop."

Leksin ran his fingers through his thick, brown hair, brushing it back in a series of short, sharp movements, allowing himself time to work through the implications of what Karpev had just told him. Then, standing up, he faced the President.

"I have to ask the obvious," he said. "The deal's been in the making for the best part of two years. Why wait until now to check it out?"

"Circumstances change," Karpev replied cryptically, without elaboration. A guarded glance at Nikolai, then he added: "Presumably Saidov told you the FSB agent we sent down to Turkmenistan to investigate went AWOL twenty-four hours ago?"

Leksin blinked at this new information. No, no one had thought to mention this. So he wasn't the first. Another surprise – as always, the best news left to last . . . A dangerous place for an outsider – was this what Saidov had meant?

Chapter Three

Tashkent, Uzbekistan

The hamlet lay between the towns of Chirchick and Gazalkent to the east of Tashkent. Once a powerhouse of Soviet manufacturing, based around a giant tractor factory, the region now languished in sluggish destitution, a victim of the industrial decay that had set in after Uzbekistan's independence. Much of the former workforce had been drafted in from Russia and the Ukraine and, uprooted to an alien state, they had built themselves wooden houses in the traditional style to remind them of home. All those who could had now left, returning to their roots in the motherland, leaving behind the rump too old or too poor to escape.

An elderly woman jammed shut the door of her tumbledown wooden dacha and shuffled with the laboured steps of a chained convict along the lane. A battered shopping trolley jangled behind her as she dragged it along the unsurfaced, potholed track. The early morning light etched the details of her shabby cotton dress and patterned scarf knotted tight at her chin.

At the fork, she trudged left towards the station. A milk-cart drawn by a scrawny donkey blocked the centre of the road, doing the rounds before the unrelenting sun took hold. Waiting his turn to fill his jug, an elderly man, hands clasped behind his hunched back, watched a group of thin children playing hopscotch. Here the old games were the only ones: no one had the money to buy sophisticated toys like city kids. The babushkas kept watch, huddling closer as the old woman approached.

One of them sucked her teeth and frowned as she passed. "Where's your grandson? He should be pulling that trolley, not you."

The old woman shrugged her sagging shoulders. "In bed. No

work for him round here, might as well stay there." She lifted the flap of her bag a fraction to show the meagre stock of vegetables inside. "I'm off to the city to sell these."

She continued slowly down the lane to the junction with the asphalted main road to Chimgan, Tashkent's chief resort in the foothills of the western Tien Shan mountains. The ramshackle station lay on the far side, and the train was due soon. As she stepped out, a gleaming black Lancia Voyager hurtled towards her on its way to some flash weekend retreat in the mountains. The brakes screeched as it swerved around her, horn blaring as she stuck to her path. The world order had changed, she grumbled into the air, but she wouldn't let that get in her way.

*

Eleven o'clock and the temperature already topped 40ºC. The horizon shimmered, even the dust had trouble moving. The old woman turned into Broadway, a tree-lined avenue in the centre of Tashkent, free of traffic and straddled at either end by a giant statue of Tamerlane and state security headquarters. She shuffled slowly through the lines of street traders, inspecting the paintings displayed on makeshift easels, sniffing hungrily as she passed the giant vats of yellow-rice plov. When at last she found an empty space, she extracted the scrawny home-grown vegetables from her bag and laid them out on the ground. No one stopped to buy, and after half-an-hour she repacked and trundled off.

The sun pounded off the cracked surface of the road as she plodded past the vast white mass of the SNB building, headquarters of one of the world's most infamous security forces. A scar showed its pale line on her cheek as she stopped to wipe the sweat off her face with the ends of her scarf. She rested for a moment before turning into a broad boulevard, shady with chestnut and chenar trees. She continued past a parade of sizeable, intricately carved, stone houses surrounded by elaborate gardens, set back from the road. Shielded behind tall railings, the top prongs wound with barbed wire, in Soviet times living here had been the perk of party officials. Now Tashkent's most influential oligarchs had taken over possession.

A little further, she left the patchy shelter of the trees and entered a newly-developed estate where the grey, faceless houses with their bare gardens were already fissured by the corrosive heat. Hauling her trolley over the sun-cracked pavement, she approached a group of women gossiping over tea outside a street cafe. Their voices hushed as she passed, and their eyes followed as she moved on.

She turned into a quiet, deserted lane where wild cannabis and spearmint sprouted along the verge. The trolley stuttered on the rutted surface, and she was forced to pick it up. She panted as she progressed and, halfway along, she paused, supporting herself against a fence. Through its cracks, she inspected a wrecked car rusting in the garden amid brightly coloured toys scattered amongst the neat vegetable beds. Pushing at the gate, she lugged her trolley slowly up the steps to a little terrace. Inside children fell silent when she knocked.

The door opened a fraction, and the harassed face of a young woman appeared. "What do you want?"

"A drink of water, please. It's so hot." The old woman flapped a dirty hand in front of her face.

"Clear off!"

As the young woman tried to push the door shut, it slammed back on her, knocking her to the floor. As she struggled to get up, the old woman brushed past, suddenly swift and upright, grabbed her daughter by the hair and flashed a knife to her throat. The other child screamed.

The scarf slipped back, revealing her short-cropped, jet-black hair. "Get the boy!" Nadia ordered. "Shut him up or this one dies."

Chapter Four

Tashkent, Uzbekistan

Nadia forced the woman and her two children over to the kitchen table, then extracting a roll of heavy-duty tape from the bottom of her shopping trolley, she started to bind the mother's hands and legs to a chair. The two children sat on the opposite side of the table, sobbing.

"If either of you make a move, I'll kill your mother," Nadia warned them, moving the knife to their mother's neck, wanting to make sure they understood.

The children stared back through terrified eyes, blinking back their tears.

"Get it?" Nadia growled at them, banging her fist theatrically onto the table.

They nodded their heads nervously.

Nadia checked their mother was tightly secured, then moved across to repeat the process on the little girl. Focusing on applying the last strip of tape, she missed the second when the girl's brother slid off his chair and made a run for the front door.

"Come back, Husan!" his petrified mother shrieked after him as she saw Nadia reach for her knife.

Too late. Husan's hand was already on the door catch when the knife spun through the air, thudding against the back of his head. The boy slumped to the floor.

His mother screamed, her face contorted in grief. Rushing over to her, Nadia slapped her hard across both cheeks, first with her palm, then with the back of her hand. "Shut up!" she ordered savagely. Her voice softened as she added: "The boy's alive, it was only the butt of the knife that hit him."

But the woman's hysterics were beyond her own control, and

Nadia tore off a strip of tape and placed it over her mouth. She finished securing the girl, then went over to where Husan lay still and picked the boy off the floor. Carrying him next door, she trussed him up before leaving him on his own to regain consciousness.

Back in the kitchen, Nadia taped a hexogen cartridge to the leg of the kitchen table, then connected it to an electronic detonator fixed underneath. She tugged gently at the wire to check it was secure. Then, taking up her position behind the front door, she settled herself to wait it out.

Footsteps outside. Her muscles tightened, a predator's reaction. Her eyes fixed on the back of the man in his mid-thirties who let himself in. His white shirt tucked loosely into synthetic grey trousers, he carried a parcel.

"Hey kids, come and see – " he began, but broke off at the sight of his wife and daughter bound and gagged around the kitchen table.

Nadia pounced swiftly from behind. Placing her left hand on his shoulder, she thrust the tip of her knife where his jaw met his ear. Together they shuffled towards the empty chair at the head of the table.

"Sit down, Alisher!" Nadia ordered.

"Who are you?" Alisher demanded through clenched teeth, his anger yet to be overcome by fear. "What do you want?"

Nadia remained silent, allowing him time to take in his new situation. Alisher stroked his forehead with nervous fingers, looking to his daughter, then to his wife, catching the terror in their eyes, feeling the weight of their lives in his hands. He noticed the explosives taped to the table leg and gasped for breath, opening and closing his mouth ineffectively as he tried to figure a response.

"What's this for?" he asked, rising from his chair and steadying himself against the table. "There must be some mistake. I . . . we .. . haven't got anything."

Backing slightly away, Nadia held out the detonator and indicated the chair with her eyes. Alisher sat down again, his eyes circling without focus around the cluttered room, searching for something that was not there.

"Where's Husan?" he asked, a new terror in his eyes. "What have you done to my son?"

"He tried to escape," Nadia replied, piling on the tension. She let a few taut seconds tick by before she added: "He's next door, he's going to be all right."

Alisher's face flexed with relief, and he stared at Nadia in dumb silence. For some moments, their eyes locked, then all at once his shoulders crumpled and the tears came. This was the moment of submission for which Nadia had been waiting.

"Your family will be fine if you do what I tell you, understand?"

Alisher raised his head, still snivelling, and his eyes blinked at her. "What choice do I have?" he asked, knowing the answer.

Nadia retrieved her trolley and wheeled it towards the bedroom. "Come through here. I'll explain."

*

Alisher jumped off the tram just before Gulyamov Street and strode towards the British Embassy where he worked. He now wore a traditional quilted robe of faded blue cotton over his loose trousers. Underneath, a layer of plastic-covered hexogen strips was strapped to his body. A hole slashed through the pocket gave access to the detonator. The image of his wife and children burned in his mind. He knew what he must do.

The embassy was set back off the road within a compound whose walls were crammed with sophisticated monitoring devices. A solid, beige and brown building, it represented a mixture of styles: the faded grandeur of imperialism crossed with traditional Uzbek architecture. A small, detached hut stood at the compound's entrance, housing the security staff who checked the papers of those who wished to enter, or opened the security barrier for those about to leave. Alisher flashed his pass to the guard at the entrance, who waved him past. Then, keying in a code, he let himself into the security hut.

23

"You're late," his colleague snapped as he entered, then looking him up and down, continued: "What's with all the gear?"

"It's my wife's birthday," Alisher replied. "I'm going straight to the party after this shift."

"Well in the meantime, keep your guard up. The ambassador's due out at any moment. Be ready to open the gate."

Alisher sat down in front of the bank of screens and waited for his colleague to leave. His eyes drilled Screen I which covered the entrance where the ambassador's car waited. Not long now. His pulse pounded in his ears as he steeled himself.

He felt a knot in his stomach as the main embassy door opened and the ambassador climbed into the Range Rover. Pressing the switch to release the lock on the security barrier, Alisher walked unsteadily out of the hut as the car eased forward. Sweat trickling down his face, he waited for the car to reach him. As it closed in, his eyes zeroed in on his target. Launching himself forward, he grabbed the cord in his pocket and tugged.

Chapter Five

Tashkent, Uzbekistan

Nadia left the water running in the shower, then wrapping a towel around her body, studied herself in the mirror. Her features were handsome in a rather boyish way, black hair worn short, eyes green and intense under prominent black eyebrows. Years of training camps in hostile climates had coarsened her skin, and a faded scar zigzagged down her left cheek, a relic of an old assignment. But a rigid regime had kept her in shape, her body firm and supple, slim without being wiry. Taking his turn under the shower, Stas looked out with approval. She liked that. Now in her late thirties, it was good to keep a sexual hold over the younger men she needed.

Gathering the pile of discarded clothing she'd worn to Tashkent, she rolled them into a ball and carried them out to the enclosed rear garden. Dousing them with paraffin, she set them alight, the flicker of the flames almost invisible in the early evening sun. Back inside, she uncapped a beer, turned on the television, then collapsed face-down on the sofa. It was demanding work acting old, it took continual discipline to execute every action so slowly, especially in the city's sultry heat. The journey back, too, had been hellish, the station clogged with security police who'd scanned papers at improvised checkpoints.

She glanced up as Stas emerged from the bathroom, his muscular body gleaming from the shower. "Anything yet?" he nodded towards the screen.

She shook her head. "Not yet." Her eyes glinted. "By the way, you know that woman with the twin kids around the corner? Well, she thinks my grandson should take better care of me."

He gave her a slow grin and slapped her bottom. "Better than she knows," he commented, perching beside her. Leaning to kiss the nape of her neck, he ran his fingers along her spine. "To be honest, I'm not surprised they fall for it. Even I hardly know you when you leave the dacha."

Nadia smiled. They'd come to the village nearly two years ago, just after a mission in the northern Siberia had fallen apart. On that occasion she'd been outmanoeuvred, and those of her terrorist cell who'd survived had gone to ground. She'd kept, and in secret equipped, this dacha as a bolthole for just such a day, and now she lived here with Stas, one of the survivors. Close to Tashkent, right in the heart of the Central Asian republics, it provided a discreet yet ideally situated base for her to continue her activities.

Stas slipped his hands around to cup her breasts just as the news began.

"Not now, Stas. I want to watch this." She sat up.

A reporter stood outside the entrance to the British Embassy in Tashkent and waved one arm towards the shell of a burnt-out car. A suicide bomber had thrown himself onto the ambassador's car, he reported, killing the ambassador and his driver outright. His bodyguard was not expected to live. No one had yet claimed credit for the assassination, although the authorities suspected the Islamic Movement of Uzbekistan, which had been responsible for similar attacks in the past.

The camera homed in on the ambassador's charred body.

"Poor bastard!" Nadia muttered softly. The man's previous posting had been to the British Embassy in Moscow, and he'd recently published a book entitled *Russia: A Slow Death*. Its subtitle – *A British Diplomat's Diatribe on Human Rights Abuses* – told it all. Nadia herself suffered no illusions about the Russian leadership: Karpev was a bastard, a despot masquerading as a democrat, who'd stop at virtually nothing to hold on to the reins of power. She knew all too well his preference for the old ways of dealing with dissent: every abuse claimed in the book was bound to contain a large element of truth. The ambassador had been rare in having the courage to speak out. In her heart, she secretly admired him. But he was not her boss, and they were.

As the camera continued to pan over the devastation, a voice-over reported a second explosion shortly afterwards at a private dwelling in the Tashkent suburbs. The police were seeking to establish a connection between the two incidents.

Nadia felt a sour taste in her throat. The image of the young woman's face still lingered, the despair in her eyes as she'd realised that, whatever happened, they were all going to die. Had her husband truly believed she would spare them? Alas, terror didn't operate like that.

Stas switched off the television. "Mission completed," he said, pulling Nadia to her feet. "Time for your reward."

She allowed him to guide her onto the bed and lie beside her. With a sudden twist, she straddled him, her hands pinioning his arms against the hard mattress. For a moment his eyes rebelled, then veered away at the chill in her stare. She was in charge: Stas was the expression of her will, and he needed to know it.

Chapter Six

Moscow, Russia

Leksin spun around and glared defiantly at Marchuk. The man was built like a tank, broad, with massive forearms, a flat nose and jutting jaw, sharp as steel. With legs spread at a slight angle, fists clenched and precisely distanced, his face was creased in concentration, betraying no fear, just a brutal confidence. Leksin realised he couldn't afford to let up for a second. Any lapse of attention, and it would all be over.

Keeping his eyes glued on his adversary as his feet side-stepped smoothly across the floor, Leksin's muscles tensed as the man approached. At the last moment, in a swift movement, Marchuk threw himself to the ground and kicked sharply upwards. Leksin was ready for this, though. Ducking to one side, he arced his leg towards the man's head. Just in time, Marchuk rolled to one side, springing to his feet.

Leksin nodded involuntarily, as if in acknowledgement. Marchuk was good – and fast. Once more the man advanced in attack, his arms powering like pistons as he threw out a flurry of punches. Leksin blocked and parried, thwarting all but the last of Marchuk's lunges. His heart pounded in the sudden rush of adrenaline, and he backed away.

Control your breathing, that was key. Maintain a distance, make your height advantage count. Leksin sucked air down to the pit of his stomach, giving his head time to clear.

For a few moments the two men studied each other, edging around the floor in an endless loop, their bodies poised at a slant. Searching for an opening, Leksin feinted, first with one leg, then the other, then the first again, trying to lure the other man into committing. By instinct, Marchuk was an aggressor, more at ease in attack than defence, and this sparring ran against his style. At the first dip in his concentration, Leksin thrust forward. In a flash he grabbed Marchuk and twisted his own body to throw him, but as Marchuk fell, he seized Leksin's arm, dragging him down with him. In an instant the advantage had switched. A contest of brute force with this man, Leksin realised, was a one-way street to disaster. Scrambling away, he pushed himself up.

Turning to re-position himself, Leksin was aware for the first time of the cordon of spectators, who seemed to have materialised from nowhere. Their intent eyes mirrored the fight, while their faces remained blank, indifferent to the consequences. If they were making any noise, such was Leksin's concentration that he didn't hear it.

Glancing back at Marchuk, Leksin didn't rate his chances of disturbing the man's composure again. Turbo-charged, his opponent could go on like this all day and eventually wear him down. Leksin would have to outthink him and, if necessary, take a risk. Marchuk sprang forward, pivoted on his right foot and lunged at Leksin's face. Leksin swayed left, but as he straightened, Marchuk committed himself fully and landed a right foot into Leksin's stomach. Leksin winced and retreated two metres. Clearly confident he now had Leksin's measure, Marchuk glided forward, the soles of his feet rasping on the floor. As Leksin skipped back, shifting out of the direct line of attack, the man let down his guard to give himself more options and went for the kill. It was the moment of carelessness for which Leksin had been waiting, and he moved fast to take Marchuk unawares. Grasping his robe, Leksin spun counter clockwise on his left leg and snatched his wrist. The shift caught Marchuk off-balance and, unable to halt his momentum, he crashed over Leksin's shoulder onto the canvas.

"*Yame!*" the FSB karate instructor shouted as Marchuk's body thumped to the makiwara mat. "Good work, Alex," he said with professional approval. "You had him walk right into that one."

Leksin smiled as he bowed to his opponent. At Cambridge he'd been in the university karate team and, soon after he moved to

Moscow, Nikolai Koriakov had used his influence to arrange for him to practise at the FSB's Sokolniki Centre – a tough school for Russia's security forces, and one that took no prisoners. He shook hands with his defeated opponent, last year's Red Star champion.

"Well done, I thought I had you there," Marchuk panted. "I'll watch out for that move next time."

Looking over the man's broad shoulder, Leksin checked the clock. Coming up to ten o'clock. His appointment at the Chestny Kombinat wasn't till two. As his breathing slackened to normal pace, he let the idea of seeing Vika again into consideration. He'd blanked her from his mind after their breakup for so long that the habit had in the end taken hold. Her face floated before him, almost unfamiliar after a lengthy absence. He shrugged, perhaps the hurt would no longer be there when he saw her later.

Anyway, before that he had another appointment he was determined not to miss. He stopped off to get a cold drink from the machine before heading for the changing rooms.

Chapter Seven

Moscow, Russia

Leksin let himself into his apartment. With a package from the Tretyakov Gallery cradled under his arm, he made straight for the study, where he stripped off the bubble-wrap. Resting the painting against the wall, he backed away to inspect his new acquisition. A self-portrait by Serebriakova, he'd accepted it from the Tretyakov as compensation for his assignment. Perhaps the painting wouldn't fetch as much as his standard fee on the open market, but no matter: as far as he was concerned, he'd got the better bargain.

Reaching across to deflect his desk-lamp's glare from the canvas, he studied the technique by which the artist had brought herself to life. Bold brushstrokes enacted the sweep of her arm, highlighting the glide of her hair as she brushed it. Once before, he'd bought a work by this artist. On that occasion, he'd given it as a gift to a friend, then lost both friend and painting. This one he'd keep.

But where to hang it? His flat in Skatertny Lane was in a pre-Revolutionary block in an ancient quarter of Moscow. Initially the hub of suppliers to the Tsar's court, they had found themselves booted out by the aristocracy who'd installed themselves there in elaborate stuccoed palaces. In Soviet times, his block had become a warren of sordid *komunalkas* where up to five families had been crammed into each unit. When Leksin first found the flat, he'd immediately realised its potential. The brief to his architect had been to give him a gallery, utilising its high ceilings, long corridors and large windows. The furnishings were to be functional, unfussy and neutral in tone. Nothing was to distract from the paintings.

His great-grandfather had been a renowned art collector in those rarefied days before the revolution. Exiled by the Soviets in 1920, he'd been forced to abandon his paintings along with

31

everything else. Seventy-five years later, when Leksin left England for Moscow, he'd set about rebuilding the collection – and he was making steady progress. Even though the process was becoming increasingly difficult as interest in Russian art exploded, attracting the attention of trophy hunters and oligarchs, the contacts he'd established in the art world had enabled him each year to recover one or two more.

He held up his new acquisition between Kustodiev's vibrant village festival scene and the cool calm of a Petrov-Vodkin still-life. Yes, here would be good, he reckoned; after all, this wall was where he kept his favourites. Facing his desk, old friends looked out for him through his job's regular all-nighters.

Logging onto his private network, he entered the painting's details on his database. Artist, title, description, year, seller, price, link to his grandfather. Job done, he sat back in his chair, and his eyes rested on the photo of Lena, his sister, on the desk corner. He swallowed hard, lost for a moment in recollection. Once so full of life and talented, Lena had spent much of the last two years in a Swiss clinic recovering from her meltdown, the collateral damage of one of his past assignments. Was there something he could have done to prevent it? Should he have foreseen the danger in which he was putting her? Had her distress been avoidable? He'd asked himself these questions time and time again. Each time he answered them in the negative, but still he blamed himself. Lena was the only family he had – she'd deserved better from him.

Too many memories were on his back today. He extracted a small Palekh box from his desk-drawer, spread a line of coke on his desk, then hoovered it up. Settling back, he closed his eyes as the rush took hold. He was still riding the wave when the intercom buzzed to announce his driver's arrival to take him to his next meeting.

Chapter Eight

Moscow, Russia

"Mr Leksin, you're expected. Come with me, please." The receptionist led him across the foyer to a bank of lifts, slipped a card into the security slot and pressed '12'. "The lift will take you straight to the top floor. You'll be met there."

As the lift started to climb, Leksin almost willed it to go slower, wary about what to expect when it stopped. Vika Usenko, now Chairman and Chief Executive of Chestny Kombinat, had been one of only a handful of women with whom he'd ever let down his guard. He'd fallen under her spell the moment they'd met and proposed to her shortly afterwards, but in the end she'd proved to be another who got away. One day the two of them had been planning their wedding, the next their relationship had been brought to an end in a single flash. He'd made no attempt to see her since, it hurt less that way.

However, when Lev Usenko, her father, had died unexpectedly shortly afterwards, it *had* come as a surprise to read in the papers that he'd bequeathed his business empire to her in preference to her elder brother, Max. No question that Vika was by far the brighter of the two siblings, but nonetheless this was Russia: business here was essentially a man's world, and it was very un-Russian to favour the daughter over the son. By all reports, ever since she'd been well enough actively to assume the reins, there had been nothing but friction in the camp. Not surprising. Max wasn't one to take such a decision lying down. According to the rumour mill, he'd adopted a policy of minimum cooperation and tried to rally support amongst his father's old colleagues. Recently, Leksin understood, Vika had axed half the board in a sudden coup, presumably a tactic to undercut Max's powerbase.

The lift pinged as it came to a halt and the doors slid open. Lev Usenko's former secretary stood waiting for him in the corridor. Leksin recognised her immediately and smiled self-consciously.

"Good afternoon, Mr Leksin," she began. "Good to see you again. Please follow me."

*

Vika came forward to greet him. Batting away his offered hand, she touched her cheek to his. Smiling as if she appreciated his discomfort, she invited him to sit down.

"You look great," he said, and meant it. Slender, her skin as smooth as the soft-textured trouser suit she was wearing, the plastic surgeon had done a fantastic job. No vestige of the scars remained. A slight limp, perhaps, if you knew to look, but nothing more.

"You remember my brother, Max."

Leksin nodded at Max. A man of cherubic good looks and a languid manner, he was immaculately dressed in a tailored dark blue suit, a pink silk handkerchief peering over his top pocket. He grunted but didn't get up. The two of them had never hit it off.

Looking around, he took in the room: still the rampart of a desk, Victorian mahogany, with scorch marks from Lev's cigars where he used to forget them and a photo of Sergei, Vika's younger brother, and the circular conference table around which they now sat. A different painting hung on the wall behind Max, though. Three peasants resting in a cornfield, Leksin's gift to Vika before they broke up. "You still have the Serebriakova," he observed.

"I always liked it."

"Me too. Sometimes wish I'd kept it." Leksin gave a wry smile as Max rose to whisk a handkerchief over the painting, as if his arrival had somehow soiled it. "I've just got another one of hers, belonged to my great-grandfather."

"You should make sure you hang onto it this time," she teased.

"I will," Leksin replied, a little more flatly than he intended.

34

Max scraped back his chair, unable to hide his impatience. "For heaven's sake, can we get on with it?"

Leksin glanced at Vika, caught the fatigue in her eyes, there for an instant, then gone. "Alex, why don't you tell us what we can do for you?" she asked, forcing a smile.

Leksin summarised the purpose of his mission.

"Well, my brother's the one to help you here," she told him when he'd finished. "He looks after our operations in Central Asia. The pipeline project's been his baby from the start."

Leksin nodded, resigned to the inevitable, and turned towards Max. "How did the company first become involved?"

Max spread his hands flat upon the table and looked up as if to deliver a lecture. "To use Jung's term, it was synchronicity," he began pompously. "Saidov's contacts in Turkmenistan alerted him to their government's intention to sell off the right to run an oil pipeline across its territory, and he immediately realised the importance of securing that right for Russia." His voice was on a single plane, a monotone without inflection, like students reading aloud in a language they don't fully understand. "But these days our country seeks to emulate a capitalist power – at least, when it suits – and the government specified that the project would have to be financed entirely through the private sector. That's where I came in. The Chestny Kombinat has very strong historical links in Central Asia, particularly in Turkmenistan, as well as contacts throughout the oil sector generally. We were ideally placed to take the lead on the project."

Leksin teetered on the verge of contradicting him. He'd once debated Jung's theory at the Cambridge Union, and Max, pretentious as ever, had got his wires crossed. Synchronicity was a theory that tried to account for coincidence. The word that Max was reaching for was synergy, but no matter. It wasn't important enough to pursue, tempting though it would be to rile Max further. Instead Leksin sought clarification.

"When did Saidov approach you?"

"About eighteen months ago, a little earlier perhaps."

Leksin thought back: he and Vika had still been together then. "Why didn't he approach Lev direct?" he continued. He hadn't intended the question to sound patronising, but fearing that it might be taken this way, quickly added: "The Prime Minister was, after all, your father's friend."

Max extracted a Black Russian from the packet in front of him, tapped it several times on the lid before lighting it.

"Saidov was a family friend," he corrected eventually, as if this explanation would do.

"But Lev must have been involved – "

"I told my father, yes." Max's uninflected tone promised no elaboration.

Leksin squinted at him through the cloud of smoke, making a mental note to follow up with Saidov, and changed tack. Keen to discern the level of Vika's own involvement in the project, he addressed her directly.

"Has it all been plain sailing for Russia, or have other countries wanted to get in on the act?"

She gave a little shrug. "As far as I know, no one else has expressed an interest." She angled her head enquiringly at Max. "Isn't that right?"

Max nodded. "All the international oil majors are operating in the Caspian," he explained in his usual flat tone. "But none of them were inclined to confront the issues surrounding the proposed pipeline."

"Like what?"

"Like dealing with the Turkmen authorities, for example. It's almost impossible to do business down there without an established network of contacts."

"And Afghanistan?" Leksin prodded.

"That too."

Leksin waited for elaboration and, when none came, addressed his next question to Vika.

"Vika, what arrangements will be made for the pipeline's security there?"

"I'm told that's taken care of." It was a lame answer, and he could see she knew it.

Leksin gave her a look that asked for more, but nothing was forthcoming. The colour rose in her cheeks, and she glanced away. So was she really unaware of the planned safeguards in Afghanistan? Given the physical vulnerability of the pipeline during its passage through that country, this seemed inconceivable - as did the scenario that she'd left such a massive and politically sensitive project as this entirely in the hands of Max. It was as if all the straight-sided pieces in the jigsaw were missing. "Max, can you shed some more light?"

"As Vika said, it's taken care of." Max sighed impatiently. "Right from the start we realised that the pipeline was viable only if we could guarantee its security. We're not fools, Alex. Dealing with this aspect was obviously No 1 priority."

"But how?" Leksin pressed.

"Well, you asked me just now whether my father was involved. Of course he damn well was. He had the contacts in the Turkmen government, and he enlisted their support. In the long term, Turkmenistan will need the pipeline for its own oil from the Caspian once it comes on stream. The country shares a common border with Afghanistan, and the two countries share a number of mutual interests. They set up a meeting in Kabul at which my father was present. Together, they negotiated a series of deals to guarantee the pipeline's security. In particular, my father agreed a profit-sharing arrangement with Afghanistan once the pipeline's operational."

"And you're confident the Afghan government can make good on its guarantee?" Leksin persisted.

"Yes," Max replied baldly. "They all stand to make a great deal of money, there's no better incentive." He blew out a series of small smoke rings, watched them ascend, then looked pointedly at his watch. "I've another meeting shortly. Was there anything else?"

Leksin left a pause before he replied. "One thing. I'd like to examine the detailed plans and budgets."

"Well, they're in Turkmenistan. That's where the project team's based."

"So who's the best contact down there?"

"Don't worry," Max replied, stubbing out his cigarette. "I'll fly down myself to take care of you."

Leksin groaned inwardly. He had little doubt he'd have more freedom to operate without Max getting in the way.

A chair scuffled as Max rose to his feet to signal his participation in the meeting was at an end.

As they walked back to the lift, Vika asked: "How's your sister? Any better?"

"Lena's still in the clinic in Lausanne, I'm afraid," he sighed. "Doctors say she's making progress."

"Give her my love when you next see her, tell her I haven't forgotten her."

The lift swished open. Stooping to kiss her cheek, Leksin said: "Good to see you again, Vika. You look really well, better than ever."

He turned to shake Max's hand, but he'd gone.

Chapter Nine

Ashgabat, Turkmenistan

Ali Orazov was a small, unremarkable man whose only distinguishing feature was a huge hooked nose, over which two sparkling eagle eyes missed very little. Over the years he had wormed his way up the slippery Turkmen ladder. The political uncertainties, the declining economy and, above all, the succession of volatile presidents had made Turkmenistan a difficult country in which to rise – and even more difficult, and dangerous, to keep a grip when you'd reached the top. But despite the odds, and with more than a little help from certain influential friends, Orazov had held on through the knocks which had unstuck the careers of so many of his contemporaries.

The doorbell rang, announcing the arrival of the car to take him to this evening's Presidential reception. Descending the stairs from his living-room, he slumped onto the back seat. His flight back from Zurich had landed in the early hours of the morning, and he'd been in meetings all day. He felt exhausted. Never mind, he consoled himself as the car pulled away, his journey had been worthwhile . . .

*

Schultzefinanze PrivatBank was situated just off Brandschenkestrasse in the heart of Zurich's banking district. Its unassuming frontage contrasted sharply with those of some better-known competitors. The main entrance, a plain plate-glass door tucked between a newsagent and a delicatessen, had a plaque to one side announcing just the street and the number. Inside, however, the hush of the lobby proclaimed old money and self-confidence. A pair of softly lit Fragonard paintings adorned cream silk-panelled walls, and a large pure silk Battier carpet lapped over the polished wooden floor.

When Orazov entered, a girl with golden hair and long legs rose behind the gilded desk to greet him, her smile on automatic. "Good morning, Herr Orazov. Good to see you again. I'll tell Herr Brennen you're here."

She led him to a meeting room across the lobby. "Can I get you anything? A glass of Bollinger, perhaps?"

Orazov raised his eyes from her perfect legs. "Just tea."

"Darjeeling, Earl Grey, Lapsang Souchong?"

"Anything. With sugar. Lots of it."

Brennen, the bank's manager, came in. Wearing an impeccably tailored grey flannel suit, a plain blue silk tie and a sober expression, he towered above his visitor.

"Shall we begin?" he asked once pleasantries were exchanged. "I have prepared the usual schedule." He handed his client a summary of his investment position. "As you can see, there has been seven per cent growth in the value of existing securities, and we have received payment of a further five million dollars."

Orazov nodded. "Just to warn you, there should be another similar payment coming in next month," he explained. "I'm in the process of finalising a major deal."

Brennen made a note, then the two men settled down for the next hour to discuss the future direction of the portfolio, tweaking it here and there as the banker recommended. Orazov himself was lost among the markets, but he revelled in these visits to Switzerland. To him they were high finance, they reinforced his sense of his own importance.

"May I get you anything before you go?" Brennen asked him when they'd finished. "More tea? Something stronger, perhaps?"

"Thank you, no. I fly back to Ashgabat later, and there's something I need to do before I leave."

"So soon?"

"Regrettably, yes. Work . . ."

Brennen nodded sympathetically. "Yes, in your position the pressure must be constant. Well, I'll look forward to seeing you as usual in about six months."

The girl with the legs reappeared to collect him. Outside he'd turned left at Brudschenkestrasse towards the taxi rank. The smell of recent rain rose from the pavements. Sunshine pierced the scattered clouds, slanting through the high-rises across the street and glinting against the windows opposite. On each side of the road, spaced at regular intervals, large wooden barrels filled with neat geraniums stood like sentries. As Orazov passed the doorway of a bakery, the aroma of fresh pastries billowed out. His mouth dropped at the corners. Pity not to stay for a few days, but . . .

Reaching the rank, Orazov told the driver to take him to the Park Hyatt in Beethoven-Strasse. A few minutes later, as he walked through the entrance, the receptionist attracted his attention.

"Your guest's arrived, sir," she told him. "I showed him into the lounge."

Slipping ten francs into her palm, Orazov crossed the lobby. As soon as he entered the lounge, he spotted the man seated by the window and headed over.

"How are you, Ramez?" he greeted the man, shaking his hand enthusiastically. "How was your trip from Kabul?"

*

Orazov blinked at the flashing lights of the paparazzi as the car pulled up outside the ceremonial palace. His driver came around to open the door and, easing out, he walked under the pillared portico and made his entrance.

Chapter Ten

Ashgabat, Turkmenistan

Nassah Rashid, President of Turkmenistan, Father of the People, extended his arms towards the delegates as he drew to the close of his post-banquet address at the recently convened International Roundtable Conference on Caspian Development. The guests, grouped at long tables banked high with flowers and forming a horseshoe around the top table, rose to their feet to applaud.

Rashid liked to put on a show, and tonight had been no exception. They were assembled in the banqueting hall of the ceremonial palace in the centre of town, the one reserved for such events. A huge green national flag hung on the wall behind him, a band of red on its left-hand side framing the five main motifs of traditional Turkmen carpet design. The floor was covered by an immense example of the craft, a rug which Saidov estimated covered more than 200 square metres. They had been served platters of plov, mounds of spiced lamb, and piles of fruit so naturally sweet that it tasted like nectar.

As Russia's Prime Minister, Saidov occupied a prominent position to the right of Rashid. He'd been slotted between the British ambassador, who'd seemed fixated on embassy security following the recent incident in neighbouring Uzbekistan, and a prominent Texan oilman, whose few comments had been as dreary as the long pauses between them. He'd treated them with his usual courtesy, but found it hard going.

Anyway, he hated these occasions. For him, not even the dancing girls with their jingling headdresses and thick braids of dark hair provided any respite from the tedium. He'd breathed a sigh of genuine relief when the President departed, his clan of bison-shouldered bodyguards waiting by the doorway to escort him.

Time to clear the lines for Leksin. Helping himself to a large glass of cognac, Saidov took a thirsty gulp and surveyed the room. It took a while before he spotted the squat figure of the Minister of Energy amidst the other delegates flocking to the bar.

"My friend," Saidov greeted him, putting an arm around his shoulder. "Spare me five minutes, will you? I need a private word in your ear."

Chapter Eleven

Moscow, Russia

Taking the lift down to the basement, Leksin descended to the library of the Ministry of Foreign Affairs. A series of cavernous rooms situated in a building south of the Moskva that housed the Ministry's overflow, this was where intelligence reports on over 100 countries were archived.

The librarian greeted him with a smile. "Hello, Mr Leksin, good to see you again. You'll find all the material Nikolai Koriakov requested for you on a table in Room B."

"Thanks, that's great," Leksin replied gratefully. "Tell me, how's your wife?"

The librarian pointed to a photograph of a baby on the counter. "We had a boy," he replied proudly.

"Congratulations, looks just like you." Leksin grinned and reached over to shake his hand, then set off towards Room B.

*

The table was piled high with background reports on Turkmenistan. Opening his laptop, he logged onto his home network and got started.

Much of the background was already familiar. In many respects, Turkmenistan represented the heart of Central Asia. Nestled on the eastern shores of the Caspian Sea, it shared borders with Kazakhstan, Uzbekistan, Iran and Afghanistan. With average summer temperatures between 40ºC and 50ºC, over three-quarters of its surface comprised the Karakum Desert, dry, inhospitable and deadly.

For a century an integral part of the Soviet empire, Turkmenistan had obtained independence in 1990 when the USSR dissolved. Although reputed to have the world's fourth largest reserves of natural gas, the country had not prospered on its own. Like many of the newly independent nations it found itself ill-prepared for the new free market conditions. For years it had been part of a Soviet command economy. Central Planning dictated what and how much each region produced, and in return they got an allocation of products from other regions. It was a crude procedure. Zhigulis might roll off the vast automobile assembly line in the town of Togliatti by the Volga, and be distributed throughout the Soviet Union, but other goods - cotton produced in southern Turkmenistan, for example - were supplied in return by central mandate. This system worked to a point so long as *every commodity* came from somewhere, and *each* province had access to all the goods it didn't itself produce. However, when Turkmenistan broke away, it had found itself not just stockpiling its production way beyond local requirements, but also cut off from essentials manufactured elsewhere.

This situation had been exacerbated by Saparmyrat Niyazov's assumption of power. The region's former communist leader, his ascendancy to the presidency had been a foregone conclusion. A demagogue - power-crazed, unbalanced, at times verging on lunacy - his first actions had been to change his own name to Turkmenbashi (literally, father of all Turkmen) and declare himself President for life. The bulk of the nation's vast natural gas revenues were siphoned off to a 'foreign exchange reserve account', reputedly held at one of Germany's largest banks, the purpose and management of which remained undisclosed. A faint smile crossed Leksin's lips: it wasn't hard to guess the identity of the account's true beneficiary.

The list of Turkmenbashi's excesses seemed endless. In a country characterised by severe water shortages, he designed a vast lake to be built in the Karakum Desert surrounded by cypress trees, a ski resort, and an ice palace close to the capital, while simultaneously allowing the fabric of the country to crumble. He banned opera, ballet and the circus for being, in his words, 'decidedly un-turkmen-like'.

On one occasion he came out against the use of gold teeth and caps. 'I watched young dogs when I was young,' he pointed out. 'They were given bones to gnaw to strengthen their teeth. Those of you whose teeth have fallen out did not chew on bones.' But health was clearly not always such a priority. Inexplicably, he'd ordered the closure of all hospitals outside the capital, sacking some 15,000 public health workers in a stroke, insisting that in future the sick make their way across the desert to the capital for treatment.

Frowning, Leksin ran his fingers through his hair, a series of short sweeps, struck by the thought that, if Turkmenbashi had been a character in a novel, reviewers would have regarded him as too far-fetched to be credible. He glanced bleakly around the room, his eyes aimlessly following the shelves of neatly stacked books, before reading on.

Not surprisingly against such a background, the press was tightly controlled and clung to the official line. The country's record on human rights continued to be one of the worst in the world. Dissenting voices were persecuted and tortured. An alleged assassination attempt had provided the opportunity to round up thousands of such dissidents and their families. Some were exiled or imprisoned. A few were freed. Others were never seen again. Russian intelligence sources suspected Turkmenbashi had stage-managed the incident himself, affording himself an excuse to clear out the stable.

Whilst Turkmenbashi had died of a heart attack in 2006, his successors had not seen fit to redress his abuses. Western companies had grown fed up with doing business in a country where the courts were heavily biased against them, and few hung on. So, when Turkmenistan - like the other countries bordering the Caspian - discovered vast oil reserves, it had proved impossible to attract the outside investment and expertise to exploit them properly. Each year in their State of the Nation addresses, successive Presidents had promised reform and economic reconstruction, but again and again these had proved empty promises. The reality was that things continued very much as before. The media were encouraged to blame the Russians for the country's ills with the result that Russian enterprises were increasingly confronted by demonstrations of protest. Meanwhile, the benefit of the country's vast natural gas revenues continued to be denied to the wider population. The present incumbent, Nassah Rashid, was no better than the rest of them.

Plus ça change, thought Leksin, it was a familiar story in this part of the world. The Soviets had imbued a culture of corruption throughout their empire, and it would take longer than the passage of one generation to eradicate it. In this respect, Turkmenistan was no different from Russia.

*

Leksin packed up his laptop and headed for the exit.

Outside, the late-afternoon breeze alleviated the relentless humidity of the Moscow summer and the Moskva river seemed to ripple with delight. Across the road, the sun lit up Dom Naberezhnaya, the apartment block they called the House of Sighs, from which officers and apparatchiks alike were once collected nightly during Stalin's purges and whisked away to summary execution.

Heading home, Leksin started across Kamenny Bridge, assimilating the information he'd just processed. As he walked, his eyes resting appreciatively on the walls of the Kremlin before him, a drunk stumbled between him and the view. Just managing to duck around him, he strode on but found himself ambushed by a long-avoided memory.

Chapter Twelve

Moscow, Russia

He clutched hold of Vika to stop her falling as her high heels skidded on the ice. He steadied her, and she giggled as he tilted her face towards him to kiss her. In the background, he glimpsed a faint red glow behind them in the portico of her father's house, and the silhouette of Max between the pale columns. Vika too seemed to sense his unseen eyes and turned away. Throughout the evening, as champagne had flowed to celebrate their engagement with family and friends, Max had made little attempt to hide his resentment at his sister being the centre of attention. But so what? After the wedding, he'd shield her from him.

Let me drive, he suggested, but Vika refused. The red Alfa Spider had been an engagement present from her father, she reminded him, and she couldn't wait to try it out.

Vika sped through the night towards Moscow as he dozed by her side. Halfway there, he woke up and stretched on the leather seat. "Slow down a bit, Vika," he yawned. "There's a speed check coming up."

"They'll stop us anyway in a car like this. I can deal with them, Alex, don't worry. Go back to sleep."

Sure enough, in the distance a white Lada was pulled up at the side of the road. Vika's foot depressed the brake. For an instant, it seemed to him, the car seemed not to notice, then just as quickly it scrunched to a halt by the GAI policeman who stood waving his white baton.

Vika lowered her window and produced a neatly folded $100 note from the pocket of her fur coat.

*

When they were nearly there, Vika changed gear and slipped the car through the interchange onto the Garden Ring, the wide road that encircled the city centre. Tall plumes of steam and smoke rose to the left from a heating plant that worked around the clock through the Moscow winter, pumping heat through the centralised system to apartment blocks and offices. As the car gathered speed again, he'd glanced ahead at the huddle of workers from the previous shift waiting at the tram stop, hunched against the cold.

A figure detached itself from the group and staggered out into the road, the vodka bottle clutched in one hand twinkling under the beam from the headlights.

Vika hit the brakes, but there was no response. Instinctively she swerved, and Leksin felt his body slammed back into the seat as the car spun around and around, revolving inexorably into the path of an oncoming lorry. He reached across for Vika, then waited for the impact, helpless.

Chapter Thirteen

Moscow, Russia

Leksin poured a cold Baltika as he reluctantly punched in the number of the clinic in Lausanne. He wasn't relishing this conversation. He was scheduled to take his sister to Italy on holiday next week – all part her rehabilitation programme – but this new assignment meant he'd have to put that on hold. As he took a swig of icy beer, the administrator at last came on the line. Yes, it was late to cancel, Leksin agreed. Yes, Lena would be very disappointed, and yes, he'd be in touch again soon. It was a practised routine, and yet again he felt guilty.

Sometimes, he suspected, they overestimated what he could achieve. Just ten days before President Karpev was due to sign the pipeline contract, and now they wanted him to vet the deal, in Central Asia of all places. What did they expect him to uncover within such a tight timetable? Turkmenistan was a notoriously difficult country in which to operate. Be careful there, Saidov had warned, and now Leksin understood why. On what basis should he succeed when their own FSB agent seemed to have failed?

Heading into his study, he took out the Palekh box and spread a line. Closing his eyes, he forced himself to take deep breaths. That was better. It was always the same at the outset of a new assignment, he reassured himself: the self-doubt, not knowing where to begin. But like stage-fright, all the uncertainty would disappear once the action got going.

Opening his eyes, he surveyed his paintings, his mouth dropping open when he spotted a jagged cross slashed through the centre of his new Serebriakova. He felt the fury rising inside him, and his face expressed pain as if he and not the painting had been stabbed. Approaching the painting cautiously, he noticed how segments of canvas hung loose as if they had been posed that way.

Extracting a remote from his desk, he pointed it towards the wall cabinet. Its small doors slipped open and a CCTV monitor rolled out. He clicked again: the tape rewound and a black-and-white picture lit up the screen. Leksin watched as a short, compact man in his mid-twenties, hair tied back in a ponytail, let himself into the hall and advanced down the corridor, a small canvas bag slung over his shoulder. Activated by movement, the picture switched to the study. Ponytail entered, examined the paintings on the walls and took down the Serebriakova. With equipment from the canvas bag, he taped a plastic canister to its rear. Using a craft knife, he sliced the cross into its centre, attached a wire from the canister to one of the flaps, then re-hung the picture. The screen then switched back to the hall. As the man let himself out, he took a key from his pocket to lock the door behind him. Thirty seconds later, with no movement inside the apartment, the screen went fuzzy.

Leksin reached for the phone – the intruder hadn't touched it.

"Nikolai? I've got a problem."

Nikolai knew the tone. "Where are you, Alex?"

"At home. My new painting, the Serebriakova – someone's wired it with explosives."

Nikolai hesitated a moment before asking: "Do you know who ...?"

"I don't know the man on the tape, no, but I can guess who's responsible."

"And?"

"I mentioned the painting on my visit to Chestny Kombinat, said it was something special."

Nikolai let out an involuntary gasp. "How'd he break in?"

"He didn't. He had a key."

"Who else has a key?"

"Only Vika, she never returned hers."

"You don't think – ?" Nikolai's voice sharpened.

"No, not her," Leksin assured him, amused at the thought. "She may have consigned me to the doghouse, but I don't think she'd put me down."

"OK, I get the picture." Nikolai commented. "I'll get a disposal team over straightaway."

Chapter Fourteen

Moscow, Russia

A timid hand alighted on Max's shoulder. Contemplating it for a moment, Max drew on his Black Russian, then placed the lighted tip against the white skin above the knuckle of the middle finger. The boy shrieked as he withdrew his hand and sucked at the burn.

"Bad timing, Pasha," Max admonished. "I've got too many other people trying to fuck me at present. Just pour me another glass of wine."

Sulkily, Pasha fetched the bottle of Chardonnay and filled Max's glass. As he returned the bottle to the wine cooler, Max's eyes surveyed his naked body. Two months since he'd picked Pasha up from the streets around Taganskaya station. He'd spotted his potential through the stupor of substance abuse, and as always he'd been right. Pasha's gratitude he took for granted, compliance was what he required in return.

"Come to bed," Pasha urged. "I've been waiting for you."

Max waved him away. "When I'm ready. Now leave me alone."

The boy screwed up his face and stuck out his tongue. "So who wants you anyway?" he demanded with a deliberate effeminate lisp. "No wonder your father put your sister in charge, you and your temper."

Max's mouth dipped at the corners. Pasha flushed and ran tearfully upstairs. He'd gone too far, but his words had found their target. Max's stomach knotted as he recalled when Olga Chernikova, his father's ex-mistress, had let rip after she'd been kicked out and warned him that the old man had changed his will. Daddy's girl, Vika, could do no wrong. His hand clenched the stem of his wine glass, then gradually relaxed. Lev Usenko was dead now, buried beneath a ton of black marble. Vika would have to learn to fight her own battles.

He drained his wine, clicked the remote to turn up the background music, then leaned back into his chair. Usually the room's elaborate luxury could sooth him. The library, as he called it. One wall all bookshelves, the pristine volumes marshalled with precision, the furnishings a blend of cream and lavender-grey, restful shades. But today he felt impervious to them. Leksin, always distinctly unwelcome as far as Max was concerned, had reappeared on the scene. The pipeline project stood to make a fortune, catapulting Max personally into the oligarch league, and he wasn't about to let his sister's ex-lover spoil the party. Perhaps the problem had been sorted this evening, but just in case he needed a contingency plan. He intended to fly down to Ashgabat himself in the morning, so that he could deal with Leksin there if necessary.

The ormulu clock on the mantelpiece began to strike the hour. Time for bed. Stubbing out his cigarette, Max crossed to his desk and slipped the key to Leksin's apartment that Vika had never bothered to return back into the drawer. Then, recalling Pasha's insult, his neck muscles stiffened. In his present mood, he didn't envy the boy one little bit tonight.

Chapter Fifteen

Moscow, Russia

Leksin's driver pulled up in front of a low-slung, two-storey building, arranged on three sides around a central courtyard. Soviet in style, concrete with square plate-glass windows, the freshly-painted playground equipment stood out in marked contrast. St Josef's Orphanage, a sign above the door stated.

"I won't be long," Leksin told his driver. "I promised the Principal I'd pass by on their saint's day, but I've got to get back to see Nikolai Koriakov this afternoon before I fly out."

Quietly, Leksin slipped into a large, high-ceilinged room where an enormous mural of the Kremlin skyline covered the whole of one wall. The chairs and tables were all pushed to the sides, like a gymnasium, and the children were grouped on rugs in the middle, crouched over their Lego-brick constructions, supervised by one of the staff or volunteers. When they had finished, he was due to award a prize to the group with the best building.

Across the room, the orphanage's Principal spotted him, but Leksin raised a hand. Let them play, he mouthed, I'm fine here. She nodded and slowly skirted the room to join him. In her usual shapeless top and skirt, her face had as always that strained, slightly vulnerable quality of someone who carries the cares of the world upon her shoulders but is determined not to show it. Leksin had nothing but admiration for her.

He whispered to her that he didn't have much time and, putting an understanding hand on his arm, she called an end to the competition. The children looked up and, noticing Leksin, rushed over to drag him off to admire their creations.

As Leksin's eyes wandered around the room, he was gratified

by the children's ready smiles. He joked with them as he did the tour, enjoying their exuberance. In the beginning, it hadn't always been like this. He recalled the strange affinity with them he'd experienced on his first visit. Of course his own background had been privileged beyond comparison to theirs, but as exiles abroad, his parents had always felt displaced and this feeling had passed onto him too. England might be where he was brought up, but somehow it was not his home. He'd always known that, if events allowed, he would end up in Russia. Yet even here he'd failed to find the sense of belonging that he sought. To Russians he would always be an outsider. Like an orphan. His success afforded him the ability to help St Josef's, but so far as he was concerned, this represented more than just giving something back in return.

He chose the winner and presented the prize, then the Principal clapped her hands to grab their attention. "On this, our saint's day, we must thank our benefactor, Mr Leksin . . ." she began.

"Toys for everyone," Leksin shouted, keen to sidestep the embarrassment of the Principal's expression of gratitude. He pointed towards the door where his driver had appeared with an overflowing crate.

"That was naughty of you," the Principal rebuked him gently, as the children swarmed around the driver. "I had my speech prepared."

"I'm sorry. I'd love to stay longer, but I can't. I'm flying to Turkmenistan later, and I have to get on."

"Well, thank you for coming, you've made their day."

As she escorted him to his car, Leksin slipped her the monthly envelope and asked: "Is there anything else you need?"

The Principal sighed awkwardly. "There is one thing, Alex, but I hesitate to ask. You've been so generous already."

"What is it?"

"Our boiler, it's on the blink. It won't last next winter."

"That won't do," he agreed. "Order a new one, get them to send me the bill."

Spotting the relief in her eyes, Leksin gave her a hug. "It's nothing, I promise you. Now go back inside and enjoy the rest of your saint's day."

Chapter Sixteen

Ashgabat, Turkmenistan

There wasn't much that singled out Borzov from the crowds of other Turkmen on this weekday morning. Olive-skinned, medium height, his check shirt hung loosely over baggy trousers, his sleeves rolled up. The difference as he made his way down Zarkainer Lane and through the swarm jostling into the market was the random path his eyes took all the time – a habit from his SNB days that had never left him.

He threaded his way through the market's labyrinth of stalls. A broad, sturdy woman with calves like tree trunks powered past, brandishing a shovel-load of foul-smelling smouldering grasses, and Borzov darted out of her way. The fumes warded off the evil eye, he'd once been told, and shielding his face from the toxic smoke, he didn't doubt it.

As he stopped to glance at a shop front piled high with blue and green local pottery, his friend, Islom, shouted across the alleyway. "Borzov, hey, come over here – I've got something to show you."

Islom held out a lacquered box, his broad grin uncovering a row of gold teeth. Sliding the lid open a fraction, Borzov peered inside, then snapping the box shut, hurriedly passed it back as if it were burning his fingers. "You trying to kill me?" he complained, not joking.

"Brought in from the desert last night," Islom told him, unapologetic. "Never seen such a large tarantula."

Borzov shook his head. "I'll never understand what you see in these creatures." Nonetheless, he looked around with morbid fascination: glass tanks of snakes, black widow spiders and scorpions. A dull grey serpent, its thick body coiled round a rock, stared back from its cage through gelid eyes.

"What's that?" he asked, inching closer.

"*Naja Oxiana*, better known as Oxus cobra" Islom replied with relish. "Lives in the foothills all along our southern border. Vicious little bastard, strikes just for the hell of it."

"Who'll buy that? Someone who can't stand his wife?"

Islom laughed and slapped his shoulder. "I pity the girl who marries you, Borzov."

Continuing through the throng of stalls until he reached the far side of the market, Borzov followed the main road towards Azadi Square. After four hundred metres he turned left into Sutaymanov Lane. A narrow leafy lane, this was an upmarket enclave, mainly residential, sheltered and quiet, lined with tidy whitewashed dachas, bougainvillea trailing over their wooden frames. Half-way along, set back in a short cul-de-sac, a high metal gate blocked entry into a covered, paved parking area and a manicured garden. Inside the enclosure stood a shining white building with inset porticos and French windows opening onto mosaic terraces: Chestny Kombinat's headquarters in Turkmenistan.

Borzov paused to exchange pleasantries with the guard at the entrance, then headed for a small bungalow set apart from the main building. A metal plaque on the wall bore the simple inscription: Security. He tapped numbers into the keypad and the door clicked open. Passing into a room cluttered with monitoring and radio equipment, a woman with a nest of dyed-auburn hair looked up from her computer.

"Bad news, I'm afraid," she greeted him. "Max Usenko's flying down today. There's an email on your desk. He wants to see you as soon as he arrives."

Chapter Seventeen

Ashgabat, Turkmenistan

It was mid-afternoon when Max's plane touched down in Ashgabat, and he headed straight for Chestny Kombinat's headquarters. Giving the receptionist a cursory nod, he raised a hand to indicate he could find his own way, and set off in short, tidy steps along the corridor.

Adam Smolinsky, General Director of the company's operations in Turkmenistan, jumped to his feet as he entered. A skin-clad skeleton engulfed in a baggy suit, his voice quivered with the timidity of someone who expected the worst. "Borzov told me you were coming. Nothing's prepared, I'm afraid. No one filled me in on what you'd want."

Max kicked a chair into place and, slipping his pale cotton jacket over the back, sat down. He felt his pockets for his Black Russians, placed the packet on the desk and, extracting a cigarette with meticulous care, lit it slowly. Then, confronting Smolinsky's anxious gaze, he said flatly: "We're terminating your contract."

Caught completely off-balance, Smolinsky's mouth dropped open, unable to find the right words. "Why?" he stuttered lamely. "What have I done wrong?"

"It's an operational decision," Max explained, as if this meant something.

Smolinsky fixed Max in a dejected stare. "But my family . . . " His bony hand pointed at the photo on his desk.

Max shrugged and opened his hands, acknowledging the inevitability of collateral damage.

"I've done whatever you asked – " Smolinsky said, his voice shrill with mounting indignation.

"And so you will now," Max interrupted with sudden ferocity, slapping his hand hard against the desk to show he meant business. "Do you understand?"

Smolinsky hesitated, verging on the edge of protest, then backed down.

Max's face relaxed into an insincere smile. "You will get one year's salary as compensation, but only if you keep these conditions." He counted on his fingers, pronouncing each syllable distinctly as if he was talking to the hard of hearing. "One, you submit a voluntary letter of resignation. Two, you leave the building by close of play today. And three, you do not break the confidentiality clause in your contract. The compensation will be paid in a lump sum twelve months from now provided you've complied."

Extracting a draft resignation letter from his holdall, he slid it across the desk and fiddled with a pencil while Smolinsky scanned through it. "The offer's not negotiable. Accept it now, or it lapses." He paused, then added deliberately slowly: "Break your confidentiality clause, well . . ." He snapped the pencil in two.

Smolinsky's eyes flitted around the room, searching hopelessly for an alternative. Finally, after fumbling in his desk for a pen, he morosely scribbled his signature on each page.

Max slipped the letter back into his holdall and looked at Smolinsky with satisfaction. "I'm sorry," he smirked. Swivelling his chair to face the window, he blew smoke rings into the air and watched them break against the ceiling. "Send in Borzov on your way out, will you?"

Chapter Eighteen

Ashgabat, Turkmenistan

A heat haze veiled the brash concrete angles of Ashgabat's modern airport when Leksin's plane finally landed after being delayed half the night at Domodedovo. On the tarmac a stewardess wearing a tight uniform and a brittle smile waited to escort Leksin to the bus marked CIT, reserved for 'Commercially Important Travellers'. As the bus moved forward, he noticed a vast white banner strung across the terminal building that proclaimed in red letters: *Halk, Watan, Rashid* – the People, the State, Rashid.

Already hacked off by the waste of valuable time, the CIT lounge had none of the comforts promised by its name and did nothing to improve his overall mood. A spartan, L-shaped lobby with stark overhead lighting, the walls were lined with cheap leather sofas and tacky adverts for local businesses. A harassed receptionist struggled to deal with the new arrivals, while overhead a television blared out last night's Presidential address to the nation on an endless loop. Leksin sped through the paperwork and handed it in. Keeping a tight check on his irritation as he waited for it to be processed, he glanced up to see Rashid, the Turkmen President, summoning ministers to the podium one by one and dismissing them from their posts. Wayward children hauled before the class, it was their unequivocal embrace of such public humiliation that Leksin found disquieting. He sat down and watched the surreal scene unfold.

"I appointed a young man, Welmedov, as Minister of Communication," Rashid was telling the nation, the crown of his head shining under the crude television lighting. "He didn't come to me even once during this short period to ask my help to solve any issue. I trusted the telecoms development to his care, but he didn't even go there and inspect it, he doesn't know anything about it. He's a nice-looking guy with a pristine white shirt, but when it comes to work, he's asleep at the wheel. I want to promote young talent. And it seems as if they work for the first spell, but after about a year they get spoiled quickly – because of their car, reputation, and so on. Welmedov, you're a good guy, but you have left me with no choice but to remove you from your position for your serious failures, for your inability to fulfil your task." The President beckoned the culprit to the podium. "Do you have anything to say? Am I giving a fair account?"

The outgoing Minister reached the podium, bowed his head and approached the microphone. "Yes, what you are saying is right." He shot a nervous glance towards his President, who waved him brusquely aside.

"Tekebay will take your position," Rashid continued. "He achieved his first success in the health business. He has his faults too. I can criticise him for his past business practices or for his daughter. I've talked about these before, if you remember. But he's enthusiastic and driven. I know that supervision is needed, or he'll run wild. It will be given. So, Tekebay, I tell you now to work honestly. Don't fall off the wire anywhere. You have food to eat and clothes to wear. Do you understand?"

A short, sinewy man seated in the front row rose to his feet, cautious and circumspect. "I'll do everything possible and work days and nights. I promise that I'll always work honestly – "

Leksin felt a tap on his arm: he turned to find the stewardess holding out his passport. A man at her side carried his suitcase. "The porter will take you to the taxi rank," she informed him briskly.

As the taxi drove along Independence Way, the wide avenue leading towards the centre of town, Leksin absorbed the full extent of the cult of personality, so meticulously fostered by the President. Each house carried a Turkmen flag like shrines to their leader. Giant posters bearing the President's image adorned the walls of public buildings. Even the vodka bottles in kiosk windows bore his picture on their labels.

Pulling up at the traffic lights on the edge of Azadi Square, Leksin glanced around with bemused detachment. The vast open space was dominated by the enormous Arch of Neutrality that soared like a monstrous space rocket over the square. At its apex towered a golden statue of Turkmenbashi. Each day, Leksin had read, the figure turned a full circle with arms spread out to harvest the sun. Enclosed by official buildings clad in white marble and topped with golden domes, this central plaza was lined with ranks of firs and plane trees. It seemed to Leksin to have the appearance of a parade ground, at once immaculate and sterile. Militia clad in dull grey uniforms stood on every corner.

As the taxi lurched forward across the square, Leksin felt the lack of sleep catching up with him. He was due to have lunch with Max Usenko in a little over an hour. At least, that should be enough time to stop off at the hotel and sort himself out.

Chapter Nineteen

Ashgabat, Turkmenistan

The security guard directed Leksin's taxi from the covered forecourt to the rear of the building. Rounding the corner, they pulled up at a flight of marble steps. As the driver opened the door, Leksin's head pounded to the beat of traditional pipes, and he noticed how the men who grasped them sweated profusely to blow the long, resounding notes on the instruments as tall as themselves. He cast a quizzical look at Max as he came forward.

"The Minister of Energy's joining us for lunch, thought we'd put on a bit of a show," Max explained. "Ah, here he comes."

Leksin turned to watch the approach of a white Toyota, stretched three times its normal size. As the Minister stepped out, he was met by a girl in a scintillating tunic of multi-coloured local Khan-Atlas silk shot through with gold, wearing an intricately embroidered skullcap as bright as her smile.

"*Assalom alaykum,*" she murmured. May peace be with you.

She offered him a tray of round naan bread, a small blue bowl of salt to one side, before turning to Leksin. He broke off a piece of naan, dipped it in the salt, tasted it, and nodded appreciatively.

Max introduced the two men.

"I'd been hoping to have a chance to meet with you," Leksin greeted him.

"Then let us make the most of the opportunity," the minister replied formally. "Come."

Taking Leksin's arm, he ushered him up the shallow steps skirting a wide arched entrance. Colonnades of intricately carved wooden pillars, curved like elongated pine cones, supported upper and lower verandas. The walls of the house were white, dappled with honey-coloured bricks laid in complex relief patterns.

Inside, they sat down on embroidered silk cushions around a low table. A young woman poured tea into a delicate bowl and handed it to Leksin. Max gestured towards the table, piled high with platters of fruit nestling between patterned bowls filled with salads and meats spiced in the local style. "Please help yourself, Minister."

Reaching for a slice of water melon, the minister gave Leksin an apologetic look. "Forgive this hurried meeting, but our President has decreed this day as one that all government workers should spend planting trees. Alas, this extends to his Cabinet too. It is good to have an excuse to put down my shovel." A wry smile, then he asked: "So how can I help you?"

Leksin started slowly, following an established pattern. Some general questions about the Turkmen business environment, allowing the minister time to make his points, testing his answers against the picture he'd compiled in Moscow. So far, so good.

Max waved a limp hand to show his impatience. "Alex, I can't see where this is leading," he interrupted, his tone dead calm. "After all, you're here to destroy the oil pipeline deal, aren't you?"

With a reproving smile, then a slight shake of his head, Leksin corrected him: "On the contrary, Max, the pipeline is potentially an excellent deal for both Russia and Turkmenistan." He addressed the minister. "Our President very much wants the project to progress, but needs to ensure all the ramifications are fully understood."

The minister opened his hands. "And how can I help him gain such understanding?" he queried. "We are most grateful to your Prime Minister and Chestny Kombinat for advancing this project."

"I'm sure," Leksin agreed, but recalling something he'd read in the library in Moscow, he asked: "But isn't a key objective of your energy policy to reduce your reliance on Russia?"

"Point taken. Beggars, though, can't be choosers. We'll need the pipeline for our own Caspian oil once it comes on stream and, from where I stand, it's only the Russians who can deliver on the project." He paused. "No one else expressed an interest in taking part."

"So I believe," Leksin said, moving to the heart of the matter. "My understanding is that the issue of the pipeline's security in Afghanistan frightened off other potential participants. Max tells me this aspect is under control. I'd like to hear your view."

The minister threw a quick glance at Max then, clasping his hands together, replied: "It may be difficult for an outsider like yourself to understand, Mr Leksin, but our relationship with Afghanistan is different from that of other countries. Afghanistan's our neighbour." He paused to let his words sink in. "Of course, like all neighbours we have the occasional disagreement, but on the whole it's in both our interests to get on. There are a surprising number of areas where we work together towards our mutual interests."

"Including the pipeline?"

"Exactly. As I've mentioned, we'll need it for our own oil in due course. As for Afghanistan, the country's impoverished – it needs not just the money the pipeline will bring in, but also the ability to trade with its close neighbour." The Minister reached across for a handful of walnuts and paused while he cracked one. "I went to Kabul myself with Lev Usenko, Max's father, to negotiate with the authorities there. Lev agreed a form of profit sharing with them, and the terms were subsequently incorporated into a series of bilateral trade agreements that I signed on behalf of the Turkmen government."

Leksin nodded to show this was in line with his understanding. To the extent possible, though, he'd like to check for himself that the arrangements were watertight. After all, given how vulnerable the pipeline would be to just one isolated terrorist incident, this was a key issue. "I'd like to have sight of these treaties, if I may."

The Minister spread open his hands apologetically. "I regret not, Mr Leksin. The documents are in our archives and subject to our strict State secrecy restrictions. But rest assured, the Afghans are as committed to securing pipeline as we are. I met with one of their representatives just recently to run through the detail."

It was a disappointing answer, but, in the context of the political environment in this part of the world, not a surprise. A remnant of the Soviet past, the concept of state secrecy was, at best, widely defined and, at worst, extreme in the restrictions it imposed. Leksin moved on to his next point.

"Did you ever consider building the pipeline yourselves without Russia or anyone else?"

"We appreciate Russia's help in this matter," the minister replied, parrying the question. "Chestny Kombinat has been a major force in Turkmenistan for many years, and we regard the company as our friend. We will do all that is necessary to protect our friends."

His message delivered, the minister rose from the table. "And now, I regret, I must plant some more trees."

Max and Leksin escorted him to his car.

"A word of warning," the minister said as he shook Leksin's hand. "Despite our government's best efforts, Turkmenistan remains very backward in many ways, not a forgiving place for foreigners. Especially Russians these days, alas. Some things perhaps are better left alone, I'm sure you understand."

*

Back in his hotel, Leksin flipped open his laptop, plugged in his Thuraya satellite phone and logged on to his Moscow server. Laptops were vulnerable, experience had taught him, too easily hacked or stolen; it was best to keep as little as possible on the hard disk. Quickly he input his notes.

Lunch with the minister had yielded no surprises. Keen that the project should succeed, he'd been on the defensive from the outset. The scarcely disguised threat on parting had been inevitable. Such warnings were an occupational hazard, Leksin knew only too well. His fee was justified only partly by his expertise; the rest was fully attributable to the risk.

After the lunch, he'd asked to meet the Kombinat's country head, a man called Adam Smolinsky, only to be informed that he'd been sacked the previous day. "Not up to the job and bit of a problem," Max had explained, swaying his fingers to suggest the man liked more than a tipple. A coincidence? Leksin didn't believe in those. He made a note to follow up.

The team responsible for the pipeline project's planning and budgeting were, Max told him, based in Tejen, a town about an hour's drive from Ashgabat. Less convenient but more secure, Max had explained, well away from prying eyes. At Leksin's insistence, Max had arranged for a driver to take him there in the morning.

Feeling suddenly exhausted after his disturbed night of travelling, Leksin lay down on the bed and flicked through the complimentary local newspaper. A famous Turkmen philosopher had just been sentenced to death in some Iranian fatwa for supposedly implying that their version of Islam was opportunistic and corrupt. In this part of the world, Leksin reflected, the Middle Ages still rolled on. Like the white marble superimposed on Ashgabat's decrepit Soviet buildings, civilisation here was just a facade, a cosmetic veneer. You had to dig deeper to find the pulse.

Chapter Twenty

Ashgabat, Turkmenistan

Tejen, Heart of Turkmen Cotton, announced the elaborate banner that spanned the road between two skewed poles painted a bright but flaking blue. After 100 kilometres travelling east out of Ashgabat, bumping along the dusty, potholed road that bordered the Karakum Canal, Leksin was glad they'd arrived. But the place looked a dump. A former behemoth of the Soviet cotton industry, all that remained were derelict factories rimmed with rusting machinery.

As they entered the town, Leksin stared from the window at the men who hung around listlessly on the pavements, alone or in groups. Young or old, their faces bore the blank expression of those with nothing to do. Outside an abandoned cinema, fading posters peeling from its walls, two dogs humped, their tongues lolling in the heat. A band of disaffected youths cheered on the only action in town.

Beyond a power station, he caught sight of his destination for the first time. The area in front of Chestny Kombinat's office was crammed with demonstrators. From what he could hear, their chants were voicing the anti-Russian sentiment about which he'd been repeatedly warned. As the car drew closer to the main entrance, they faced a barrage of insults and, when the gates swung open, the beleaguered security guards had difficulty clearing a path through.

The car pulled up in the forecourt. Leksin got out, and a bald, pot-bellied man waddled over to meet him. "Mr Leksin?" he shouted, hitching his trousers over his paunch. "I'm Kodir, head of the pipeline project team. I'm sorry about the welcoming committee." He signalled towards the demonstrators. "There's a lot of anti-Russian feeling in the country at the moment. We just have to live with it."

*

Sealed off from the unrest outside, Leksin spent the rest of the day with Kodir and his team, working his way methodically through the project plans and budgets. Having neither time nor inclination to check the detail, he'd concentrated on the big picture. Did the project make sense as it was currently designed? Were the assumptions on which it was based reasonable? Had the principal risks been identified and evaluated?

In general, he'd been impressed by what he'd found. Based on the figures presented to him, the pipeline would prove to be a massive cash cow for decades, even assuming Saidov and his Turkmen counterparts took a decent slice for their part in guiding the project through – an inevitable facet of business in Central Asia. In particular, it would be a game changer for Chestny Kombinat.

Kodir had brought out a file of detailed pipeline design drawings, then at Leksin's request explained in layman's language the basis of route selection and hydraulic and mechanical design. The line pipe selected was the type most commonly used for cross-country pipelines, API 5L. For the most part, it would run underground at a minimum depth of one metre. At regular intervals along the way there'd be pump stations to boost pressure and valves to allow sections of the pipeline to be isolated if there was a leak.

In Afghanistan, Kodir had mentioned, the difficult geography meant that large stretches of the pipeline would have to run overground, but there was no way around this. Leksin had taken the opportunity to question him on the pipeline's security as it transited that country, but clearly the negotiations on this matter were outside Kodir's pay grade. Interestingly, he'd mentioned that Afghan geologists had done the route mapping there, and the current plan was to use local Afghan labour to lay the actual pipeline. Other than that, he'd nothing new to add on the matter, other than to confirm that, right from the time he started working on the project, he'd been assured that security was not an issue. To be honest, Leksin reflected, he might well be right. Max, and then the Minister, had outlined details of the arrangements, and these seemed plausible enough under the circumstances. Nonetheless, he'd have preferred to have had the chance to review the relevant treaties himself, just to make sure.

His thoughts were interrupted by Kodir's return. Out of breath, his face dripping with sweat, he patted his pockets for a handkerchief before passing over a folder.

"As I say, Mr Leksin, security prohibits me letting you take any budgets or plans out of the building," he puffed. "But you'll find the other stuff you asked for in the folder."

Leksin emptied the contents on the table. Picking up a map, he unfolded it, then spread it out.

"It's the proposed route of the pipeline through Turkmenistan," Kodir informed him. "The despatch terminal's close to the Caspian, linking up with both the Caspian oil fields and an undersea pipeline running down from Russia. It goes inland across the Karakum desert – the symbols indicate the location of pump stations and valves – then heads south to skirt the Garabil Plateau before entering Afghanistan."

Leksin traced the route with his finger, then nodded his understanding. Pulling out a second map, he asked: "And this one?"

"That shows all Chestny Kombinat's locations in Turkmenistan," Kodir explained. "Mind you, I'm not sure why you want it, it doesn't really tell you much."

"You're probably right," Leksin agreed, non-committal. Shuffling the papers back into the folder, he stood up. "Now, I'm afraid, I'd better head back to town."

*

As they came out onto the forecourt, the roar from the protesters caught Leksin unprepared. Weighing them up through the railings, he could see their numbers had at least doubled during the day. Glued together in one heaving mass, their placards jabbed the cloud of dust that hovered above them, rising and falling in time with their chant. The message on them was clear.

'Russians go home.'

'Kremlin is evil.'

'Save us from the Russian oppressor.'

"Is there another way out?" Leksin asked.

"'Fraid not," Kodir replied placidly. "But don't worry, they're harmless. The driver'll get you past."

Opening the car door, he instructed the driver to take Leksin back to Ashgabat.

"Goodbye. Let me know if there's anything more I can do."

From the rear seat, Leksin watched him retreat into the shadows as the car pulled away. The gates opened and the clamour intensified. As they edged slowly forward, the protestors blocking their path were shunted aside. Suddenly a whistle blew and the mob lunged forward, hemming in the car, crashing their placards against the exposed bodywork. On either side, the doors rattled as hands tried to force them open. In front, angry faces pressed against the windscreen and screamed obscenities.

The car's engine cut out.

"Back up!" Leksin yelled at the driver. "Reverse through the gates!"

The man sat still.

A metal bar smashed through the rear passenger window, spraying glass over the back seat. An arm reached in to pull up the lock and the door swung open. A bearded assailant leaned into the car. Built like a sumo wrestler, forearms as broad as most men's thighs, he wrapped his massive fingers around Leksin's arm.

"You're coming with us," he shouted, tugging hard.

Leksin swivelled in his seat and cracked his fist into the man's face, breaking his nose. With a loud grunt, the man tightened his grip and hauled Leksin towards him. Leksin struck out with his foot, but with little room to manoeuvre, his kick lacked force. As he felt his body slide inexorably towards the door, the man emitted a shriek and let go. Behind him Leksin glimpsed a thickset figure, one hand with a chokehold on his attacker's neck, the other clamped on his groin. Yanking him backwards, the newcomer rammed a knee into his face, then jumped into the car.

"Get going!" he barked, holding a gun to the driver's head. "Run over any shit who gets in the way!"

The driver hastily switched on the ignition and slammed his foot on the accelerator. The car lurched forward, bouncing over those in its path as if they were speed bumps. As it sped away, Leksin looked back and saw the injured spreadeagled in their wake. He glanced back through the railings into the forecourt. The round figure of Kodir still hovered in the background, pensively drawing on a cigarette.

Leksin turned to inspect the craggy face of his rescuer.

"Name's Talgat," the man said, hardly out of breath. "Nikolai Koriakov asked me to keep an eye on you."

Chapter Twenty-One

Tashkent, Uzbekistan

Stas lay on the bed, stripped naked and bored stiff. The vague breeze from the shoddy plastic fan scarcely stirred the heavy midday heat, and had no effect on the thin layer of sweat that covered his body. God, he hated this place, the stifling atmosphere, the permanent haze of insects, the decayed squalor of the village in which they lived. How could he not resent Nadia when, even with the constant demand for their services, she seemed determined to deny him any role in the action? She kept herself busy, of course, and her work got her out of here. Unlike him. He felt doomed to waste away in this hell hole without any chance of escape.

Propping himself up on one elbow, he flicked through the channels on the television at the end of the bed. Given her need to monitor events in the outside world, particularly in Russia, Nadia had permitted a satellite dish. Tucked away in an angled alcove between the chimney and the eaves of the rickety attic, it was well hidden and provided Stas's only respite. Some quiz show flashed up on the screen and held his attention. As the contestants flummoxed question after question, Stas bellowed the answers. He let out a frustrated sigh. Could people really be that thick?

As the credits rolled, he reached for a paperback beside the bed – a biography of Pushkin that Nadia had recently picked up for him second-hand in Tashkent – and started to read.

The buzz of his phone jolted him from Pushkin's cool St Petersburg canal-side mansions. He immediately realised it had come through on the mobile they specifically reserved for business. He recognised the voice.

"Nadia's out at the moment," he said. "Give me the details."

He scribbled fast as the caller methodically recited his

requirements.

"I've got that," Stas stated at last. "The escape route?"

He listened to the reply, writing down the answer.

"And timing?" he asked finally. "That's a bit tight . . . No, no, we'll manage."

The line went dead. Pouring himself a beer, Stas felt more alive than he had since they'd come to this shithole. He sat on the edge of the bed and ran through the conversation in his mind. So Nadia's boss had a new job for them, and this time it was right up his street. He glanced up at the wall clock: Nadia wouldn't be back for at least two hours. That should give him time to get things up and running, take over and own it as *his* assignment.

Sliding the bed to one side, he lifted a loose floorboard, then extracted a small brown notebook from the gap underneath. He flicked through, noting down the contact details of those of their former cell who'd survived the debacle in northern Siberia. This mission was going to require a team of professionals, and who better than those with whom he'd worked and trained in the past? He would trust them with his life.

One by one, he called them, explaining the objectives in detail, the composition of the team and, of course, the financial arrangement. No one refused.

All he had to do now was to convince Nadia to let him run with it.

Chapter Twenty-Two

Tashkent, Uzbekistan

"You can't accept a job without my permission, you know the rules," Nadia rebuked Stas. Her manner was disapproving, an irritated mother telling off a wayward child. "No way we can do what he wants, I'm sure you realised that the moment he called."

"*You* don't have to do anything," Stas corrected defiantly. "This one's mine, nothing to do with you."

"Stas, it's far too dangerous." She shook her head in frustration. "We've no obligation to take it on, it's way outside the deal."

Stas ran his hand through the day-old stubble on his chin. "Well, it's all planned," he asserted with an air of finality. "I've already assembled the team, they're all set to go."

"Then you'll just have to un-assemble them. It's not happening." Her voice was now hard and belligerent, and her eyes flashed with resolve.

"It's not, eh? So what would you rather I do, Nadia?" Stas rejoined with sudden aggression. "Hang around in this dump, waiting to screw you whenever you feel the need? I didn't spend years training just to end up as your toyboy."

Nadia fixed him in an incensed stare. For a moment her wide green eyes bore into him, disconcerted by his bluntness, and Stas drew back as if she'd strike.

"Fuck you, Stas! One thing those years of training should have taught you is obedience," she let fly through clenched teeth. "You're not taking this job, that's an order." She rubbed her hands together as if she was brushing off sand. "Ring him now and put an end it," she ordered as she turned towards the bathroom and ran the shower.

Some moments later, she felt Stas's hands rest lightly on her naked shoulder, and she moved away. "It's alright, I've told him," he said, as his hands pursued her, running slowly around her body. Gently he twisted her towards him. Kissing her lightly, he took her hand.

"Come to bed," he whispered, and she followed.

Chapter Twenty-Three

Moscow, Russia

Max glanced at his Rolex. Already 5.30pm. At least an hour from the airport into town at this time of day, he still had to collect the tickets before meeting Pasha on the steps of the Bolshoi. At this rate he'd be lucky to make the start of the ballet. He rapped the driver's shoulder.

"Hurry up, man. Get a move on!"

He sat back in the seat and took a long breath. Calm down, Max, nothing to be done about the situation. Closing his eyes, he settled back against the cushioned leather and reflected on the events of his trip to Ashgabat.

*

Things had not gone according to plan. Leksin was like teflon: danger just seemed to rub off him. Twice now plans to end his interference had been thwarted.

When Leksin had first turned up at the company's Ashgabat headquarters, Max had managed to distract him with lunch with the minister, who'd said all the right things. Later, Leksin had asked to meet Smolinsky, the former head of operations. Thankfully, Max congratulated himself, he'd foreseen this eventuality and got rid of Smolinsky the previous day - before Leksin could get to him. Not before time too, he suspected.

But when Max had put a call through just now, shortly after landing, he'd discovered that Leksin's visit to Tejen had proved a different story. As arranged, Kodir had taken Leksin through the plans and budgets. No problem there. Then, at Leksin's request, he'd been provided with two further documents. The first was a map of Chestny Kombinat's operations in Turkmenistan, unabridged courtesy of Kodir's stupidity. Why did Leksin want it? Was he just fishing, or was he looking for something in particular? The second was a map of the pipeline's proposed route through Turkmenistan. Interesting. Which direction would his enquiry take next?

Afterwards, the stage-managed demonstration had failed to achieve its objective. If he'd got the gist of Kodir's stutters, some stranger had appeared from nowhere and intervened, compelling the driver to move on and force a path through the protestors. Unfortunately, yet again, Leksin had escaped unscathed.

Max opened his eyes and focussed. One thing was certain: Leksin had to be stopped. The man might encapsulate everything Max disliked, but there was no doubting his ability. Like a hunting dog, he had an unerring nose. Too dangerous to leave him at large. Lighting up a Black Russian, Max let the smoke escape slowly through his lips. Borzov had better make a better fist of it next time. The issue needed to be quickly resolved.

Chapter Twenty-Four

Moscow, Russia

Volodya stuck his head around the door and, beckoning him into her office, Vika pointed to a chair. She flashed him a smile as she continued her phone call.

The two of them had first met at university. The grandson of a Korean family resettled to Kazakhstan during the Great Patriotic War, St Petersburg had been a long way from home and he'd missed his family desperately. Vika had taken him under her wing and they'd grown close. Two years into his course, Volodya's father had needed the sort of operation to save his life only available to people like her, the New Rich. Vika had pulled strings: the father had been whisked up to Moscow, cared for in the Kremlin's own hospital, and recovered. Since then, she knew, there was nothing he wouldn't do for her.

Volodya was a computer geek. Awarded a Red Diploma, Russia's top degree, in computer science and communications, he'd been snapped up by a US financial services company in St Petersburg. A few years after graduating, Vika's father had put her in charge of their own operations in St Petersburg, where she'd thrived amongst her close college friends, overhauling the local business. One of her first moves had been to recruit Volodya to update the IT systems. He'd exceeded even her expectations, so when Vika's father had recalled her to Moscow to join the main Board, she'd had no difficulty in persuading him that Volodya should come too.

When her own father died unexpectedly not long after her accident, she wasn't up to assuming her new role as Chairman of Chestny Kombinat. Reluctantly she'd had no choice but to leave much of the day-to-day management to Max. By this time, Volodya had already been put in charge of IT for the entire operation, so she'd asked him to be her eyes and ears. He had his own ways of monitoring remotely the directors' meetings and emails, including her brother's. It had taken a few months for her to rebuild her own physical resources so that she could take a fully active role herself, and during this period Volodya had been her principal source of information. With Max going out of his way to keep her in the dark, she'd never have managed without him.

Slipping the phone into its cradle, Vika glanced at her desk clock. Quarter past six. Tonight was a gala ballet at the Bolshoi to be attended by President Karpev and his new girlfriend. All the company's senior executives were going, so they'd have left by now. The two of them should have the place to themselves.

"Ready?" she asked, meeting her friend's eyes. "Let's go."

*

As expected, the corridor outside Max's office was deserted. Vika dangled a bunch of keys.

"These were my father's," she explained to Volodya. "He never really trusted his directors, so he kept a set of spares to all their offices."

The keys were unlabelled. She tried several before one turned in the lock. They slipped in, locking the door behind them.

Vika wrinkled her nose at the waft of stale tobacco and aftershave, which was in marked contrast to the room's otherwise sterile atmosphere. Everything in its place, and a place for everything. It had always needled her, her brother's compulsion for neatness, unchanged since his childhood. Prissy in the extreme.

"OK, the computer's yours. I'll start on the filing cabinets."

Volodya tapped in Max's network password, then his fingers darted over the keyboard as he programmed a subroutine to copy emails, both sent and received, to a separate address he'd set up on the network. He sent a brief test message to confirm it. Next, he opened the hard disk's directory and scanned through.

Vika rifled through the wall cabinets, looking for anything

relating to the pipeline. With Leksin now on the case, she had to discover whether Max was hiding something from her and, if so, what. Along with the project's magnitude as a potential coup for the company came extreme political sensitivity. Any hint of impropriety could cause irreparable damage. Karpev was well known for the disdain he extended towards oligarchs – since her father's death, she was counted as one of them – and he would take advantage of any sign of weakness to topple their business empires. Two of her late father's closest associates had fallen prey to this strategy: one still languished after ten years in a Siberian jail, the other had fled the country and died in exile. Whatever it took, she had to protect Chestny Kombinat from a similar onslaught.

Like everything else, the cabinet drawers were tidy, orderly and well-organised – but absolutely nothing there about the pipeline. "The cupboard's bare," she told Volodya, frowning.

"Same here, Vika," Volodya replied, getting up from the computer.

Vika took Volodya's place at Max's desk. Moving aside an envelope marked for Max's attention, she rummaged through the drawers, pulling out their contents to flick through them. Again, nothing. She replaced them as she'd found them.

About to give up, she spotted a low filing cabinet tucked into one corner. She'd never noticed it before. She tried her father's keys, but none fit – it must be new. Fetching a paper clip from the desk, she unfolded it to fiddle with the lock, finally eliciting a click. A useful trick her ex-fiancé had once shown her, she explained to Volodya who watched in amusement. Pulling open the top drawer, her mouth tightened when she found its stash of gay porn. Slamming the drawer shut, she caught Volodya's eye and they gave each other a knowing look. Gay was one thing; Max was another, and neither of them harboured any illusions about his real depravities. She opened the second drawer. More of the same. Another blind alley.

In the silence they heard the lift doors ping open. The two of them waited motionlessly until it became clear the footsteps in the corridor were heading their way. Vika pointed urgently towards Max's private cloakroom. They scrambled across the room, shutting the door behind them just as a key turned in the lock. Holding their breath in the darkness, they heard someone cross to the desk. The footsteps started back towards the door, then paused. Instinctively Vika shrank back into Volodya. It seemed an age before the footsteps continued and the door clicked shut. Vika let out a long sigh of relief. She hadn't reckoned on Max returning from Ashgabat so soon.

*

He'd stopped off at his office to pick up the Bolshoi tickets and found the lower drawer of the new filing cabinet a fraction out of line. But his was the only key. Something felt wrong, so he'd made for the stairwell across the corridor and waited in the darkness.

It hadn't been long before Volodya emerged, closely followed by Vika. To be honest, he wasn't surprised: Vika had always been an interfering bitch, for ever poking her nose where it wasn't wanted. So what was she after this time? And Volodya too, as usual in on the game and on her side.

Well, whatever their purpose – and he could guess – they'd been wasting their time. There was nothing in his office relevant to the project. Same with his computer. Emails had always been kept to a minimum, and the few there were utilised a private account. If, as Hemingway said, the best way to find out if you can trust somebody is to trust them, then he preferred just not to risk it.

Chapter Twenty-Five

Moscow, Russia

The man patrolling the perimeter with two leashed Dobermanns waited as Vika's car approached. Shielding his eyes from the late morning sun, he waved when he spotted Vika seated next to the driver. The electric gates rolled open, and the car drew up in front of the house. A vast red-brick pile of ugly design and awkward angles, two turrets tacked on each end, her father had commissioned it in the late 90s as a mark of his new money and status. Vika hated it. Many times she'd vowed to find somewhere else. She would too – when time allowed.

Sergei, her five year old half-brother, was splashing about with his English nanny in the pool in the centre of the lush green lawn. He climbed out as soon as he saw her and came dashing across, dripping wet. "Vika, Vika, you're home early."

She hugged him gingerly as his nanny swooped on him with a towel. "I've got a surprise," she chanted, in that tone parents reserve for announcing treats. "We're going away for a few days."

"Where? Tell me."

"It isn't a surprise if I tell you, is it?" she teased. "Now go with Jenny and pack some things. Hurry up, I want to leave in half-an-hour."

As they set off, Vika felt the familiar ache in her leg that, since her accident, nagged her whenever she felt stressed. It was a long shot, she knew, but somehow she had to persuade Olga, her father's ex-mistress, to help her see the whole picture. Max was keeping something from her, that was certain now. The pipeline was by far and away his largest project, and it was inconceivable that they should have found nothing connected to project in his office unless he was purposely keeping anything associated with it off-site, something he'd only do if there were aspects he wanted to keep secret. There was a piece of the puzzle without which she could never make sense of the whole, and she was pretty sure Olga held it. During their time together Vika had often envied Olga's closeness to her father and the lack of secrets between them.

One problem, though: Vika could be certain of a hostile reception. With a single exception, Olga had no call to love the Usenko's. A one-night stand one drunken night after a row and Lev had kicked her out without a word, refusing her any further access to Sergei. Vika had fought hard against this at the time - it wasn't right to separate the boy from his mother - but her father had been adamant. Vika had kept on at him until the double blow of her accident and his death, after which she herself had depended on Sergei's company and affection to help her through the resulting trauma. Under the circumstances, perhaps Olga had a point: even if there were excuses, Vika had, like her father, deprived Olga of her son. Now Sergei was all Vika had to bargain with. In any case, whatever the outcome, it was time to right the wrong.

As the Volvo S80 nosed through the crowds around Danilovsky Market, her driver swapped curses with a gnarled babushka who'd taken the early train to Moscow to sell raspberries from her dacha. She stood her ground, determined not to give an inch to some fancy foreign car.

Vika slid down her window. "Here, let me buy them from you," she called out, as exhaust fumes flooded in. "They look delicious." She held out a wad of rouble notes.

The old woman snatched the money, and her complaints turned to blessings when she saw how much. Quickly she passed Vika the cartons of fruit, then stepping clear, made the sign of the cross.

The car moved on. When it reached the dual carriageway, it started to pick up speed. Sergei leaned his head against Vika's shoulder, and she ruffled his hair absently, trying to dispel memories that were never far from the surface.

*

She opened her eyes and there was her father sitting by her bed. It was as if she were looking down a tunnel, with his image clear in the centre but the edges blurred. He rested his hand on her arm and spoke, but the sounds only echoed, making no sense. He disappeared and Alex took his place, a bandage around one arm. He too spoke words she couldn't understand.

She tried to turn over, but couldn't. In panic she looked towards Alex for help. He stroked her hair back.

"You're all right, Vika." Each word came separately. She had to concentrate to string them together. "There's nothing to worry about."

But there was, wasn't there? Where was she? What was she doing here? Her head seethed with the struggle to remember. The brakes . . . she'd slammed them down . . . nothing had happened. The car was spinning round and spinning round, then . . . What came then?

Alex was hurt, she could see that. "Are you OK?" she whispered.

"I'm fine. Don't speak, you should rest."

"I should've let you drive."

Her father came back into view. "How is she, Alex?" His voice was a growl of concern, but his eyes held a rage she couldn't place.

Alex's hand closed around hers. "She's fine."

The two men sat in silence watching her. She tried to pull herself upright, but couldn't move. Her leg ached.

"What am I doing here?" Her throat felt scoured with sandpaper.

"You had an accident. You were injured. You're in hospital."

"What have I done?"

"Rest now, Vika."

Fuck, what have I done? Why won't they tell me? "Help me up, Alex."

"Better to lie still, Vika."

She searched Alex's face for a comfort she could not find. His eyes wouldn't quite meet hers.

"Help me. Why won't either of you help me up?" She was angry now.

The two men raised her just enough to look around the room. On one side of the bed, there were wires and machines with lights that flashed and jumped. Lower down, a frame over her legs held off the bedclothes. A harness dangled from the ceiling. What had she done?

She caught sight of Max for the first time, sitting alone in the corner, silently watching. There was something strange about his expression.

She tugged the sheet until it fell away. Then she shut her eyes. Oh no, not that. Please God, she didn't deserve that.

*

"Are we there?" Sergei asked, pulling at Vika's sleeve as they turned into a quiet road lined with trees that partially screened the rows of grey apartment blocks on either side.

Vika's eyes flew open, her senses overloaded by the memory of that moment of realisation in the hospital. Her leg ached, a ghost of the agony then. She forced herself back to the present as the car slowly rolled past the identical entrances before pulling up in front of Entrance 23B, and she squeezed Sergei's arm affectionately. Such a warm and open-hearted boy. So unlike Max.

"Yes, darling. Now stay here while I pop inside," she said as the driver opened her door. "You'll get your surprise very soon."

Chapter Twenty-Six

Moscow, Russia

The cramped apartment with its brown furniture and worn upholstery was far removed from Vika's Moscow and added to her sense of unease. The low ceiling brooded over her as she perched on the edge of an armchair and stared at the framed photo of Sergei on the wall. A small gilded icon of the Vladimir Virgin hung just underneath.

Olga emerged from the kitchen. She was thinner, fine lines shadowed her eyes and mouth, but the familiar elegance was still there, at odds with her surroundings.

"Still take it black?" she asked, handing one of the two cups she carried to Vika.

Vika nodded.

Olga sat down opposite her. "Forgive me, Vika, if I'm doing you an injustice," she began, making no effort to conceal the bitterness in her voice. "But given that I haven't heard from you since your father kicked me out, I'm assuming you want something."

Accepting Olga's directness as more than fair, Vika gave a half-apologetic smile as she considered her response. To be honest, she was fishing, not entirely sure for what she was looking, certain that she'd recognise it when she found it. Her understanding of the circumstances surrounding the Kombinat's initial involvement with the pipeline project was scant, to say the least. For some reason her father had never discussed it with her. Sometimes it had almost seemed as if he was trying to avoid doing so, and she'd been too wrapped up in Alex at the time to work out why. Now she needed to discover how the company was first brought in, why Saidov approached Max rather than her father in the first instance, how her father had reacted . . . anything, in fact, that might help her get a more accurate picture.

If it came down to the wire, she could of course do a straight trade: Sergei for information. But this really wasn't her preferred route. Until the split, she'd always got on well with Olga, often confiding in the older woman, seeking her advice. Now she sought not confrontation, but information - and, perhaps, reconciliation. She'd much prefer to separate the two matters if possible, although she realised that just for the moment Sergei had to be kept in reserve.

"I'm ashamed to say you're right," Vika admitted at last, feeling her way. "I'd like to ask you about something that happened when you were still with my father."

Olga raised one eyebrow in surprise. She studied her cup silently, turning it in the saucer to one side, then the other, then back again. Finally she looked up and gave a little nod. "What do you want to know?" she asked bleakly.

*

As the lift descended to the ground floor, Vika sorted in her mind through the answers Olga had just given her, trying to make sense of the new information. The timeline of events might still be incomplete, but Olga had undoubtedly filled in some important gaps. Why hadn't her father told Vika himself before he died? Had he held back to protect her? Until today she'd always assumed her father changed his will out of some misplaced feeling of guilt or pity, this was the first time she'd realised he'd done so before, *not* after, the accident. She felt as though a fog had lifted.

The lift slid open, and Vika was suddenly overcome by a sense of panic. Even though, thankfully, she hadn't been forced to use Sergei as a bargaining chip, she was nonetheless on the verge of opening a door no choice of hers could ever close. Her hand moved instinctively to the ache in her leg and she brushed at her trousers with her fingertips as though that would make it better.

With more than her usual limp, she led Olga over to the car.

The driver opened the rear door, and Sergei emerged. He looked at Olga with bemusement for some moments before his eyes lit up, and he threw himself into her arms. A tear rolled down Vika's cheek as she watched the scene. A boy needed his mother, and she couldn't take her place.

Chapter Twenty-Seven

Moscow, Russia

The basement bar of Angels wasn't Max's favourite place: too loud and too garish, useful only for the occasional pick-up. Enclosed in a bubble of Perspex and chrome, the dance floor heaved with sweaty bodies writhing to the music. Around the room, men huddled in pairs, rapt in each other. On a giant screen, silent pictures of President Karpev played out like ancient newsreels. Gleaming and bare-chested, he performed a selection of he-man antics on an endless loop. Despite his regime's homophobic stance, the President himself – with his muscular and often exposed physique – remained an icon within the gay community.

Denis, the fair-haired boy Max had picked up last week, sat with a middle-aged man in a silk shirt at the next table. He looked bored. Catching Max's eye, he gave him an enquiring look. Max shook his head, and the boy pouted.

The music stopped, and Max glanced up expectantly. A loud cheer arose as the DJ announced the evening's main act. Yelena, a lithe young man in perfect make-up and an sequinned dress, took to the stage. Taking the microphone, his husky voice began a classic ballad. Max watched through the blue haze of smoke. There was something about Yelena beyond the beautiful voice that intrigued him. His lips were sensual and inviting, but his eyes seemed vulnerable and wary of pain.

When the performance finished, Max left money on the table, then climbed up the steps to Tverskaya Street, where an open air rock concert was playing in front of the town hall. City elections were coming up, and Moscow's mayor had declared an extra public holiday to rake in some more votes. The heavy beat affronted Max's eardrums as he threaded his way through the massed spectators towards home.

"Don't look back, Max!" He recognised the voice behind him at once and stopped.

"Your young boy told me where you were," the voice continued, then added with a chuckle: "He sounded rather cross with you."

Max lit a Black Russian and said nothing.

"I'm concerned about your sister," the voice declared without further explanation.

"You mean, searching my office?" Max asked, unfazed. "It's under control. She's for ever poking her nose where it's not wanted. But there was nothing there for her to find, I'd made sure of that."

"No, not that," the voice corrected him. "Vika's been to see your father's ex-mistress today. How much does she know?"

Too much, Max suspected, the corners of his mouth drawing down in frustration. Olga and her father had been very close. He couldn't be sure how much he'd have told her, or how much she'd be prepared to share with Vika. But there was a definite risk.

"I'll deal with my sister," he announced calmly. Sucking smoke deep into his lungs, he exhaled slowly. "How did you find out?"

No answer.

Max spun around to find no one there. Some twenty metres away, engulfed by the crowd, he glimpsed the back of a familiar figure.

Chapter Twenty-Eight

Ashgabat, Turkmenistan

"So, nothing so far," Nikolai summed up succinctly once Leksin had finished his update. "I'd been hoping to have some news for Karpev. He's been continually on my back, checking on your progress."

"Tell the President it's early days yet," Leksin said, realising this was cold comfort given how few days were left. "Talgat's organising a helicopter to take me over the pipeline's proposed route across Turkmenistan this afternoon. Perhaps something will come out of that."

"Well, let me know."

"Of course. I'll call you as soon as there's anything." Leksin rang off and moved back to the map spread out on the table.

His eyes traced the pipeline's route across Turkmenistan, but his thoughts were elsewhere. Nikolai was right: progress was nil so far. But what did they expect? Perhaps, in actual fact, there wasn't anything to find – had they thought of that? Was Saidov in fact right, and Karpev's doubts unfounded?

Weighing against this, of course, were the two attempts to choke his investigation – the booby-trap in his flat and the demonstrators in Tejen. These were both real, and they suggested a different conclusion. But even this wasn't certain: they might be no more than Max's spiteful reaction to what he saw as meddling in his business. A bit far-fetched perhaps, but Leksin wouldn't put it past him.

Mechanically he spread a quick line, then turned up the TV volume to catch an interview with the Afghan President, as the coke kicked in. There had indeed been a surge in Taliban activity following the American withdrawal, the man was saying, but

94

these days the army was far better trained and equipped than ever before. He had no doubt they could cope with the Taliban threat. In some areas the army had actually gone onto the offensive in a new 'seek and destroy' strategy.

*

Leksin sat down at a table shaded by an arc of chestnuts in the hotel's poolside restaurant. He'd no idea how long the journey would take – almost certainly, it would be late by the time he got back from his survey of the pipeline route – so it was best to eat while he could. A waiter invited him to survey the platters of skewered meat stacked next to the *mangal*, a trough-like barbecue. As he made his choice, he watched the cook raking red-hot embers from a pile of burning wood into an even layer, then spacing the kebabs at neat intervals over them. A tourist wearing Bermuda shorts, sunglasses and a broad-rimmed straw hat hovered at his side snapping photos before ambling around the pool to take a table on the far side of the terrace.

The bleep of a text message interrupted Leksin as he ate. *Lev Usenko wanted to pull out - pipeline flawed.* Instinctively he looked around the restaurant, but there was no likely source. Only the lone tourist, a group of Japanese women, the waiter and the barbecue man remained. He tapped a reply: *Who r u?* A minute later, another bleep: *Here 2 help.*

Leksin ran his fingers through his hair. Who'd sent this message? Not Nikolai. Nor Talgat. Neither required anonymity. An employee with a grudge? Possible, he supposed, especially given that Vika had sacked a number of Lev's cronies. It wouldn't be the first time he'd been helped by a tip off.

Wanted to pull out. Everything pointed to the deal being a game changer for Chestny Kombinat - its potential profitability was staggering. Lev Usenko had never been one to look a gift horse in the mouth, so why would he have wanted to pull out? *Pipeline flawed.* But in what way? After all, it had been Lev himself who'd met with the Afghan authorities to broker the deal that guaranteed the pipeline's security. What had he subsequently discovered that made him change his mind?

Leksin was still struggling to make sense of the message when the icon in the top corner of his screen started to flicker. Damn, the battery was running out, he'd meant to charge it last night. He'd better go back to his room and plug the phone in.

Catching the waiter's eye, he made a sign for his bill. As he was signing it, someone called his name, and his head snatched up to find Talgat.

"Come on, Alex," he urged. "We need to get going."

*

From his table on the far side of the terrace, Borzov, in his over-the-top tourist get-up, looked up from *America Today* and watched the two men depart.

He tapped a number into his mobile. "They're on their way," he announced softly.

Chapter Twenty-Nine

Karakum Desert, Turkmenistan

As they set off from the hotel, Talgat's phone rang, and he depressed the switch on the Bluetooth hands-free speaker. The caller was his normal helicopter pilot. They'd met some years ago and quickly developed a good understanding, since when Talgat had relied on him whenever he needed to get somewhere fast, no questions asked.

"I'm at the hospital, my wife's had an accident," the man explained hurriedly. "My cousin, Safir, will take my place today."

He rang off abruptly.

Talgat threw Leksin an uneasy glance. "I'm not sure about this, Alex. This is sensitive stuff we're doing, and I've no idea how reliable this Safir is."

Leksin hesitated, weighing up the options, before finally making the call. "We have to get on with it, Talgat, and there's a lot to cover before it gets too dark. I can't see we have much choice."

Talgat shrugged, but continued to look doubtful as he drove out of the city.

*

Encircled by a framework of barbed wire and derelict watchtowers, the military airport was situated to the southwest of Ashgabat on the edge of the Kopet Dag mountains that formed the border with Iran. Next to it lay a smaller, fenced-off compound from which *Transporta Airways* operated its private helicopter charter company, mainly serving the Caspian oil rigs.

As their car pulled up outside the hanger, a lumbering figure with receding grizzled hair and grease-stained overalls emerged.

He wiped his hands with a cloth as he approached.

"I'm Safir," he explained. "Everything's ready. Let's get going."

The helicopter circled over the patchwork of wind-blown ruins that was all that remained of Nissa, the ancient capital of the Parthians, and banked eastwards along the path of the mountains. To their left, the Karakum canal stretched into the distance, a boundary between the mountains and the edge of the desert. Fifteen minutes later they circled over the border settlement of Tagtabazar.

"That's Afghanistan over there," Talgat told Leksin, pointing south. "This is where the pipeline will cross over." He paused to give Leksin a chance to take it all in, then continued: "It's not safe for us to stray over the border unannounced, so we'll follow the proposed route back from here to the Caspian."

Heading north, the helicopter swept through a steep valley separating the crest of Kopet Dag from the Garibil Plateau. As they emerged over flat ground, the Karakum desert unfolded before them, the air pulsating in the heat as if it were alive. Splintered and fierce, the landscape was nothing like the glistening sandy deserts Leksin had seen portrayed in the cinema. By contrast, it was desolate and dark. *Kara* was black in Turkmen and *Kum* meant sand: this desert took its name from the layers of dark saxaul and tree-like juzgun bushes that extended their sun-parched branches over the sand.

As Safir soared low over the wilderness, a movement caught Leksin's eye. "What's that?" he shouted to Talgat, pointing below.

Talgat examined the ground, taking a while to pick out the reptile. "Ah, that. Locals call them *zemzens*. Caspian monitor. You only find them here, though they're a distant relation to the komodo dragon. They're shy, rare to come across one at all, but just like the dragon, be wary if you do. The bastards move at a hell of a pace – jaws like dinosaurs, you're in real shit if they sink their teeth into you."

Leksin watched the creature veer away, then turned to inspect the map Kodir had given Leksin, that was now spread across

Talgat's knees.

"We're here at the moment," Talgat said, tracing with his finger. "The pipeline'll stretch north away from the canal, then in about five minutes it'll turn west to the Caspian."

Leksin stared from the window as the helicopter skimmed the desert floor, unsure what he was looking for. In Moscow, then once again in Tejen, attempts had been made to put an end to his involvement, but what were they afraid he might find? To be honest, he was fumbling in the dark at the moment. He found the sensation unsettling. For the time being, though, he had no choice but to follow a methodical approach – review plans and budgets, check out the pipeline's proposed route, talk to key people and see where it led. Hopefully somewhere along the way, he'd come across a chink of light which would lead him forward.

Talgat interrupted his thoughts. "That's the Door to Hell." He pointed towards a giant fiery crater to their right, spewing smoke and flames. "About forty years ago the ground below a drilling rig collapsed, ripping the top off a cavern full of poisonous gas. The geologists had the bright idea to burn it off. They thought it would peter out after a few weeks, but it's still burning."

As the crater disappeared from view, they continued over white salt marshes that smudged the ochre of the dunes. Leksin watched with fascination as a herd of double-humped Bactrian camels scattered, startled by the helicopter, their long legs wavering in the heat haze.

"Tell me something," Leksin shouted above the judder of engine noise to Talgat, keeping his eyes focused on the desert. "What's the lowdown on the Minister of Energy?"

"One of the so-called gang of two, he and Rashid," Talgat yelled back. "Both bought up in the same orphanage, friends for life. Made a killing when the railways were privatised – bought up all the rolling stock on the cheap, then rented it straight back to the new company."

"Not exactly above board, then?"

"Of course not. In fact, the scandal nearly did for him – until

99

the President himself took a hand."

Leksin arched one eyebrow at Talgat. "You mean Rashid knew all along?"

Talgat's face creased into a benign smile. "Alex, nothing happens in Turkmenistan without the knowledge and consent of the man who lives in the pink palace."

They flew over the single railway track.

"Where's that go?" asked Leksin.

"Links the Aral Sea with the capital," Talgat replied. "Used to be one of the busiest lines in Central Asia before the sea dried up. Now the region's struggling. The train's still run every hour, but nowadays they're almost empty."

Leksin took a compass reading, glanced at the map to see precisely where the pipeline and railway would cross, then stared thoughtfully west following the pipeline's course towards the Caspian. Out here, the desert was at its hottest, and the scrubby black carpet of saxaul and juzgun gave way to rolling sand dunes.

Suddenly the helicopter alarm started to whine, and Safir shouted over his shoulder for them to come forward. The edge in his tone betrayed concern. They moved into the cockpit, where Safir nodded towards the flashing lights on the instrument panel. "We've got a problem, I'll need to fix it before we go much further."

Their eyes trawled the landscape, looking for somewhere to put down. In the north the jagged peaks of the Yangikala Canyon loomed like giant white teeth incising the skyline. Ahead, the vast expanse of undulating sand dunes shimmered uninvitingly in the heat.

"Leave it to me," Safir told them. "I'll find somewhere to land."

They returned to their seats, but a few minutes later Safir recalled them to the cockpit. "Nomads. Tekke tribe. I'll put down there." He pointed towards a group of brightly-coloured yurts about a kilometre ahead.

The helicopter set down two hundred metres from the yurts, and they jumped out. Instantly the concussive heat assaulted them, and Leksin gasped for breath. He sheltered in the helicopter's narrow overhang of shade while Safir opened up the chassis.

The verdict wasn't long in coming. "Particle separator's knackered," Safir declared. "Sucking sand into the engine. Not a chance in hell I'll manage to fix it before it gets dark."

Leksin kicked the skids in frustration. His timetable was borderline impossible as it stood, and right from the start he'd reckoned the odds were against him unearthing anything useful within it. Now the situation was to be exacerbated by being holed up uselessly in the desert. As he glanced around dejectedly for any way out, he saw the Tekke tribesmen coming over to investigate. Their leader shouted a greeting as they got closer.

The pilot stepped in to explain the situation in Turkmen. The leader nodded his understanding before turning to Leksin and Talgat. The sunlight glinted off his gold teeth as he smiled.

"Come out of the heat, my friends," he said in flawless Russian, putting his arms around their shoulders. "We are honoured to offer you shelter for the night."

Chapter Thirty

Karakum Desert, Turkmenistan

A guttural hiss woke Leksin, and it didn't sound friendly. Unable to locate the source in the dark, his heart beat faster as he turned over. Then a soft scrambling on the ground, and something nudged his leg.

"Talgat!" He reached across to shake him. "Talgat, wake up! We've got a visitor."

A torch beam snapped on. As Leksin's eyes adjusted to the light, two masses lying on the ground rugs resolved themselves into pairs of clawed legs, long tails and gaping mouths from which forked ribbons of pink tongue projected. Nearly two metres long, the monsters' heavy bodies were armoured with grey and black scales, cross-banded with broken dark stripes. One blocked the entrance, the other homed in on Talgat, its colourless eyes fixed on the torch beam. Its tongue flickered in and out through jagged, conical teeth as though tasting the air.

"Zemzens!" Leksin could hear the fear in Talgat's voice. "Stay still, Alex. They'll rip you apart if they attack."

The one by the entrance took a step forward. Its tail beat the air, as if preparing for takeoff. Leksin drew slowly back into a crouch as Talgat reached for his pistol. Sensing the threat, the two creatures lunged forward in unison, fast as sprinters leaving their blocks. Talgat sprang back and, grabbing the side of his bed, upended it as a shield just as the two animals pounced.

The ferocity of their attack stunned Leksin. Trapped against the side of the yurt, Talgat strained to hold the bed in place as best he could while the two animals literally shredded it. Leksin realised he had to do something fast, or they'd have him. Springing forward, he clenched his fist into a ball and drove it hard against the eye of the nearest animal. A dull thud, but the horny rim of the socket stopped the blow. Bare hands weren't going to make any impression, that was clear. Scouring the yurt in desperation, he spotted a pair of crossed scimitars hanging on the wall. Four steps to stride across and grab one. Three long strides to unsheathe it and launch himself back across the yurt full-force, spinning with his momentum. The blade sliced deep into the creature's skull.

The zemzen convulsed onto its back, its legs treading air. Its mate stood poised, watching the final death throes. Spinning around, it let out a melancholy cry. Staggering toward Leksin, it halted a scarce metre away. Tail sawing from side to side, it stared at him through blank eyes. Leksin backed up slowly, holding the scimitar high, braced for attack, until without warning the creature circled and darted out through the canvas doorway.

"What's going on?" a voice outside shouted.

Leksin emerged from the yurt to find the nomad leader heading his way, the other tribesmen in a pack behind him. In the distance an engine coughed into life. He watched with sudden understanding as the lights of the helicopter slowly lifted from the ground and swooped away across the sands.

*

The nomad leader accompanied Leksin back to the yurt. As he pulled back the canvas flaps and entered, he found the barrel of Talgat's Makarov aimed directly at his head.

"Don't make a sound!" Talgat ordered. "Face-down on the rug, hands behind your head."

For a second the nomad wavered, tempted to flight, then seeing the fierceness in Talgat's eyes, thought better of it. He lay down on the ground as instructed.

"Alex, keep an eye on what's going on outside. I'll deal with this."

Talgat approached the nomad leader and kicked him hard just below the ribs. As the man wheezed, Talgat expertly ran his fingers down his body, stopping when he found something strapped to his leg. Pulling a small knife from the sheath, he threw it across the yurt.

"Now roll over."

He waited until the man lay on his back before nuzzling the Makarov under his cheekbone. "Name?" Talgat spoke in Turkmen.

"Fariq," the man groaned.

"So tell me, Fariq, who put you up to this?"

Fariq didn't reply, but raising his head, spat into Talgat's face. Calmly wiping the back of his hand across his cheek, he fired a bullet through the nomad's knee.

A rumble of angry voices erupted outside, and Leksin on look-out saw a powerful figure shove his way through the other tribesmen towards the yurt. Leksin signalled to warn Talgat, then shifted to one side as the man burst in. The sight of Fariq, clutching his shattered leg, halted him. It was the instant Leksin needed: the point of his elbow crashed just below the man's ear and he slumped to the ground.

Talgat forced the pistol harder into Fariq's chin. "Tell them you're OK!"

"It's all right," Fariq shouted to the tribesmen outside. "It was nothing, just an accident."

As they backed off amid the ringside murmur of discontent, Talgat placed the tip of the pistol against Fariq's other knee. "You have till ten to tell me who put you up to this. One . . . two . . . three . . . four – "

"Some stranger, don't know his name," The words spilled fast from Fariq's mouth. "Your pilot brought him."

"When?"

"Two days ago. He came unannounced, left quickly."

"What did he want?"

"He told me the helicopter would be back with another man, possibly two."

"And?"

"You'd be forced to stay the night. We were to capture the

zemzens, push them in . . . make it look like an accident."

"What was in it for you?"

No answer.

Talgat rested his foot on the injured knee.

Fariq's face contorted in pain. "Said it was worth five thousand dollars."

Reverting to Russian, Talgat filled Leksin in and things began to fall into place. It wouldn't have been rocket science to guess that at some point he'd follow the proposed pipeline, especially since he'd specifically asked for a map showing its route. But what did come as a surprise was the fact that someone knew about Talgat. Leksin said as much.

"Few secrets in Turkmenistan," Talgat replied.

"Anyway, no time to dwell on it now," Leksin said, shrugging it off. "You notice those camels tethered behind the next yurt?"

Talgat nodded.

"Our way out of here." Leksin hauled Fariq to his feet, ignoring his groans as he twisted the shattered knee. "We'll take him with us. You've got the pistol. I'll carry him, and you cover me."

Outside the tribesmen had hunched together to wall off their exit.

"Move away!" Talgat waited a few seconds for them to part; when they didn't, he aimed at Fariq's other knee. "Next one will cripple him. Third one will kill him."

Reluctantly, the tribesmen broke apart and Leksin walked through the gap, his eyes fixed on the camels ahead. A gibbous moon cast a soft glow over the desert. Out of the corner of his eye came the glint of movement. "Talgat – "

Talgat dropped to one knee as he swivelled around to face a man rushing at him, a small kard knife held high above his head. A single bullet blew out the man's left eye. "Anyone else?" he challenged, making a slow sweep with his pistol. Again, they backed off.

At last they reached the post where the camels were tethered. They selected two, then firing a couple of shots into the air, scattered the others. Leksin grabbed hold of Fariq and threw him over his camel's neck, then mounted.

"We'll dump him when we're clear," he told Talgat, then pointed eastwards. "That way."

"Straight into the heart of the desert?"

"No time to explain, but I have an idea."

Chapter Thirty-One

Karakum Desert, Turkmenistan

They'd been riding for nearly an hour when Leksin told Talgat to stop. He raised a finger to his lips, a sign to keep quiet and listen. In the desert at night sound travels huge distances and, straining to hear, they could just make out the faint, but steady, shuffling of the camels pursuing them.

"They're on our tail," Talgat said.

Leksin nodded. "Three, maybe four, kilometres at most. Need to get a move on. Pass me your compass again."

He squinted to take another reading in the moonlight which, as they continued across the undulating terrain, dimly illuminated the way ahead. Leksin was struck by the eerie calm of the stillness. Here and there dark, angular boulders rose from the sand in the scant silver light.

Little by little the yielding surface gave way to a rubble-strewn desert floor. Saxaul and juzgun bushes grew here, first thinly spread, then more concentrated like a carpet of nails. Somehow, though, much to Leksin's amazement, the camels remained sure-footed, picking their way through even in the dark, but they had to be more careful, and slower, than before.

After a while, they halted again and listened. The patter of the camel's hooves was closer now, and Leksin realised that time was not on their side. With nowhere to hide out here, it wouldn't be long before their pursuers caught up. The desert was their land, it held no fear or secrets for them. For the time being all he and Talgat could do was keep plodding on. Could they reach a way out, or were they just delaying an inevitable confrontation in which they were unlikely to come out on top?

Eventually they found themselves on a salt stream, the remnants of a dried up river that once had wound its way through the desert. The surface was baked hard, even and without obstacles. The camels picked up speed. In the distance a huge dark shadow loomed ahead. Gradually the image sharpened into a tall elongated ridge. As it rose, pointed pinnacles of rock clustered its surface, effectively barring the way.

"Hell," Talgat muttered bleakly.

"We'll follow the stream's path," Leksin told him. "Somewhere it'll have cut a way through."

Sure enough, about a kilometre north, they reached a point where the ancient river had etched through the ridge, which dipped enough to allow them to pass. By the time they emerged the other side, the sun had edged over the horizon, and the desert was revealed in all its vastness. Surveying the endless flatlands, Leksin realised the extent to which the odds were against them. Now they were even more exposed, pinned down under the sun's searchlight with nowhere to hide, and their pursuers steadily narrowing the gap between them.

"Why don't we make a stand on the ridge?" Talgat suggested, sensing Leksin's hesitation. "At least we'd have a better chance than on the flat."

Leksin shook his head. "It'll get too hot once the sun gets up. We wouldn't last long." He reached over to place a hand on Talgat's arm. "Come on, Talgat. We'll get out of here, trust me."

As they rode on, the sun climbed higher on a landscape that shone and shifted like shattered glass. Suddenly there was a loud snap. Talgat's camel bucked and toppled him over, narrowly missing his head as its feet crashed back upon the stony ground. Leksin circled around to inspect.

"Leg's broken," Talgat said, getting to his feet. Pulling out his pistol, he shot the animal in the side of its head. Leksin felt nauseous as the camel buckled in slow motion, its body trembling on the ground for a few moments before at last lying still.

In the distance they could now see clearly the dust churned up by their pursuers. Leksin caught Talgat's eye, recognised the anxiety on his face, and for a moment regretted not having followed his suggestion to make a stand at the ridge. They might have struggled to hold out there, but now with just a single camel, what chance did they have? Even with the sun still low in the sky, the heat was building rapidly. It would only get worse. Surely they couldn't last long here either?

Talgat climbed onto Leksin's camel and they continued. With the weight of two, its movement was laboured and its breathing heavy. Talgat glanced repeatedly over his shoulder, and each time the Tekke seemed to have made up a little more ground.

A tap on the shoulder, and Talgat followed the direction in which Leksin pointed. "See that over there?" Leksin asked. "That's what we're heading for."

In the distance Talgat could just make out a black shape, deeper than a shadow, approaching from the horizon.

"A train," Leksin answered without waiting for the question. "We flew over the track in the helicopter, remember? We must get there before the train passes. It must be close now."

The camel trudged on, oblivious to their kicks and encouragement, as the train drew nearer, too close for comfort. It got them across the track with seconds to spare, and snorted with relief as they quickly dismounted. A shot rang out behind them. Spinning around, Leksin saw the tribesmen only a few hundred metres away, brandishing their rifles and closing in fast. Grabbing Talgat's arm, Leksin pulled him behind the camel for cover. A further hail of shots thudded into the camel, whose knees gave way. Just in time, the train rumbled between them and their pursuers, slowing down to allow them a few vital extra seconds. A hand extended from an open carriage door and hauled Leksin aboard. A second later, Talgat swung in too and landed next to him, sprawled at the railway guard's booted feet.

Chapter Thirty-Two

Ashgabat, Turkmenistan

In Ashgabat, the importance of an official is measured by the size of his office and the opulence of its furnishing. Ali Orazov's office left no room for doubt. The members of his tribe were numerous, but there was room for all of them here. Behind the huge desk hung a life-size portrait of President Rashid. Facing it on the opposite wall was an intricately woven rug that pictured Orazov himself in ceremonial robes. A Yomut carpet lay on the marble floor, rich purple and intricately patterned with gul motifs, a recent gift from a grateful businessman. Orazov appreciated its value at least as much as its beauty.

Between the row of brocade-draped French windows, an array of air-conditioners contended with the midday heat. Despite them, Orazov felt his temperature rise as he listened to his aide's report.

"What do you mean, they escaped?" he yelled, jumping to his feet. His black, gypsy eyes bore into his aide. "This is what happens when you rely on peasants. If it had been left to me, I'd have shot the man and be done with him." Pacing the room, he demanded: "Where the fuck's Leksin now?"

"Back in Ashgabat."

"The agent still with him?"

"Yes."

Orazov grunted and kicked a wastepaper basket across the floor.

"We're tracking their progress," the aide interjected desperately.

Orazov's face glared with contempt. "Don't lose them again, or you'll regret it!"

The aide nodded and scurried off. With his boss, it never paid to be the messenger.

Chapter Thirty-Three

Tashkent, Uzbekistan

With the careful gait of the elderly, the shabbily dressed old woman wove a slow path through the gravestones of the Botkinskoe cemetery. Emerging from the scant shelter of its trees, she reached the steps of the Russian Orthodox Church and stopped for a while in a patch of shade. It was a sweltering day, well over 40°C. Only the misguided devout would be in church today. She rummaged in her shopping trolley and, taking out a bottle of water and a tin cup, poured a splattering. As she sipped, her hunter's eyes surveyed the graveyard.

Taking out a black cotton veil, she draped it neatly over her head. Then, holding onto the stone banister, she dragged herself and her trolley up the steps, past a pair of tall icons and into the church. A sprinkling of elderly pensioners, deep in their private prayers, teetered around the nave, where wafts of incense permeated the air. Shuffling across the stone floor, she stood before the iconostasis and extracted a rosary from her pocket. Running the beads through her fingers, her lips began to move.

A few moments later, the priest in attendance spotted her and inclined his head almost imperceptibly. A broad-shouldered man with a thick greying beard and an ornate crucifix dangling from a chain, he approached each worshipper in turn and whispered his message. Gradually the church emptied. When the last one had gone, the priest locked the carved wooden door.

"OK, Nadia, we're alone now," he told the old woman. "I wasn't expecting to see you so soon. What can I do for you?"

She handed him a list and waited in silence while he scanned through it.

"Remind me, which Makarov do you use?"

"The PMM."

"Soft-point or armour-piercing bullets."

"Armour-piercing."

The priest grabbed the handle of her trolley and wheeled it towards the sacristy. "This'll take about an hour," he said over his shoulder. "Come through. Have a cup of tea while I put it all together."

*

Nadia took her cup into the priest's study. Settling into an armchair, she clicked on the TV and froze as the picture clarified and she took in the full implications of the scene that appeared. On screen a reporter holding a microphone stood in the road outside a grey-stone building set back about fifty metres behind her. Above her head, a banner inscribed 'Islamic Democratic Freedom Movement' was spread edge to edge on the walls. Left of screen, two columns of men in black kevlar jackets were drawn up ready for action.

"To recap," the reporter began, "just after midday a group of terrorists stormed School No 86 in Pechatniki, a rundown suburb in Moscow's South-east. At the time the attack occurred, the children and their teachers were having lunch in the cafeteria and they have all been taken hostage."

The camera panned the scene. The area in front of the school was deserted, save for a cluster of soldiers who'd managed to reach the school unseen and take cover, their backs now pressed hard against the walls. Two terrorists on lookout duty were positioned at upper windows, their features hidden by dark balaclavas. From his extreme height, Nadia recognised one of them as a member of her former cell.

"We're now going to my colleague, Oleg," the reporter continued. "He's in the command centre."

The picture switched to a grave-faced man inside a vehicle filled with monitors and laptops. An officer from the security service stood at his side. For a moment Oleg stared back silently at the

112

camera, then realising he was live, began: "I'm standing with Captain Petrev, the officer in charge of today's security operation. His men have succeeded in inserting tiny cameras through the school wall, so they can monitor what's going on inside. Captain, could you talk us through what's happening?"

The picture flickered, then clarified into the scene in the school cafeteria. The children were grouped in the middle of the room, cross-legged on the floor, their terrified faces turned towards the three armed women who watched over them. The black skullcaps over scarves exposed only their staring eyes and emphasised their menace. The children's teachers were lined up in stiff ranks against the far wall, their hands on their heads. Wires linked to explosives packed around their bodies were clearly visible.

Another camera showed explosives mounted high on the ceiling beams. The windows below were also rigged with booby traps.

Stas, you fool, she mouthed, I told you not to get involved, it was far too dangerous. Get out of there now before the trap slams shut.

Chapter Thirty-Four

Tashkent, Uzbekistan

The priest returned with Nadia's trolley, stopping in his tracks when he saw the news report on television. Sensing Nadia's anxiety, he immediately put two and two together.

"Stas?" he asked.

Nadia nodded without looking up.

"So that's why he wanted all the explosives the other day?"

She turned towards him as she let this information fall into place. "What explosives?" she asked automatically, already sure of the answer.

"He came here and nearly bought up the shop, you'd think he intended to start a small war." He paused, before adding: "I thought you knew."

Nadia shook her head.

"Why this?" the priest asked, motioning towards the screen. "What's in it for him?"

"The Russians want an excuse to crack down on dissidents," she replied, her eyes still fixed to the screen. "Too much bad publicity recently about human rights abuses. What better than an attack on children to make the public look the other way?"

The priest blinked, unsure whether she was serious.

Almost on cue, the reporter at the scene began to interview President Karpev who had just popped up at the scene. Nadia's body stiffened as she heard him spew out the stock phrases: "The sense of public outrage . . . Need to protect our people from terrorism . . . Catch and destroy these thugs whatever the cost . . . Treacherous activities of the ISIS followers within our borders . . . Need to support the existing regimes to prevent its further spread . . ."

Catching the priest's eye, Nadia explained: "I ordered Stas to have nothing to do with this, but the idiot's ignored me." She paused to purse her lips. "It's all a sham, of course. The school building used to be KGB – there are underground tunnels leading out from the basement. Any moment now, the idea is that Stas and his team will make a run for it. No one's actually supposed to get hurt."

A second later, though, she realised she'd spoken too soon. As a background explosion drowned out the President's voice, the picture tilted and the scene took on an air of panic. The camera swung round to zoom in on the children's school where smoke gushed from a hole in the wall on the ground floor. Two commandoes crouched either side, yanking children forward as they scrambled through and ran pell-mell towards the awaiting soldiers.

The camera panned up to a first-floor window. Nadia felt physically sick as the tall figure leaned out and opened fire on the fleeing children. Back in the days when they'd worked together, she recalled, she'd had her doubts on this man's resilience. Now under extreme pressure, the maniac had gone rogue and blown the whole operation. She watched aghast as, emptying the magazine, he fumbled to replace it. The camera switched back to the road, where the small bodies lay in pathetic heaps.

"Not like that, Stas," Nadia whispered. "Not like that." She blinked and wanted to look away as her worst nightmare grew real before her eyes.

An armoured car veered across the centre of the road, acting as a shield for the soldiers in Kevlar jackets who sheltered behind it. As they fired furiously upwards, a row of tanks thundered behind them. There'd be no escape now. Stas, you fool, if only you'd listened to me.

A small girl, dark-haired and in a blue dress, stood weeping in the road. Rooted by fear to the spot, she stared helplessly back at the school. As the camera flashed in on her, a bullet struck and shattered her skull into a halo of tiny red fragments.

115

Immediately, the screen blanked. Television had done its job, Nadia understood; any more would be overkill. No one would dare criticise Karpev's clampdown on dissidents now.

Chapter Thirty-Five

Moscow, Russia

Seated bolt-upright at his desk, Nikolai Koriakov, deputy minister at the Department of Overseas Development, jotted down notes as he listened to Leksin's update on speakerphone. A couple of interesting developments, but a lack of anything that could really be described as progress. Something *had* to crack soon: there were just six days until the official signing ceremony.

Leksin, Nikolai realised, was treading dangerous waters. Several attempts had been made on his life, each time thwarted. So far. But how long before one succeeded? He gave Leksin the details of an FSB safe house in Ashgabat. "Note the address down in case you need it, entry code's 4389D," he told him, then asked: "What next?"

As he listened to Leksin's reply, his secretary appeared at the door. She seemed flustered. He gave her a look that asked why.

"I'm sorry to interrupt, but – "

Before she could finish the sentence, President Karpev brushed her aside. Saidov followed, one step behind.

"I'll call you back," Nikolai murmured, and switched off the phone.

As he moved to greet his visitors, Karpev waved him back into his seat. "We've just been to the school in Pechatniki – or at least, what's left of it after this afternoon's fiasco," he explained. "Fucking mess!"

Nikolai nodded. He'd followed the incident on the TV screen in his office, seen the children's bodies scattered in front of the school, learnt with horror that the terrorists had subsequently blown up the school rather than risk capture. The current estimate of the death toll approached two hundred.

"It's got to stop," Karpev stated resolutely. "The FSB are rounding up all suspected terrorists as we speak." He paused before spelling it out: "I intend to eradicate them."

"So what can I do?" Nikolai asked.

It was Saidov who answered. "We were passing on our way back, Nikolai. Thought we'd take the opportunity to get an update on Leksin's progress."

"Still nothing concrete, I'm afraid, Prime Minister. Leksin's been through the detailed plans and checked out the pipeline's proposed route. They all seem in order." Nikolai paused before adding: "But a couple of developments suggest all may not be quite as it seems."

Karpev took note.

"Someone seems determined to block Leksin's progress at every turn," Nikolai explained.

Karpev's eyes asked for more detail. When none was forthcoming, he prompted: "So what are they concerned he might discover?"

"At this stage, we still have no specific knowledge," Nikolai replied. Shifting in his chair, he chose his next words with care. "One interesting fact, though, has come to light. Leksin's learnt that, before he died so suddenly, Lev Usenko wanted to pull out of the pipeline project."

"How did he learn?" Saidov asked, surprised.

Nikolai hesitated before continuing. It was the obvious question, and he was reluctant to admit the answer was an anonymous text. Saidov would simply dismiss that as a hoax. Leksin's instincts, though, told him the message was genuine, and his instincts were not often wrong. "I'm not sure," Nikolai lied at last. "But he's convinced this was the case."

Saidov shook his head in disbelief. "I think someone's deliberately misleading him. It was Lev Usenko himself who went down to Kabul with the Turkmen Minister of Energy to negotiate the terms of the pipeline's safe passage through the country. I'd like to know Leksin's source, see you if you can find out." Standing up, he stared thoughtfully from the window. As he deliberated, he noticed a guard outside the Ministry shooing away a stray cat as if it threatened national security. Turning back, he asked: "So what now? What's Leksin's next move?"

"He's trying to locate the former General Director, a man called Smolinsky. Max Usenko terminated his contract before Leksin flew to Ashgabat. Leksin wants to know why. He suspects the man might know something."

"Well, Nikolai, keep me informed," Saidov said, checking his watch. "We need to go. I've got another meeting, and . . ." – looking at Karpev – ". . . the President's holding a press conference shortly."

As he made towards the door, Karpev remained seated.

"You go ahead, Erlan," he told Saidov. "There's another matter I want to discuss with Nikolai while I'm here. I'll see you back in the Kremlin."

Chapter Thirty-Six

Moscow, Russia

"Shit!" Max muttered, looking through the spotter scope. A 480 score, way down from the 550 of his Olympic shooting days. An assistant offered to wind in his target, but he waved him brusquely aside. No need to rub it in.

His thoughts were scattered all over the place today, and concentration was in short supply. Not for the first time Vika was the problem. What was his sister up to, searching his office, then sneaking off to see Olga? Even as a child she was for ever sticking her nose in his affairs. So what did she hope to discover now? On whose side was she? *What did she know?* No wonder with all these questions on his mind, he couldn't focus on the target. Added to which, he reflected, shoving the TOZ35 back in its case, these Russian pistols were crap anyway.

Stowing his kitbag neatly in his locker, he went through to the club bar and ordered a glass of Chardonnay. Calm down, Max, he told himself. Wherever there's a problem, there's always a solution. He shouldn't let Vika get to him, he knew, but she always did. Especially since she'd stolen his birthright as chairman of the Kombinat. Whatever happened, she couldn't be allowed to get in the way now. Not when he was so close.

Downing his wine, he passed through Reception on his way out. The bronzed young man behind the desk smiled at him invitingly. Another time, perhaps. Outside his driver held open the car door, and he jumped in with unaccustomed vigour. It was time to set things in motion.

*

The house was empty when he got home. Pasha was out, no doubt still smarting from the battering Max had dispensed the night before. Poor boy, it hadn't really been his fault. He'd just caught Max at a bad time and borne the brunt of his frustration with Vika. Never mind, Max reflected, the boy'll forgive him when he stops sulking. He always did, he had nowhere else to go.

The doorbell rang. As soon as Max opened the door, he could feel his own distaste surfacing inside him. With a curt nod of the head, he acknowledged Dima and Viktor, father and son. Both ex-KGB, small fry specialising in muggings and abductions, now part of Moscow's seedier underworld. Max brought them in when he needed their particular skills, but they were still scum.

The two men sat across the dining-table from Max. The elephant and the mouse, he reflected: Dima bald and lumbering, Viktor compact and thin, his hair tied back in a ponytail.

"So, Mr Usenko," Viktor began, rubbing his hands as if he were about to tuck into a feast. "You've another job for us."

Max nodded and got straight down to business, keen to spend as little time with the two of them as possible. "I need you to warehouse someone temporarily. My sister."

Scratching the back of his head, Viktor exchanged quick glances with his father. For a moment he seemed so confused he couldn't think of anything to say. "Your sister?" he spluttered eventually. "We'll have the police down on us like an avalanche. They'd have you marked as their prime suspect straight off."

"On the contrary." Max let out an impatient sigh. "It's just because my sister is who she is that makes this fool-proof," Max answered without inflection, as if he were reading the weather. "Being kidnapped for ransom is an occupational hazard for the mega-rich in Russia. The police will assume this is just another instance of the same." His lips tightened as he pushed an envelope across the table. "You'll find what you need here. Photo, address, plan of the house. Two keys – one gets you into the garden from the back door, the other into the kitchen. My sister and the English girl who looks after my half-brother are the only ones in the house at present. Their bedrooms are marked on the plan. The servants are quartered in a separate building some distance from the main house. They won't be a problem. Be careful not to disturb the dogs, though. Routinely they're kept leashed, my sister's afraid of them around our young half-brother. But he's not there at present, so they'll have no hesitation letting them loose at the slightest hint of an intruder."

Dima thumbed through the envelope's contents, pulling out a smaller, stamped, addressed envelope wrapped in cling film. "What's this?"

"That's the letter to the police demanding a ransom. Once you've kidnapped my sister, post that in the central post office in Tverskaya, so it can't be traced. Don't touch the envelope with your bare hands, wear gloves. The letter will make them think it's a genuine kidnap."

"And will you pay the ransom?"

"Of course not." He sighed again. They really were idiots. "I just want her kept out of the way for a few days, no more. I'll let you know when to release her, but it'll be long before the ransom deadline expires."

"And when's this to take place?"

"Tonight." Max silenced any protest by standing up to signify the end of the meeting. "Let me know as soon as it's done."

As he led his visitors out into the hall, the front door opened and Pasha lurched in. He reeked of cognac, and a mottled purple bruise stained one cheek. He teetered as he faced them, his angled head inviting some reaction. His gaze switched from one to another before resting on Max. His brow puckered as he struggled to remember, then he stalked across the hall until their faces were close enough to kiss.

"Bastard!" He spat at him.

Dima and Viktor watched dumbstruck as Pasha clambered upstairs, clutching the banister for support.

Chapter Thirty-Seven

Moscow, Russia

A little after midnight, the Lada turned off the main road and followed a dirt-track through the forest. Reaching a clearing used during the day by woodcutters, it pulled up under a tall birch. The headlights went out. Dima and his son remained seated while their eyes got accustomed to the dark.

"OK, let's go," Viktor said eventually. "Don't forget the bag."

Reaching across to the backseat, Dima grabbed a small, canvas hold-all, then climbed out.

"This way," Viktor told him, heading into the forest. Earlier he'd cased the area, identifying this isolated clearing as a discreet place to leave the car. From here, it was just a five minute walk to the house.

The faint beam of Viktor's torch threw a dim trace of light on the way forward. Nevertheless they walked slowly, feeling their way along a barely visible trail through the undergrowth. Above the shuffling of their feet through the woodland detritus, they could hear the rustling of small animals rooting in the bushes. The tall firs grew steadily denser, closing in around them, claustrophobic and threatening. Here, the moon's light made only tiny stars in the dark expanse of foliage above their heads.

Viktor recoiled and pulled up short as four fierce animal eyes suddenly glinted in the torch beam, and the solid mass of two female wild boars came forward. Pitched above their angry snorts were the squeaks of their young. Viktor snapped off the torch, and they backed away until they stumbled over the sprawling roots of a broad tree. Crouching behind it in the dense carpet of pine needles, they waited for the boars to move off.

Viktor got to his feet. "Come on, we're wasting time."

"Ssssh!" Dima cautioned as he rose stiffly, grunting with pain. "They're still close."

Viktor set off again and Dima reluctantly followed, relieved when, a little further on, the forest came to an abrupt end. A path wound its way beside the wall surrounding the Usenko residence, taking them to a metal gate that led into the garden. Viktor slipped one of the two keys Max had furnished into the lock and exhaled softly as it turned. Dima elbowed him aside as, his bulk blocking the way, he opened the door with extreme caution and inspected the scene. About thirty metres away, separated from them by a lawn, stood the dark shadow of the main house. To the left, on the far side, a much smaller house. The servants' quarters, according to the rough plan Max had sketched.

"The lights are all out," Dima observed. "Everyone's asleep. Let's go."

The two men moved silently across the lawn, then using the second key, opened the kitchen door. Inside, the modern fitments and Italian tiles gleamed under the torch beam.

"So this is how an oligarch's daughter lives," Victor muttered dryly.

"Shut up," his father panted. "Sign language only, remember?"

Dima led the way through the kitchen to the entrance hall, a massive circular space with a high ceiling and a central domed skylight. Two bronze lions guarded the front door. Without a word, they climbed the staircase that curved its way to the next floor. At the top, they stood still for a moment, checking no one had been disturbed. Satisfied, they crept along the corridor towards Vika's room which, according to the plan, was at the far end.

"Ready?" Dima whispered.

Viktor extracted a syringe from his carry-case, squirted a little into the air under the torch beam, then nodded. As Dima swung open the door, he rushed past and ran towards the bed. Empty, the duvet spread neatly and undisturbed. No one had slept here tonight.

"What the fuck . . . ?" Viktor hissed under his breath.

Dima put a finger to his lips, then made a sign to indicate they should check the other rooms. He'd do one side of the corridor, Viktor the other.

Together they checked each room in turn. All were empty until Viktor reached the last one. Its door ajar, he could just make out the sound of regular breathing. Catching his father's attention, he gently pushed the door open. Moonlight streamed through the open curtains, its blue-black light outlining the lush contours of the girl's naked body stretched full length on the bed. Her hair was fanned out on the pillow, and her legs were spread apart, sprawled in sleep. As Dima pulled his son back into the corridor, neither caught her eyes blink open.

*

"Stop just there!" a voice rang out in the dark. "Move and I'll set the dogs on you."

Their heads whipped around. A man was advancing across the lawn, struggling to hold two huge dogs that strained at the leash.

"Shit!" Dima exclaimed. "Run for it, boy, get going." He shoved his son forwards.

Viktor sprinted towards the garden gate, Dima doing his best to keep up behind. In his panic, Viktor fumbled the key in the lock, just managing to open the door and get through as the first of the snarling Dobermans pounced. Dima was less fortunate. The two dogs pinned him to the ground, one of them tearing at his arm, the other clamping its jaws around his throat. Viktor stood momentarily paralysed until their handler caught up, then clanging the door shut, he scurried off like a rat into the forest.

Chapter Thirty-Eight

Moscow, Russia

In crisp white blouses and black skirts that showed off their long, sinuous legs, two fair-haired women in their early twenties with fixed smiles stood behind the reception desk set up on the deck of the Patriarch. Max Usenko had chartered this sumptuous river cruiser for the day's events. Constructed in Sweden to the highest standards, its owners had added extra chrome and designer highlights to bring it in line with the Russian market.

All but one of Max's guests had arrived, and they were now taking coffee and pastries in the salon. Max himself waited to receive his last guest. Lighting a Black Russian and inhaling slowly, he was infused with a glow of satisfaction. Over the last year he'd held a series of meetings relating to the pipeline's financing. Investment bankers, lawyers, oligarchs, equipment suppliers, potential investors and other interested parties had all been approached, in groups or individually, as part of a meticulously planned campaign to raise interest in the project. Today was the turn of key oil executives. The outcome would be crucial, and Max was relying on their greed for new markets to bring about an opportunity to turn the screw during the meeting and the lunch that would follow it.

A pretty girl in sailor's uniform appeared at the top of the gangway and nodded. Max stubbed out his cigarette. Instructing the receptionists to warn the other guests they were ready to start, he checked his appearance in the chrome while he waited for Saidov to come on board.

*

"Sit down, gentlemen, please," Saidov said as he entered the salon, where Max's visitors were all now in place around a vast boardroom table specially brought in for the occasion.

"Good to see you, Anatoly," he said, hugging Anatoly Grekov, head of the mighty Kamneft, one of Russia's largest privately-owned oil companies whose operations spanned Western Siberia. "How's Galina?"

"She's fine, Prime Minister," Grekov replied. "She told me to ask when you were next coming around for dinner."

Saidov pushed out his thin stomach to make it look larger than it was, and patted it. "You know me, Anatoly. I never turn down an invitation to a good meal."

Grekov laughed. "I'll be in touch."

Next, Saidov greeted Valery Zabov, the oligarch who'd acquired massive oil reserves in the Krasnoyarsk region during Yeltsin's ill-fated privatisation programme. "How's your son doing at school in England?" he asked. "His mother must be missing him."

Zabov gave a little grimace. "She does, Prime Minister, she never tires of telling me. But the boy's very happy at Eton."

"Give her my regards," Saidov said, before moving onto Leonid Komzin, the recently-appointed head of Lozneft, the state-backed concern that ranked as one of the world's largest vertically-integrated oil companies. "Good to see you back," he welcomed him. "How was Cap Ferrat?"

"Sunny, but so full of Russians nowadays," Komzin replied. "It didn't feel like a holiday."

Saidov laughed, then continued around the table, stopping to greet each one of the oil executives in turn. At last he took his position at the head of the table. Max Usenko sat down at his side.

"Gentlemen," Saidov began. "This is the third time we've met as a group to discuss the proposed pipeline. Max Usenko and I would like to start by updating you on events since our last meeting and take your questions, then I intend to set out the government's terms for licensing the pipeline's capacity once it's built." He turned towards Max. "Perhaps you could summarise where we are at present?"

Max slowly lit a Black Russian, then stood up. For the next hour he ran through the progress made by the project team in Tejen and the various discussions that had been held with the Turkmen authorities.

Saidov resumed the floor once Max had finished. "President Karpev will sign the contract with the Turkmen President in five days," he announced. "Gentlemen, there is nothing that can stop this now." His eyes drifted around the table. "Any questions before I go on?"

Valery Zabov waved a hand to attract his attention. "Prime Minister, are we sure no other country's been angling for the concession?"

Saidov nodded. "No problem there. The only possible competitor might have been the Americans, but they've had all sort of problems with the Turkmen government and realised they'd be on a hiding to nothing."

Anatoly Grekov caught Saidov's eye. "What's the position in Afghanistan?"

"The Chestny Kombinat has been involved for the last eighteen months on this issue, so perhaps Max you should answer this question," Saidov replied.

Max reached across to pour himself a glass of mineral water. "We have no problem there, Anatoly," he said flatly at last. "You must understand that this is a difficult question for me to answer. Significant negotiations have been progressing behind the scenes, most of them secret, so my hands are largely tied."

"I can appreciate that, Max," Grekov acknowledged. "But you too must accept that without adequate arrangements for the pipeline's security, it would be very difficult for any of us here to convince our boards to invest in the project."

There was a murmur of agreement from the other oil executives, and Max gave a resigned smile. "Let me say this," he began slowly, his monotone for once seemingly laced with sincerity. "You all knew my father for many years, and have dealt with Chestny Kombinat regularly. Throughout all your dealings with my father not one amongst you ever had any cause to doubt his judgement. The Afghan government's been severely strapped for cash, to say the least, and my father himself agreed terms with relevant parties to guarantee the pipeline's safety. I ask you, please, to accept his judgement on this."

He searched the room for protest, then when none came, he asked: "Any other questions?"

"I've one." All eyes turned on Ivan Yesipov, the head of Stroyneft, the State-owned oil transportation services conglomerate. "When do you envisage work on the pipeline will start?"

"Good question, Ivan," Saidov interrupted. "And it serves as a good introduction to the next part of today's meeting." He nodded towards Max who handed out folders. "The answer to your question is almost immediately," Saidov continued. "The project team have drawn up detailed plans and feasibility studies, the route's decided, and all costs are fully analysed. The only thing that remains is the financing." Saidov ignored the ripple of soft laughter, and went on: "As you know, we've held discussions with the money men already, and we've outline agreements in place for most of the funding. As I've already mentioned, a key purpose of today's meeting is to explain to you the government's proposal for licensing the pipeline's future capacity." He paused to ensure he had everyone's attention. "Put simply, we will be auctioning ten-year licences within the next three months. The ten-year period will commence once the pipeline is operational, but the upfront payment for the licence will be payable immediately and complete the funding gap."

A murmur of disapproval ran throughout the room, and Saidov raised his arm to stem it. Everyone in the room wanted access to the pipeline. Saidov's negotiating position was exceptionally strong, and he knew it. All of a sudden, a stern expression replaced his practised smile.

"The President has decreed that the pipeline must be entirely financed by the private sector. So that, gentlemen, is how it is."

Chapter Thirty-Nine

Moscow, Russia

Soon after nine-thirty, the main gate opened a crack and a young woman emerged in a flowery cotton dress. The nanny. She waved to the guard before heading off towards the village. Viktor made a wide berth and followed.

He pulled up when the girl stopped to talk in broken Russian with a middle-aged woman coming towards her. From her gesticulations and the direction in which she pointed, it was clear that she was trying to explain about the break-in at the house last night. The woman looked both intrigued and horrified. In a small village like this, such an event would be the main talking-point for many weeks.

Once their conversation finished, Viktor kept a discreet distance as the nanny strolled on past the bus stop. Just beyond, she turned off the road and took the shortcut through the forest towards the village shop. The path was overhung with thick foliage, screening out the light of the sun, and the spread of roots from the huge trees either side made the surface uneven.

Through the trees, he watched her halt as she spied a couple of wolf cubs playing in a clearing about fifty metres away. She left the path and crept closer to get a better view, shielding herself behind a tree. From somewhere the two animals had found a rubber tyre and were intent on ripping it apart. A twig snapped behind her, and she turned around just as Viktor's arm encircled her neck, choking off her scream. The wolf cubs darted away.

Kicking his shin, she struggled free and tried to make a run for it. Catching hold of her arm, he yanked her back and sank his fist hard into her stomach, doubling her up. Throwing her writhing body over his shoulder, he clutched her tightly and lugged her deeper into the forest. Dumping her on the ground, his boot hit her ribs with an audible crack. He seized her hair and jerked her face towards him.

"Where Vika Usenko? Tell me and I stop," he hissed in bad English.

The nanny's body lay still under him as she tried to understand. "Ashgabat," she said, fumbling over the unfamiliar word. "She's in Ashgabat. Please don't hurt me."

Relaxing his grip, he started to unbutton his belt. Pretty girl. Pity to waste this opportunity. He could kill her later.

Chapter Forty

Ashgabat, Turkmenistan

It was Sunday. Vika had donned her new Armani dress, and felt better than she'd done for a long while. Next month, the plastic surgeon would start to correct the scars on her cheek. Her leg still troubled her at times, but the prosthetics centre was working on that. Just a few more weeks, they'd promised her, and it would all be sorted out. Not a moment too soon. It was time to be herself again. Huh, what was she saying? She was herself now, of course – but, still, it would be good to feel complete once more, back in charge of both mind and body.

Lunch, just the family. Alex and her father were discussing the FSB's increasing influence over the business community. Sergei, bored, had long ago trotted off. Vika was deep in thought, sipping a second cup of coffee. She herself might be coming to terms with what had happened; Alex was another matter. Over the last few months he'd struggled to cope. It was as if his world had fallen apart as much as hers. To be honest, she'd grown tired of trying to lift his spirits while maintaining her own – it never seemed to do the trick, or at least, not for long. The whole experience had tested him to the limits, and she knew in her heart he was failing. Again and again she'd reassured him that it made no difference. She'd no intention of leaning on him now, any more than she had before the accident. Try to convince Alex of this, though! He seemed determined to treat her as another problem to be solved.

Her father took his leave to see to business. Vika watched as he left, unwilling to look Alex in the eye. Her gaze stayed fixed for far too long on the closed door, then glancing back at Alex, she touched the crown of her head in a small gesture of nervousness.

"Alex, we need to talk."

Alex shifted in his chair, sensing what was coming. "Vika, don't." His lips barely parted as he spoke.

She placed a finger over his mouth. "No, Alex, let me talk. We can't go on like this. The accident was terrible, but it happened. It's over. I've tried a thousand ways to tell you it doesn't matter, but I know you – it matters to you. I'm damaged goods and you need your toys in working order."

"That's not fair, Vika," Alex protested.

Vika's face relaxed into a faint smile. "You're right, Alex, and I apologise. The problem's me, not you. If we went ahead with our wedding, I'd never know whether you felt trapped into it or did it out of pity." She paused as if in the hope of contradiction, then continued when none came. "Either way, I couldn't bear it. I need to find someone who's known me only as I am, not as I was. Do you understand?"

Alex shook his head, looking genuinely confused.

"Come on, Alex, I know you get what I'm saying. It's been fun, and, God knows, I appreciate all you've done for me since the accident. I really do, I promise. But . . . " She stopped in mid-sentence, swallowing hard. Pulling herself to her feet, she leaned across to kiss Alex's forehead. "I'll show you out."

"Vika . . . "

As she turned away, her leg buckled and she sprawled onto the floor. "Not now," she begged silently. When Alex rushed to help, she shrugged him off. She'd done without him before, and by God, she could do it again.

At the front door, Alex turned to say goodbye. "I'm sorry, Vika . . . "

"Goodbye, Alex." She stepped back as he made to kiss her. "I'll send for my things at your flat."

She watched as his car drove off, then went into the drawing room where, despite herself, she surrendered to tears. Minutes later, her father came in.

"What's wrong, my girl?"

She wiped her eyes with her sleeve. "I'm all right, daddy. Believe me, I am . . . "

"Alex?"

"Gone."

Nodding as if he'd seen this coming, her father held her closely.

*

She jolted awake as the stewardess gently shook her shoulder. "Vika, we'll be landing in Ashgabat in twenty minutes," she said softly. "You'd better fasten your seat belt. Can I bring you anything?"

Vika managed a smile. The stewardess had worked on the company's jet since her late father first acquired it. They were old friends. "No, thanks," she replied, rubbing her eyes. "I must have nodded off."

Chapter Forty-One

Ashgabat, Turkmenistan

Standing in the taxi queue outside his hotel, Leksin looked across at the sparkling new building opposite with mixed feelings. Late yesterday afternoon, he'd checked out the location of the safe house Nikolai had mentioned – no need of it yet, but better to be prepared. The sun on his back, he'd walked back to his hotel, exploring parts of the city that he hadn't seen. As he'd neared his hotel, approaching this building clad with shining blue-painted frames of reflective glass, his eyes had been drawn to a beautiful young woman heading towards the entrance. She wore a vivid tunic, and her long dark hair hung in thick plait to her waist. She'd glanced at him as she passed, her oval face neutral, accustomed to admiration, then disappeared into the building. He'd stopped for a few seconds, then on a whim decided to follow her in.

This had been the first shock: registering that, like everything else in this city, the elaborate frontage was merely a facade. Encased within, away from public view, lay a squalid tenement, paint peeling off its walls, pipes rusted, staircases littered with garbage and wreaking of stale urine. A sign on the wall had delivered the next shock: 'People's Orphanage No 312'.

He'd negotiated the debris to the shabby, wooden entrance, introduced himself and asked to be shown around. Her first reaction had been to ask him to leave, but when she'd realised his proposal involved possible funding and not just flirtation, she'd invited him in. Tamara, she was called, and she'd assumed responsibility for the running of the orphanage after her mother had fallen ill. She'd taken him from room to room, proudly showing off her charges, constantly apologising for the conditions in which they lived. She did her best, she'd told him, but resources were scant. It was a battle just to keep the children clothed and fed.

Her cool green eyes had flushed sudden delight when Leksin had handed her $1,000. She'd smiled when he asked for her number, but she'd given it to him. And he'd meant it when he'd said he'd be in touch.

The doorman touched his arm, bringing him back to the present. He'd reached the front of the taxi queue. He told the driver to take him to Chestny Kombinat's HQ.

*

Logging onto his Moscow server, Leksin scanned through his notes, searching for some clue that might point a way forward. Unsure which direction to turn, he felt disquiet that he still had no tenable leads. The various attempts to stop him indicated there *was* something to find, but if only he knew where to look . . . What had convinced Lev Usenko of the need to pull out? Find this, Leksin suspected, and he'd have the key.

In the meantime, as he'd been shown to his office this morning, he'd identified one potential avenue of investigation. Across the corridor, Adam Smolinsky's name had yet to be removed from his office door. There had to be a chance his papers hadn't been cleared away either. It was definitely worth a look. He sneaked out, checked no one was around, then slipped into the former General Director's office.

Heading straight for the two metal filing cabinets, he found them locked. He rummaged in the desk drawer for a paper clip, then twisting it into shape, used it to tease the locks open. He thumbed through the files inside: monthly accounts . . . management reports . . . credit reviews . . . staff appraisals . Finally he came across a thin folder headed 'Pipeline'. He took it over to the desk to examine it.

Smolinsky was evidently a very methodical man. The majority of the file's contents were meeting minutes in the form of 'to do' lists, each item ticked off with completion date noted. Others were minutes of conversations between Smolinsky and members of the project team. All very innocuous. Given the project's significance to the company, Leksin would have expected to find more.

As he slipped the folder back in the drawer, a folded sheet of paper fell out. He opened it to find a printed copy of an email. His eyes were drawn immediately to the signature. He read through. *"Adam, thanks for alerting me to your concerns. No need for you to worry, I have the situation in hand. I'll be in contact soon. Regards, Vika Usenko."* Leksin slipped it into his pocket.

Back in his office, Leksin leant into his chair, his eyes fixed on some distant point as he ran through the implications. What did Smolinsky tell Vika? Equally significant, when? He pulled out the email to check the date. Nearly three weeks ago. Whatever information Smolinsky had imparted, Vika had been made aware of it some time before Leksin's initial meeting with her and Max in Moscow. Why hadn't she said anything?

He felt a sour taste in his mouth as he recalled Vika's words. *My brother's the one to help you here. He looks after our operations in Central Asia. The pipeline project's been his baby from the start.* Yet here was evidence to the contrary, that she was herself involved. What was she playing at? How much did she know?

One thing was sure. It was now more crucial than ever to meet Smolinsky face-to-face. He'd get his home number from the receptionist later.

*

Vika ... Now this was a move he hadn't expected. She was sitting in the company's reception reading a newspaper, cool and relaxed in a cream trouser suit. Sensing his stare, she turned and caught the surprise in his eyes, there for an instant, then gone. She gave him an awkward look that was almost a smile.

Leksin kissed her cheek. "What brings you here?"

"Oh, this and that. I decided it was high time I came down here myself and took a look at our operations."

Leksin studied her face, making an effort to act normal. First the email to Smolinsky, now she'd turned up in person. Coincidence. Unlikely – Leksin didn't believe in those. So what was she up to?

The lift opened, and a man emerged and approached Vika. His face folded into an easy smile as he introduced himself as Borzov, head of security. "Miss Usenko, good to meet you. You should have warned us, I'd have sent a car to collect you." He glanced at Leksin and looked puzzled to find him there. "Anyway, Miss Usenko, I've made an office ready for you. Let me show you up."

"Alex, nice to see you," Vika said, rising to her feet. "By the way," she added casually, "how's your assignment? Any progress?"

"This and that, you know."

Vika half-smiled, then turned to follow Borzov, stopped again when Leksin asked: "How long are you staying here?"

"Not really sure. A few days, I think."

"Dinner tonight?"

Vika hesitated a moment, smoothing the collar of her jacket. "Yes, that works. I've got a suite at the Sheraton."

"I'll pick you up at eight."

Waiting until they were safely installed in the lift, he approached the receptionist. "Do you by any chance have a home number for Adam Smolinsky?" he asked carelessly.

The receptionist tapped on her keyboard and a number appeared on the screen. Jotting it down, she passed it to Leksin.

Chapter Forty-Two

Ashgabat, Turkmenistan

Catholicism in Turkmenistan hadn't prospered during the Soviet era. Back in 1904 Ashgabat's Catholics had been given permission to build their own neo-gothic church, and a decade later the Catholic community had swelled as Polish immigrants, mainly trained professional people, fled wartime atrocities to a country hungry for their skills. However, the church had been closed by the authorities during the 1920 purge and physically destroyed by God during the great earthquake of 1948. Thereafter, all religion was effectively suppressed until the approach of the millennium, at which point the Vatican was given permission to set up an Apostolic Nunciature in the city.

Leksin showed his passport to the guard at the Nunciature's entrance, then followed the signs to the 'Transfiguration of the Lord', the chapel inside the embassy. Earlier, when after some persuasion Smolinsky had finally agreed to meet him, the former General Director had explained he was attending a funeral service for a member of the Polish community that afternoon. The chapel will be full of mourners, he'd told Leksin. Take the aisle up the left side of the nave until you reach a small side-chapel. Sit down there, and I'll join you when I can.

As Leksin slipped through the back door, the requiem mass was already in progress. An open coffin rested at the head of the aisle, a single white lily on the stone floor in front. Mourners filled both sides of the nave, their eyes fixed on the priest in a black chasuble who addressed them from the chancel. Leksin watched as, with a histrionic flourish, the priest spread his hands in a wide arc and drew them together.

"*Misereatur vestri omnipotens Deus, et, dismissis peccatis vestris, perducat vos ad vitam aeternam,"* he began. May Almighty God be merciful to you and, forgiving your sins, bring you to life everlasting.

A muttered Amen, then the priest made the sign of the cross.

Leksin tiptoed along the left-hand aisle until he reached the Lady Chapel, a small recess where two rows of pews enclosed a simple altar. On a tall pedestal to one side stood a statue of the Madonna and child. He sat down near the altar.

"In memoria eterna erit Justus: ab auditione mala non timebit," the service continued behind him. The just shall be in everlasting remembrance; he shall not fear the evil hearing. Chair legs scraped against the stone floor as the congregation sat and the small choir began the *Dies Irae*.

A whisper reached his ear. "Mr Leksin?"

A gaunt man stood at the end of the row, his face set in deep furrows.

"Mr Smolinsky?"

He nodded, glanced around nervously, then sat down next to him.

"Walk away from this, Mr Leksin," he started. "You don't know what these people can do."

"I need your help."

Smolinsky looked away, rubbing a curved finger backwards and forwards across his lips, occasionally squeezing his lower lip between finger and thumb. "What do you want to know?" he asked eventually, as if there was nothing more he could do about it.

Realising the man could lose his nerve at any minute, Leksin went straight to the point. "What exactly was your role in Chestny Kombinat?"

"I was General Director."

"I know that, but what did it entail?"

"I was responsible for all the company's activities in Turkmenistan."

"Including the pipeline project?"

Smolinsky faltered.

"Did the scope of your responsibility extend to the pipeline?" Leksin asked again.

"That was handled out of Tejen," Smolinsky replied, evading the question.

"But they reported to you as General Director?" Leksin persisted, recalling the file he'd found in the man's former office. "You knew what was going on there."

Smolinsky didn't reply, but beads of sweat appeared on his forehead.

"Tell me, Mr Smolinsky, why were you sacked?"

"Mr Usenko wanted a change."

"Is that what he said?" Leksin asked, unconvinced. "Did you in fact know something that he wanted kept secret?"

Smolinsky's head snapped around. "What do you know?" he blurted.

Just then there was a rustle in the row behind them as a woman, her head covered in a black veil, sat down and started to pray. The two men waited in silence. *"Hoc est enim corpus meum,"* intoned the priest holding up the thin white wafer that was now the body of Christ. The chair behind them scraped as the woman stood up, and they turned to watch her disappear through the half-light into the crowd of communicants.

Turning back, Smolinsky noticed a plain brown envelope that had suddenly appeared on the chair beside him. He tore it open. His body stiffened as he examined its contents. Without a word he sprang up, toppling his chair in the process, and made to leave. Leksin reached across to catch his arm, but Smolinsky shook him off. "Please don't try to contact me again," he entreated, and darted away.

Leksin grabbed the envelope. 'Smolinsky' was marked on its face in big capitals. A photo slipped out onto the floor. Leksin picked it up. A plump woman with a little girl. Two red crosses scrawled over their faces.

Chapter Forty-Three

Ashgabat, Turkmenistan

Leksin had chosen Asuda Nusay restaurant for its proximity to the Sheraton, where Vika was staying. Ashgabat, Nikolai had warned him, was no gourmet's paradise, but the food here had proved a pleasant surprise. Seated at the apex of the tastefully furnished room, their table was lit by a single candle. Piped Turkmen music now played through invisible speakers, soft enough not to be intrusive. On the far side, an army of chefs had laboured over vast grills behind a picture window. He and Vika had both chosen *cigar borek*, cheese-filled filo pastries, followed by sturgeon shashlyks with a stack of wafer-thin lavash, and it had been delicious.

The room had emptied now. Only a matronly Turkmen woman reading a book at the next table remained. Even the small group of folk singers who'd performed on and off during their dinner had packed up and gone home.

So far, the evening had been uneventful. Conversation had been polite, a little distant but without recrimination. Both of them had studiously avoided talking about the past, fearing it might stray onto the circumstances surrounding their split. The wounds, at least the emotional ones, still rankled, and small talk was the inevitable defence. If there were things to be said, by tacit and mutual consent they'd been left unsaid.

"Are you still involved with the orphanage?" Vika asked, filling in a lull in their conversation.

"Which one?" Leksin replied with a smile. "I seem to have two now."

"I was thinking of Moscow."

"Yes, that's doing much better. It's amazing to see how far a little spare cash can go."

Vika nodded. "And this second one?"

"Actually it's not far from where we're sitting right now." He told her about his visit to the orphanage opposite the Nissa Hotel. "Conditions were terrible. Pretty young woman called Tamara runs it, lovely girl – "He paused when he noticed the inquisitive look on Vika's face, flushed, then added hurriedly: "She's really struggling. A little extra will make an enormous difference."

Vika smiled as she squeezed his hand, then asked: "And the art collection? What's new there?"

"Quite a lot since . . . " The words tapered off as he rephrased his reply. "I bought a Vrubel earlier this year. Portrait of the swan queen. Really striking. You should see it, the bright colours and bold brush strokes are quite remarkable." He took a sip of coffee. "And of course the Serebriakova self-portrait. I got that as payment for some work at the Tretyakov."

Vika angled her head in curiosity. The Tretyakov had hit the headlines recently. Rumours had abounded for years that a number of its paintings and artefacts were somehow finding their way into private collections. Quite recently the acting director had been identified as the culprit, but before the police could arrest him, he'd thrown himself from his office window. Could Leksin have been involved? Quite possibly, she reflected: it wouldn't be the first time someone on the border of his life had ended up as victim.

"By the way," she went on, matter of fact. "There's an exhibition of Turkmen art at my hotel. Much of it's probably not to your taste, I suspect, but there are one or two interesting pieces. You should take a look."

For some moments they sat in awkward silence. Sensing that Leksin was holding something back, Vika raised the subject of his current investigation. "You realise, Alex, how much is at stake with this pipeline deal," she declared. "It would be an enormous money-spinner for the company."

Leksin nodded. "Quite a feather in Max's cap, isn't it? Given the problems your father had with him in the past, Lev must have been delighted." He studied Vika closely, searching for some reaction, but none came. Just a slight flicker of her cheek, barely noticeable and fleeting.

Touching his arm, Vika looked him straight in the eye. "Alex, have you discovered anything I ought to know?"

The directness of her question took him off-guard. Leaning back in his chair, he flicked his fingers through his hair in swift, uneasy movements. All the evidence so far suggested she knew something he ought to know, not vice versa. However, he wasn't ready to confront her yet. He shook his head and tested her further. "Actually, there's something I wanted to ask you. I spent much of today trying to track down the ex-GD, a man called Smolinsky. Your brother fired him just before I arrived. I was thinking it might be useful to have a word. You wouldn't know how I can find him?"

"Smolinsky?" Vika repeated the name as if she was trying to recall it, then shook her head. "Can't help, I'm afraid."

"No matter," Leksin said, acting unconcerned. Inside, though, he felt his muscles tighten: the email he'd found in Smolinsky's office earlier that day indicated she was lying. For some reason she seemed to be playing both sides against the centre. On whose side was she, though? Now deeply troubled, he brushed his napkin over his mouth and excused himself.

Vika observed him as he headed towards the men's room, sensing the change of mood. Catching the Turkmen woman on the next table staring at her with apparent disapproval, she met the woman's gaze until she looked away. Toying thoughtfully with her cup, she swivelled it around the saucer, moving the handle sideways and then back again, until Leksin returned.

As soon as he sat down, she recognised the sparkle in his eyes, the subtle change in his manner. "Oh Alex . . ." she said with a hint of her old reproof, realising he hadn't kicked the habit. "Still?" She placed her hand over his and squeezed.

Leksin looked past her. He needed neither her sympathy nor censure.

Chapter Forty-Four

Ashgabat, Turkmenistan

The exhibition of Turkmen art was set up in a conference room off the mezzanine of the Sheraton Hotel. At nine-thirty in the morning, the room was sparsely populated: a small group of Japanese women on a guided tour while their husbands attended to business, a young American couple dressed in matching tee-shirts and fraying denim shorts who repeatedly ignored the no-photographs signs liberally posted around the room, and one or two others.

Leksin passed quickly through the display of social-realist works produced by Turkmen painters during the Khrushchev and Brezhnev years – strident figures marching several abreast into factories and farms, clenched fists aloft, all glory to the Soviet experiment. Definitely not his thing, it sent a shiver down his spine like someone crossing his grave.

He stopped at a portrait of a young Turkmen woman by Camille Muralimov, one of the Mary School. Now this was more like it. The woman dressed in soft pink silk, her expression one of patient acceptance, reclined on a Beshir rug in her garden, its emptiness sweeping behind her, a cat watching over her as it licked its paw in the background. He noted down the reference number.

A bespectacled woman, with peroxide blonde hair and too much rouge, manned a desk by the entrance to the room. More intent on her knitting than security, she peered irritably over her glasses as Leksin approached.

"I'd like to buy this," he told her, handing over a slip of paper.

She got up to attach a small, circular red sticker to the frame, then rummaged through her desk for something she couldn't find. "I need to get the invoice book," she sighed. "Wait here."

As Leksin did another circuit of the room to fill in time, his mind drifted to the dinner with Vika last night. It was never easy meeting a former partner and lover – especially one who'd ditched you just before the wedding you'd planned together. However, the evening had proved less of an upset than he'd feared. The two of them had both avoided sensitive areas and kept to small talk, though if he were honest, he still found Vika's small talk a thousand times more interesting than earnest conversation with most other people. She'd seemed a little distant, and he himself had felt more detached than he'd anticipated. For the first time, the list of things he'd stored to say to Vika one day no longer seemed quite so crucial. It was just good to spend some time with her again.

One question, though, had kept him awake most of the night. Why was she in Ashgabat? Knowing her as he did, she wasn't someone who played at the edge of the rules. In this respect she was the exact antithesis of her brother. Nonetheless, there was no denying the evidence. Without thinking, his hand checked his pockets for her email to Smolinsky. Surely there was some innocent explanation?

The woman returned with the necessary paperwork, and Leksin hovered impatiently by her desk as she meticulously filled out his invoice. Finally, tearing it off, she handed it over. "We need to get a certificate enabling you to take the painting out of Turkmenistan," she told him. "I can get that organised this afternoon. If you'd like to pass by some time tomorrow, you can pay for the painting then and take it with you."

Leksin thanked her and checked his watch. Nearly ten-thirty. Later than he'd intended. It was time to go to the Chestny Kombinat and finish going through the routines before he headed off with Talgat this afternoon. In the absence of any lead, he'd fallen back on a process of elimination: remove the possibilities one by one and see what's left. A slow procedure, perhaps it would pay off in the end. Somehow, though, he doubted it. With each passing day he was becoming increasingly convinced that the answer lay elsewhere.

From the top of the staircase leading down from the mezzanine, he spied Vika crossing the lobby. He waved frantically to attract her attention, then called out her name which she didn't hear. Charging down the stairs, he darted across the lobby. As he passed through the swing doors, he could see her getting into a taxi.

"Stop her!" he shouted to the doorman as he emerged. "We're going to the same place, we can go together."

But it was too late. The taxi had already pulled out and was halfway down the ramp out of earshot.

"I'm afraid you'll have to take another, sir," the doorman said, holding a taxi door open.

Leksin got in, and the taxi headed off, pulling up behind Vika's at the main road. As the traffic cleared, he was surprised to see her turn to the left. The company's headquarters were in the other direction. So where was she going? His instincts told him to find out, and he instructed the driver to follow.

*

Tucked into a discreet corner of the Sheraton's lobby, Borzov sat slunk into a leather armchair shielded by a solid marble pillar, ostensibly reading a copy of America Today. Yesterday evening, just as he was about to head home, the office receptionist had informed him that Miss Usenko didn't require the office driver to collect her in the morning. There were things she needed to do, Vika had apparently told the receptionist.

Watch her like a hawk, that had been the instruction from Max Usenko when he'd discovered his sister had flown to Ashgabat. "Make sure you know what she's up to at all times," Max had stressed repeatedly. So when Borzov learnt Vika wasn't coming into the office, he'd headed for the hotel early that morning to keep an eye on her.

It was around ten-thirty when he finally spotted Vika emerge from a lift. Raising his newspaper a little to hide his face, he watched as she exchanged words with the desk clerk before crossing the lobby towards the forecourt. Where was she going? He needed to find out. As he rose to follow, though, a loud voice shouted her name from the mezzanine. Looking up, he saw Leksin waving frantically at Vika, then hurling himself down the stairs and across the lobby. Borzov held back until Leksin disappeared through the swing doors, then set off after him. In the distance, through the window, he could see Vika driving off in a taxi, then Leksin slipping into the next one.

He rushed out. Handing a $50 bill to the doorman, he jumped into his car and tailed them.

Chapter Forty-Five

Ashgabat, Turkmenistan

As Vika's taxi emerged from the city's industrial suburbs, it began to pick up speed. A large roadside poster proclaimed that they were just twenty kilometres from Goek Tepe, the site of the decisive battle against the Tekke tribe in Russia's conquest of what was now Turkmenistan. Each year, the driver told her, the descendants of the Tekke army commemorated their dead, slaughtered by their Russian conquerors in one of the worst massacres of the nineteenth century.

Vika stared blankly out of the window, deep in thought. She'd found the dinner with Leksin last night a little awkward, at least in some respects. They'd talked of this and that, cocktail party chit-chat, avoiding anything that might touch a nerve. Inevitable really. You can't recapture the old days - she realised that, but wondered whether Leksin did. Life had moved on, at least for her.

They reached the village of Gypjak, dominated by the mammoth mosque built to house the tomb of Turkmenbashi, its golden dome and four gold-tipped minarets set amidst immaculate formal gardens and fountains thrusting water high into the air. Just beyond, they passed a madrassa, a place of learning where groups of old men wearing ragged beards and sheepskin hats sat cross-legged on wooden divans. At its iron gates, two pale-robed students clutched books to their chests and lingered in conversation.

At the far side of the madrassa, the taxi turned left, passing through endless rows of multi-coloured, dilapidated wooden dachas, their gardens littered with a strange mixture of chickens, goats and bric-a-brac. Eventually they reached a small complex of modern houses, more Western than Turkmen in style. Here, the taxi slowed down as the driver inspected the building numbers before pulling up.

"The house you're looking for's through there," he said, pointing through a thin, pointed archway.

Vika looked around. Fifty metres along the road was a kiosk serving refreshments, where tables and chairs spilt out onto the pavement. "Why don't you grab a coffee? I'll meet you there when I've finished," she told the driver. Easing herself off the back seat, the heat blasted into her like a furnace, and she paused for breath.

Passing through the arch, she entered an elliptical open space. A children's playground surrounded by neatly painted benches was set on a central island, bordered by a series of identical semi-detached brick houses. Vika inspected the house numbers. The one she sought was on the far side, and she set off along a stone path around the edge.

Her mobile rang. Nikolai. Vika's smile vanished as she listened to what he had to say, and she stood dead still to reply.

"The office called me yesterday about the break-in. A couple of burglars chancing their arm, the police thought. They said there'd been similar incidents in the area recently." She felt tears welling in her eyes. "But the nanny . . . the poor girl . . . What exactly happened?"

Her leg throbbed. She reached down to massage it as she listened to Nikolai's account of events.

"What do you mean connected?" she interrupted, incredulous. "You don't really think the burglar hung around all night and murdered Jenny the next day?"

"That's exactly what I'm suggesting," Nikolai replied frankly, clearing his throat. "Vika, I believe it was you they were looking for." He paused to let his words sink in. "Where are you staying?"

"The Sheraton."

"Listen to me carefully," Nikolai said in a tone that brooked no argument. "If I'm right, you're in very serious danger. You must do exactly – and I mean exactly – what I say, understand?"

Chapter Forty-Six

Ashgabat, Turkmenistan

As soon as the two taxis ahead of him turned off the main road at the Gypjak Mosque, Borzov knew precisely where they were headed. Fuck. He should have followed his initial instincts and eliminated the problem at the outset. He'd said as much to Max Usenko, but failed to convince him. Now he'd have to hope the threats they'd made would prove an adequate deterrent. He cursed again. He could kick himself for not forcing the issue.

Keeping his distance, he pulled up as the first taxi, Vika in the back, slowed down and came to a halt by an arch. He watched as the second taxi pulled into the kerb a hundred metres behind. Leksin seemed to wait until Vika disappeared before getting out to follow her. Then he slowed down as he neared the arch, peering cautiously around the edge before going through.

Borzov parked in a quiet, leafy lane, then went in pursuit. Passing under the arch, he pulled up as soon as he spotted Leksin some twenty metres ahead. Hiding behind a municipal electricity hut, the man's eyes were fixed on Vika as she proceeded along the path. Borzov edged forward cautiously to get a better view.

Vika clamped her mobile to her ear, then stopped. As Borzov waited for her call to finish, he tried to make sense of what he was seeing. When he'd spotted the two of them leaving the Sheraton, he'd assumed that they were acting in concert and going somewhere together. A disturbing combination in the present circumstances, he'd decided to follow. But a very different scenario was emerging. Far from working together, Leksin was actually following Vika without her knowledge, and from the way he was keeping himself concealed, he was keen it should remain that way. But why? Only last night the two of them had dined together at Asuda Nusay.

According to the report Borzov had received, the dinner had been amicable, mostly small talk. The subject of Leksin's assignment had been raised only briefly. Hardly at all, the old woman had reported. So why was Leksin following her now? What did he suspect?

As Vika slipped her mobile back in her bag, she was clearly agitated. Stooping to rub her hand down her leg, she'd looked around nervously, almost as if she sensed danger. Reaching a house set back behind a creosote wooden fence, she rang the bell and waited.

A plump, anxious-looking woman opened the gate a crack. She listened to Vika for a few seconds, then started to remonstrate with her. Waving her arms frantically and shooing Vika away, she tried to slam the gate shut as Smolinsky emerged from the house. Eying Vika, he looked apprehensively around the courtyard, then pulled her inside.

As he lost sight of Vika behind the fence, Borzov ran through his options. There weren't many. Smolinsky was a frightened man, Borzov had made sure of that, but he was also bitter about the way he'd been treated. Even before Max had fired him, Borzov's intelligence had indicated that Smolinsky was, to say the least, uneasy about the direction the pipeline project was taking and his own involvement in it. God knows what, if anything, he might tell Vika. It was time to remove this risk once and for all. Even then, who knows? He might well be swinging his fists after the fight was over. What a mess.

Leksin suddenly turned around. Borzov ducked back, just in time. Darting through the arch, he started to walk in the opposite direction to where Leksin's taxi waited. A little further on, he glanced over his shoulder and saw Leksin slip onto the rear seat and head back towards town.

Chapter Forty-Seven

Ashgabat, Turkmenistan

Smolinsky sat in an armchair in the corner of the living room, his body sagging, his shoulders slumped, as he watched his wife wrapping presents for their daughter's birthday the next day. The rims of her eyes were red as though she'd been weeping. From time to time she glanced back at him, her eyes rich with accusation, and he looked away.

Pushing himself to his feet, drained and stressed-out, he crossed the room to the window. Outside their daughter was playing nurse in the garden, tending her doll. His fingers fiddled with his wedding ring as he watched her, moving it up and down his thin, bony finger, twisting it, pushing it back. Involuntarily, his mind superimposed a red cross over her image, and he steadied himself on the window ledge. He felt close to breaking down.

Fumbling in his pockets for his cigarettes, his hands shook as he lit one. This had to stop; they couldn't live like this. Turning around, he faced his wife with sudden resolution, and when he spoke, his tone was that of someone emerging from a mist and suddenly able to see the way forward. "We're going to your sister's in Serdar."

His wife's chubby fingers froze, and she squinted at him, closing one eye. "When?"

"Right now."

"But that's over two hundred kilometres away," she protested. "What about the birthday party?"

"We must leave today."

For some moments she stared at him in dumb silence, struggling to hold back tears. "I'll call around," she said at last.

"No, no one must know."

She moved towards him and laid her head on his shoulder. Waiting for him to comfort her, she retreated when he didn't.

"If only you hadn't talked to her . . ."

"Just go and pack," Smolinsky told her, tight-lipped. "I'll tell our girl we're going on holiday as a birthday present."

*

The sun was now high in the sky, and the temperature was nearly 45°C. Taking a handkerchief from his pocket, Borzov brushed it over his forehead as he ambled casually along the lane. One side was bordered by antiquated, rundown dachas, the other by the rear garages attached to the modern semi-detached houses of Smolinsky's complex. Wild cannabis intermingled with horsetail ephedra along the side of the road.

A little way ahead, a milkman trundled his cart laden with empty churns back towards base. Otherwise the lane was deserted. At this time of day, no one was foolish enough to brave the heat.

Borzov jumped back when a Rottweiler threw itself against the tall wire fence to his right and snarled viciously. Composing himself, he approached the dog and stared back. For a moment their eyes locked, then the dog whined and backed away.

A car pulled out into the lane some way ahead. Borzov depressed the remote detonator in his pocket and, a second later, the force of the explosion almost knocked him off his feet. A cloud of grey smoke and flames rose into the sky as debris flew in all directions. Instinctively he ducked as the ragged stub of a child's foot slapped down on the tarmac beside him. Picking it up gingerly, he tossed it over to the excited Doberman, and walked briskly away.

Well, that's one problem solved, he thought, back in his car. No one survived that. But had the damage already been done? There was no way of knowing. Was Vika now the problem? Quite possibly - and if so, how would Max deal with it? He looked at his watch: nearly one o'clock. He'd better head back to the office, report in and get instructions. He had a feeling he was going to be busy.

154

Chapter Forty-Eight

Ashgabat, Turkmenistan

Whichever way he looked at it, the evidence seemed to lead in only one direction. He ran through the points on his fingers. First, at their initial meeting in Moscow, Vika had stressed that she was not involved in the company's Turkmen activities. *My brother looks after the operations in Central Asia, the pipeline's been his baby from the start.* Second, despite this, she'd turned up suddenly in the Ashgabat head office, which hardly supported her contention. Then third – he pressed his hand hard against his middle finger – there was the email from Vika in Smolinsky's file. The man had clearly alerted her to certain concerns, but – fourth – when Leksin had asked about Smolinsky over their dinner last night, he'd drawn a blank. Perhaps he should have confronted her with the email, forced her to come clean? For some reason, he'd held back, and he wasn't quite sure why. Had he felt it best not to alert her to his suspicions at this time, or simply been afraid of doing so? Well, no matter, the fifth and final point was the clincher: her clandestine meeting with Smolinsky this morning. Presumably she'd gone to warn him off talking to Leksin. What other explanation was there?

A thin layer of sweat formed on his brow, and he wiped it off with the back of his wrist. Going into the bathroom, his hand was shaking as he splashed water over his face. For a moment he stared at himself in the mirror, turning his head back and forth as though he had a stiff neck, searching for composure.

How could he have envisaged this outcome? He'd been engaged to Vika, would have married her if she hadn't ditched him. He'd loved her then, perhaps still did a little. Certainly the wounds of their breakup still niggled. How could she lie to him so blatantly? There was nothing for it, he realised, he'd have to tell Nikolai now.

Pressing speed dial, there was no answer on Nikolai's mobile, so he dialled his office. Nikolai's secretary came on the line. Mr Koriakov was out. No, he wouldn't leave a message, just ask Nikolai to call him as soon as he returns.

Leksin extracted the small plastic sachet from the packet of Brazilian coffee in the sleeve of his suitcase, and drew a line. As he sucked in deeply, he found his hand was still trembling. He needed to calm down. Normally at this stage of an assignment, he'd expect a clear idea of the way forward, but not this time. To be honest, he was running out of places to look and wasn't at all sure where next to turn. Above all, he needed to alert Nikolai to this latest development and gain his input.

Turning on the television, he sat back and half-listened to an interview with the head of the Afghan army. His troops were struggling to deal with the sudden coordinated attacks by the Taliban across a broad front, and they'd been forced to relinquish several areas previously held by the occupying armies. He appealed to the Americans for assistance.

Leksin slumped back in his chair as the coke took hold. If the civil war in Afghanistan worsened, that wouldn't bode well for the pipeline's security, surely? How had they factored this in, he wondered, as on screen the news switched to the next item, an opposition rally due to take place in Ashgabat in a few days time. The first such event since the fall of Communism, crowds were already streaming into the capital from all over the country. Half the world's press, the newscaster said, seemed to have descended on Ashgabat, keen not to miss any aspect of this unique event – and, Leksin suspected, no doubt hoping to witness a violent struggle between demonstrators and government forces at first hand.

A chime signalled an incoming text, and he took a deep breath as he read the message.

Answer in Garkent on Garabil Plateau?

He frowned in confusion. Anonymous as before, who was the sender? Garabil Plateau? Hadn't they flown by this the other day?

Pulling the map of Chestny Kombinat locations in Turkmenistan from his briefcase, he spread it over his lap. It took a minute or two to locate the Garabil Plateau in the country's south-eastern corner. Sure enough, one edge of the plateau skirted Tagtabazar and the route inland of the proposed pipeline, another edge bordered Afghanistan. The village of Garkent looked to be just a few kilometres from the border. Chestny Kombinat didn't have a location anywhere near, hardly surprising given its remoteness.

Answer in Garkent on the Garabil Plateau? This single question led to a stack of others. Was this just a hoax, sent to mislead him? After all, time was running out – only four days before President Karpev was scheduled to sign the pipeline agreement. Was the sender of this text, whoever he was, simply trying to get him out of the way?

He tapped into the screen. *What in Garkent?*

A moment later the reply came through. *Unsure.*

Leksin scratched his head, pushing back his dense brown hair in a series of abrupt movements, caught in a genuine dilemma. If this was a hoax, wouldn't the sender have a more convincing response than that? *Unsure?* He studied the map again: was it just coincidence that the Garabil Plateau was so close to the pipeline route and the Afghan border? Perhaps – though coincidences always made him feel uncomfortable.

Another chime, and he glanced at the message on the screen. *Be careful. Much at stake. Watch yourself.*

Leksin let the expression on his face fade into a puzzled smile. Who the hell was sending these messages? He keyed in a number, and Talgat answered almost immediately.

"Talgat, I'll explain when I see you," Leksin began, almost defensively. "But in the meantime could you get Moscow to check something out . . ."

Chapter Forty-Nine

Ashgabat, Turkmenistan

"You were right," Talgat acknowledged. "Satellite pictures show a cluster of buildings – possibly some sort of plant – just outside Garkent. Right by the Afghan border. Army camp close by." He gave Leksin a hard look. "How on earth did you catch on?"

Leksin passed over his mobile and let Talgat read the texts.

"A long shot," Talgat commented.

"True," Leksin admitted. "But given the satellite pictures, it adds up." A slight shrug. "Anyway, it's a lead – and they've been in pretty short supply lately."

Talgat regarded Leksin thoughtfully, then placed a hand on his arm. "Let me go, Alex. The plateau's no place for civvies, there's military there too. More my line of work than yours."

"Stop right there, Talgat!" Leksin gave him a slight, crooked grin. "Think I'm going to let you take all the credit? No way!"

With a shrug Talgat gave in. "Then bring something warm, it gets cold up there at night."

Leksin stuffed a jersey and anorak into a lightweight backpack, placing a camera and pair of binoculars on top. "Let's go," he said, zipping it shut.

*

The scene around the station was complete pandemonium. All morning, crowds had continued to pour off trains in anticipation of the opposition rally. Most had nowhere to go and milled around the junction in a state of nervous excitement. Traders selling shashlyk and dried fruit crammed the pavements.

Talgat edged his 4x4 Blazer slowly forward, then turned onto the M37, the arrow-straight route east out of Ashgabat parallel to the Karakum Canal. In 1948 an earthquake had pulverised this whole part of the city, and as they drove through the suburbs, Leksin was struck by how the modest, squat buildings gave an impression of transience. Only the depressing, grey-brown edifice of the country's main typhoid sanatorium stood out as permanent. Built more like a prison than a hospital, it fought but failed to control the disease that, even today, was a rampant killer in this backward country.

Surveying the chaos, Leksin sighed in frustration at their slow progress as they met one hold-up after another. Every available form of transport, no matter what its condition, had been commandeered by would-be protestors. The roadsides were littered with clapped-out cars, ancient tractors and rusting motorcycles that hadn't made the grade. Tempers were running short in the stampede to get to the capital. Those left stranded were stepping out in front of cars to demand a lift. Next to a lopsided donkey cart with a shattered wheel, a group of men apparently brawled over who should continue on the donkey itself.

The scenes repeated themselves as they drove on, and through the turmoil Leksin observed the gradual shifts in landscape. Little by little the cement and asbestos factories intermingled with distilleries, then faded into scrawny vineyards and cotton fields. Here and there an ancient Soviet mural still proclaimed the glory of hard labour and urged workers on to greater efforts.

A little further on, all signs of human activity seemed suddenly to vanish. It was, Leksin felt, as if a line had been drawn on the ground, beyond which nothing should disturb the sand and saxual. To one side the land banked, sloping up to the contour of the Karakum Canal out of sight beyond the crest. On the other the Kopet Deg mountains stretched out along the southern border, a frieze of jagged peaks with foothills tumbling in a series of natural terraces towards the road.

Reaching the outskirts of Artyk, a shanty village of tin siding and asbestos roofs, the traffic came to a halt. Leksin jumped out of the car to see what was causing the hold-up, and swore when he saw the long tailback from the single police post where officials were checking papers of travellers in both directions.

"It'll be like this all the way, Alex" Talgat warned. "No hurry to process people today. All designed to slow progress."

As they edged towards the checkpoint, a fierce-looking police officer flagged them down, and Talgat pulled into the kerb. Taking their place at the back of the queue, unprotected from the soaring afternoon heat, they shuffled slowly forward. Leksin shook his head in disbelief. These checkpoints were a relic from Soviet days, when even locals were obliged to obtain a permit in order to travel from one region to another. Now this requirement no longer held, but the checkpoints survived, keeping soldiers employed and travellers under surveillance. With the extra crowds today, it was going to be hell.

At last, their turn, and they entered a grubby metal cabin where a single fan barely stirred the heat. Leksin perched on a rickety wooden chair by the registration desk and handed over his passport. The policeman studied him, then gestured towards his mobile and grinned.

"Not much good out here, no reception for another hundred kilometres."

"It's a Thuraya," Leksin volunteered in a moment of careless frankness. "Automatically takes on a satellite link if there's no GSM reception."

The guard's eyes lit up and he held out his hand. "Can I have a look?"

Leksin watched while he turned the gadget this way and that in his hand, examining it minutely. "It's so small, incredible. Mind if I show the others?" Without waiting for an answer he disappeared into the back of the hut.

"Big mistake," Leksin mouthed to Talgat.

"Patience, Alex. Like I said, they're in no hurry today, it's all part of the game."

The guard re-emerged minutes later and handed the Thuraya

back. "Amazing what it can do." He waved them on.

Back outside, Leksin returned to the car. As he slammed the door behind him, an emaciated boy, his hand deformed into something more like a foot, tapped on the window. Leksin reached into his pocket for a few manats, but as he wound down the window, a guard whacked his baton brutally against the back of the boy's knees and toppled him.

"Clear off, you fucking beggar!" the guard screamed at the boy.

Leksin reached for the door handle, but Talgat's grip held him back. He felt the fury boil in him as he watched the guard drag the boy off the road and sink his heavy boot into his ribs, aiming the kicks to do damage, not merely to hurt.

"It was better when we kept these fucking cripples locked away," Leksin heard the guard declaim to his colleague when he was done.

Chapter Fifty

Garabil Plateau, Turkmenistan

Half-an-hour later they hit another police post. By this point the torrent of would-be demonstrators heading towards the capital had thinned to a steady stream, and the queues to process their papers moved much quicker than before. As they reached the front, the policeman regarded them with mild disinterest, barely scanning their papers before waving them on.

Outside, two guards peered through the Blazer's windows. One of them patted the car's boot as Talgat approached.

"Open it!"

Talgat depressed the side of the key and the boot clicked open. One of the guards pulled it up, undid the flap of Leksin's backpack and spread its contents across the roof of the car. Picking out the camera, he passed it to his colleague who weighed it in his hand. "Fuji, light," he said, nodding his cheerful approval. "Very good." He slipped it into his pocket.

The other guard took the binoculars from their case and surveyed the mountains to the south. "Zeiss. Excellent." He hung them around his neck, then looked sternly at Talgat. "Your papers were not in order. We'll take these."

Leksin's shoulders rose stiffly into his neck as his fists clenched

"Let it go, Alex" Talgat whispered, his mouth fixed closed like a ventriloquist's. "Trust me, it's not worth it."

They drove off, continuing for several hours through the baking crust of the desert. Beyond the police post, the road deteriorated rapidly, and Talgat was forced to slow down to negotiate its broken surfaces and gaping potholes. On either side, the clay surface had fractured into a network of cracks that formed a rough honeycomb pattern. *Takyr*, they called it, Talgat said. No one seemed to live here. Even the sporadic impoverished villages on the desert's edge seemed abandoned and soulless, just the occasional camel meandering aimlessly through their sand-strewn streets.

At one of these, they stopped, and Talgat supplied a drink and sandwich from the boot. Leksin took the opportunity to try calling Nikolai again, but when he pressed speed dial on the Thuraya, nothing happened. He checked the battery: no problem there. He checked the signal: non-existent. Odd, the phone was designed to switch automatically to satellite if there was no GSM. Rebooting the phone, he input his password. Still no signal.

"Problem?" asked Talgat.

Leksin nodded.

"Explains why the policeman was keen to show the others. Clearly they'd planned to find a way cutting you off from the outset." Talgat shrugged. "Never mind." Depressing a small button at the side of the boot, he pulled out a panel behind the rear seat to reveal a rucksack and two water flasks.

He handed Leksin one of the flasks and a pair of goggles. "You'll need these for your eyes, if the wind gets up." He extracted a compass from the rucksack. "And this too, if we get split up."

Leksin pointed at the concealed panel. "Couldn't we have kept my camera and binoculars there too?"

Talgat shook his head. "Road tax, Alex. Had to lose something, or they'd have torn the car apart." Opening the rucksack, he displayed its contents. "We've got all we need in here – some hard biscuit to keep us going, binoculars, various tools that might come in handy, emergency medical stuff, even anti-venom. Don't worry, Alex."

It was late afternoon when they resumed their journey, and the sun hung heavy behind the mountains casting menacing shadows over the flatlands. Without warning Talgat swung off the M37 and headed towards Tagtabazar. As they bumped along, Leksin interpreted Talgat's terse commentary. Once a main artery for Russian troops during the Afghan war, the foothills were cluttered with the skeletons of derelict tanks and troop carriers left behind in the dash following the bankrupt Politburo's decision to pull out its forces. Even now, with the region's enormous gas deposits, the area was kept under constant surveillance for terrorist activity, and as the road twisted south through the valley, Leksin spotted soldiers perched high in the crags on lookout. A single helicopter spun circles above them.

They followed the road until the Garabil Plateau loomed ahead, a patchwork of pale and dark green, with shrubs and larches skirting hidden streams on a corrugated platform of land beyond which stood the Paropamisus Mountains across the border. The village of Garkent lay on the far side, and they slipped onto the dust track that corkscrewed through the steep foothills supporting the plateau.

Talgat pointed north, out into the desert. In the distance a dark shadow blotted out the horizon like a wall of brown sand stretching high into the sky. "Better get a move on," he said crisply.

"What is it?" Leksin asked.

As he looked across for an answer, the car turned a sharp bend. Talgat slammed his foot on the accelerator, thrusting Leksin violently back in his seat.

"What the . . . ?" Leksin exclaimed.

Less than fifty metres ahead a jeep parked across the track blocked their path. Two armed men stood in front and waved them down.

"Hang on!" Talgat shouted, his eyes sharp with concentration.

As the Blazer powered forward, the two men, taken by surprise, dived apart. At the last second, Talgat's deliberate skid clipped the jeep's front wing and sent it spinning round. For a moment the Blazer slid on the sand, then the tyres bit again and they lurched forward.

Leksin glanced through the rear window. The men were scrambling into the jeep and a second later sand spurted up as it moved.

"They're on us."

"OK. Few more minutes should do it," Talgat replied, pointing out towards the desert again. "That brown thing? Sandstorm. Be all over us shortly, we'll lose them then."

As they drove on, the sky dimmed with sand, and the wind rose rapidly, tossing torn-up saxaul in front of them. A moment later the day turned a lurid orange, then pitch black as if the power had cut out, and the road even a few metres ahead disappeared.

Chapter Fifty-One

Garabil Plateau, Turkmenistan

Leksin was relieved when the sandstorm finally passed over as quickly as it had overtaken them, leaving behind a thin veneer of dusty sand. They'd taken advantage of its cover to climb the steep foothill onto the Garabil Plateau. Talgat had scampered up the rock face like a mountain goat, but Leksin had struggled for a grip on the flaky stone.

Removing his goggles, Leksin was momentarily blinded by the glare of the sun, now lying over the distant Paropamisus mountains in Afghanistan. His throat felt scoured from the sandstorm, and he sipped slowly from his flask as he took in the full scale of the plateau. Ahead the land rolled in long undulations, like waves of a sea that had set solid. Beyond, serrated stone ridges rose one after another, each one higher than before, until eventually these merged into the mountains whose pinnacles stood on the horizon.

The surface was swathed with coarse grass, sparse at first but growing into a rich green further into the plateau. Here and there, tortured dwarf firs grew out of tiny fissures like emaciated Christmas trees.

"Better get a move on," Leksin urged. "Those bastards'll be right behind us, that's for sure."

The terrain immediately ahead pitched up and down, intercut with gulleys, and they hurried on as best they could. The scree tugged at their feet as they scrabbled up the slopes, and gave them no option other than to avalanche down. As the gradient bucked again, Leksin extracted binoculars from Talgat's rucksack and, clambering onto a high mound, surveyed their rear. As he'd suspected, the two agents were following, now too close for comfort. They'd separated to extend their search, a distance of several hundred metres between them. Leksin scrambled down to rejoin Talgat.

"One's right behind, other's over there," Leksin told him, pointing towards a rocky slope to their west. "You take him before he gets into the open, then double back. I'll keep the one behind us busy by leading him in the opposite direction."

As Talgat dashed off, Leksin turned and ran across the flatlands, heading for the cover on the far side. Reaching a depression in the ground, he rolled into it and, looking back, was dismayed to find that the agent had already scaled the bank and was sprinting across the plain after him. Leksin frowned with the realisation that he'd never manage to outrun this man. He'd have to find a better hiding place.

A hundred metres away he saw a broad dome-shaped boulder of immense proportions, its summit shingled with slate-like rocks. Time and climate had carved into it a labyrinth of broken crevices and small tunnels, like a giant anthill. Crouching low to the ground, Leksin dashed towards it. He slipped through a narrow fissure in the stone and entered a cramped inner cave, silent as a tomb. He kept quiet, listening for his pursuer.

A loud hiss issued from somewhere too near and sent a shiver down Leksin's spine. Reaching into his pocket, he turned on his Thuraya to cast a glimmer of light on his surroundings. A cobra lay curled under the stone ledge that formed the threshold of his bolthole, its mottled head drawn back and poised to strike. Beads of sweat stung Leksin's eyes as he realised he was trapped. If the snake didn't get him, then the agent would.

Pressing his body hard against the wall, he racked his brain for ways to defend himself, but drew a blank. Talgat had warned Leksin about the oxus on the journey when he'd questioned the need for anti-venom in the rucksack. *Cripple you in seconds*, Talgat had told him, *kill you inside an hour. My advice, Alex*, he'd said, *is keep away from the buggers.*

The seconds ticked by, seeming like hours, as Leksin and the snake surveyed each other from opposite sides of the cave, like a one-sided Mexican standoff in which there could be only one winner. All the time, the snake continued to hiss, rolling its head in slow elliptical movements, as if it wanted to hypnotise him, its half-evolved eyes willing him to make the first move.

Suddenly there was the scrape of feet outside, and Leksin took a deep breath. The agent or Talgat? Should he stay silent, or shout for help? A voice, not Talgat's, demanded to know if there was anyone there, then the thin ray of a torch beam shone through the crack. As the man started to shuffle through the gap, the snake became increasingly agitated, its head rotating from right to left, from Leksin to the entrance, like a spectator at a tennis match. Spotting Leksin, the agent stepped forward and raised his pistol just as the snake lunged. Again and again it struck his leg. The man screamed, then dropped both gun and torch. Leksin seized his chance and, rushing forward, crashed his clenched fist into the man's jaw. The man clattered to the ground, face-forward, and as the snake struck out once more for the easy target, this time sinking its fangs into his left eye, Leksin stepped around him and slipped out.

Chapter Fifty-Two

Garabil Plateau, Turkmenistan

"See that peak sticking up? Cat's Claw, they call it," Talgat told Leksin, holding a compass in one hand and pointing towards the Paropamisus mountains with the other.

Leksin nodded.

"That's the marker to follow, Alex." He held out the face of the compass for Leksin to see. "Memorise the reading. Anything happens to me, head for Garkent on your own."

The plateau had proved tough going, and they'd stopped for a brief rest on a bowl-shaped rock-shelf, its smooth granite surface sheltered from the dipping sun. Talgat had produced a thick hard biscuit from his rucksack, tough to chew but strangely satisfying. Gradually Leksin felt his energy renewing, and he scoured the terrain. Immediately below them a shallow valley twisted through the rocks. A herd of red-brown, short-haired moufflons grazed on its steep inclines, surefooted, their horns curved in almost a full revolution. Overhead swallows dipped and surged in a cycle of endless spirals. Beyond, the land rose in a series of small ridges and canyons, their skirts shaggy with sagebrush and fractured boulders, against the mountain backdrop now orange and violet in the early evening sun.

Setting off again, they followed the line of the valley. Not as direct as the Cat's Claw route, but it provided the best cover, and Talgat was wary of exposing them to patrols on higher ground. The sun was fading into a hazy twilight, obscuring the vista and making it difficult to judge distances. But as the light began to fade, the temperature also fell, making the going less sapping than before, and they made good progress. One side of the valley was covered with kara tau garlic, its pale pink star-shaped flowers

169

standing out in the gathering gloom, releasing a pungent aroma into the still air.

Leksin felt the rush of adrenaline build as they progressed. When this journey had started, the evidence that it would be worthwhile was extremely thin. A text message and a hazy satellite image. A long shot, as Talgat had put it. However, the sequence of events since pointed to there being something. They – whoever they were – had removed his ability to communicate, made off with his camera and binoculars, and finally tried to ambush the two of them in the middle of nowhere. The agents that had followed them after the sandstorm had meant business: they'd not been looking to take prisoners. No, Leksin reflected, there was something they were hiding, and now at last he was closing in on it.

The valley turned sharply east, so they heard the helicopter before it arced around the bend into view, the deafening throb of its rotors reverberating in the enclosed space. Talgat ducked behind a rock as the beam of its searchlight sliced the settling dusk and raked the ground. Leksin lay prone near the valley's edge, and the cone of light passed some fifteen metres to his right.

"Too easy to find ourselves trapped here," Talgat concluded once the helicopter had roared by. "Best get the hell out."

But, Leksin soon realised, this was easier said than done. The valley's steep slope was littered with loose stones, and for each upwards step, he found himself sliding back an equal amount. Still only half-way up, he eyed Talgat bounding ahead with an ease and fluency he couldn't match, and he swore in frustration as he renewed his own efforts. A shot rang out, and he saw Talgat sprinting along the spur, away from him. Maybe eighty metres behind, two figures silhouetted in the dusk were chasing after him.

Another shot. Talgat lurched forward and fell out of sight.

Leksin hugged the hillside, struggling to stay focused. His first thoughts were to go in pursuit, but, he realised, this would be an empty gesture. He didn't reckon his odds against two armed soldiers out here in the middle of nowhere. The likely result would simply exacerbate the situation. His lips tightened as nonetheless he fought back the instinct to go to his colleague's aid and recalled Talgat's instruction. *Anything happens to me, head for Garkent on your own.* Leksin shuddered as the reality of the words sunk in. *On your own.* What would he find in Garkent, and how could he possibly deal with it alone? Wary and tense, he waited for the figures to disappear, then crept over the hill and reluctantly headed south.

Chapter Fifty-Three

Ashgabat, Turkmenistan

Number 93, Magtumguli Street, is a tall, imposing building located in the heart of Ashgabat. At its front stands a towering statue of Turkmenbashi, framed against the skyline by a white marble arch inlaid with turquoise and yellow tiles. A wide arc of steps at one corner leads up through a labyrinth of columns to the control centre for State Security operations in Turkmenistan.

The Toyota pulled up and the diminutive figure of Orazov climbed out. Scurrying up the steps, closely followed by his aide, he handed his papers to the security guard, who inspected them unhurriedly. When he reached the bearer's name, he sprang quickly to attention and ushered them through with elaborate respect.

Orazov strode into the duty room, where Captain Gutov awaited them. Square jaw set rigid and eyes bulging warily, he stood stiffly, his back arched like a soldier on parade.

"What the hell happened?" Orazov demanded fiercely, dispensing with formalities. "Where did *you* lose them?"

"Let me show you, sir." Gutov took a step back to reveal a map on the wall. He traced the route with his finger. "Each checkpoint reported in as they passed. Our initial objective was to slow them down as much as possible, but as we agreed, when they turned towards Tagtabazar and their objective became certain, we set out to stop them altogether. We set up a roadblock just here, an isolated track right on the edge of the plateau."

"And?"

"They ran the roadblock, then we lost them in a sandstorm. It was bad luck."

"Bad luck, huh!" Orazov slapped his palm against the side of his head in exasperation. "Bloody incompetence, more like!"

"We found their abandoned vehicle once the sandstorm blew over, and our agents are in close pursuit. I'm expecting an update any moment," Gutov continued. "They're good men, sir, they'll catch them."

"They'd better, Captain. No more slip-ups, is that clear?" The edge of Orazov's tone made clear the price of failure. He nodded to his aide, who passed the officer a file.

Gutov leafed through the pages. A confidential FSB report from Moscow on Alex Leksin. He flicked through what was an impressive track record, to say the least, then glanced up at Orazov for guidance.

"Keep going," Orazov snapped.

Gutov read on. As he flipped the page, his eyes widened when he reached the item on Leksin's coke habit. Someone had pencilled in the margin: *'No action now, archive for future use'*.

"Put the word out that Leksin's a dangerous drug dealer," Orazov ordered. "I want posters everywhere. Make sure to stress the penalty for harbouring such people. There must be nowhere for him to hide."

Spinning on his heels, Orazov headed for the door. "I'll see you later, Captain," he warned over his shoulder. "By that time, I expect to find the problem's resolved, or you'll pay for it, believe me."

Chapter Fifty-Four

Ashgabat, Turkmenistan

Confronted with chaos, the manager of the Nissa Hotel struggled to keep his cool in front of the mass inflow of guests. With the opposition rally just a few days off, the lobby teemed with visitors who'd descended on the capital to witness the forthcoming historic event. Out of the price range of would-be demonstrators, the Nissa was booked solid, the usual influx of summer tourists heavily swelled by the arrival of reporters and television crews from across the world, all anxious to discover whether this would prove to be the start of another revolution like the one in Kyrgyzstan that forced out the old guard, or simply an escape valve for hot air, soon to be extinguished.

He'd drafted in extra help to cope with what he'd anticipated being an exceptionally busy evening, but still long queues had formed at the front desk, where a team of receptionists struggled to cope with the steady stream of arrivals, some with actual reservations, many simply hoping to bribe their way into a room. His head swivelled as he glimpsed the arrival of a uniformed KNB officer he recognised, accompanied by two plain-clothes agents. He watched as, with their usual finesse, they barged their way to the front of the queue, and he manoeuvred towards them as fast as he could. Too late.

"Get me the manager!" he heard the officer demand loudly, and he watched with dismay as, besieged by voices, the harried receptionist continued to process a guest on her computer.

"I'm busy, wait your turn," she snapped back without glancing up.

"Now, girl!" The officer shouted, thumping his fist down.

Startled, the receptionist looked up. Seeing his uniform, she went pale and jumped to her feet just as the manager caught up with them.

He flashed a practised smile at his visitor. "Good day, Captain Gutov. What can I do for you?"

"You have a guest here. Leksin. Take me to his room."

He turned to his receptionist, who inspected her screen. "Number 634, sir." She handed him the key.

Across the hall, guests thronged around the lifts, resigned to a long wait as the queue edged slowly forward. The two plain-clothed agents manhandled them aside and, ignoring their objections, purloined the next lift. As they got in, Gutov frowned at the printed timetable for the opposition rally stuck on the wall.

The manager snatched it off with an apologetic murmur. "They put them up as fast as we can take them down."

The lift pinged open, and he led the way as they marched in silence down the long corridor to Room 634, where the two agents elbowed him out of the way as soon as he'd unlocked the door. Without a word they ransacked the drawers and cupboards, tipping their contents onto the floor.

"Perhaps if I knew what you were looking for?" the manager ventured.

They ignored him. "We'll take the laptop too," Gutov told his agents, who placed it by the bedroom door before moving into the bathroom.

A minute later a voice called out for them, and Gutov led the manager in. The side panel had been removed from the bath to reveal three plastic bags containing a white powder. The officer pierced one with a penknife and wetted his finger to taste its contents.

"Cocaine."

The manager waited apprehensively as the captain rubbed the back of his hand along the line of his jaw and glared at him sternly.

"You've been harbouring a drug dealer here," Gutov said at last.

The manager swallowed hard. "How were we to know?" he suggested tentatively.

"It's a crime to conspire with pushers."

"But – "

"Shut up!" Gutov spoke into a transceiver. "Send them in now!"

A slick of sweat had formed on the manager's brow, and he dabbed a handkerchief discreetly over his face as two men appeared at the door. He recognised one of them as a local television news reporter. The other held a video camera.

"It's on the bed." Gutov indicated the bags of cocaine. "And this is the manager. He was present throughout the search."

The manager grabbed at the lifeline. "Of course, of course," he hurried to confirm. "I watched the whole thing. The three bags were hidden in the bathroom. I saw the agents uncover them."

Chapter Fifty-Five

Ashgabat, Turkmenistan

Borzov leant against the Tahiti's marble bar, absently studying the froth on his glass of Klassiki in the blue neon light. A girl half his age approached, come-on eyes, showy breasts, her hips swaying to the music. Slipping her arms around his neck, she tugged him towards the dance floor. Pretty little thing with a tight arse and an empty head – for Borzov, a winning combination. He pulled her close, but sent his mind elsewhere.

It had been a difficult conversation with Max Usenko when he'd got back to his office after the Smolinsky incident. "Why the hell didn't you take care of him earlier," Max had challenged, "before Vika could get to him?" It had taken all Borzov's self-control not to let fly. Right from the outset, he'd wanted to remove Smolinsky from the equation – it had been Max himself who'd resisted. Just frighten the man off, Max had urged, no more. It had been an accident waiting to happen – and now it had.

Then, when Borzov had raised the thorny question of Vika, yet again Max had prevaricated. The man was a weak little shit, Borzov despised creeps like him. But he was the paymaster, there was no other option than to play by his rules. What did Smolinsky tell Vika, Max had asked persistently. A look of sheer pain had crossed Borzov's face. How the fuck was he meant to know? At best, nothing, he'd replied; at worst, nothing good. In any event, what did Max want him to do now?

It had taken till late this afternoon for Max at last to come back with a decision, then a couple of hours to make the necessary arrangements. Afterwards, he'd come to the Tahiti to fill in time.

He checked his watch as the music changed. Time for business. He shrugged the girl away. A pity, but there'd always be another.

177

Taking a $100 note from his back pocket, he tucked it down her cleavage. "Keep it warm, honey," he shouted over the music.

She pouted back synthetic disappointment as he turned away and walked out.

*

Borzov pulled up two blocks down from the Sheraton, continuing the rest of the way on foot. Even at this hour, the pavement heaved with people, many sheltering for the night in car parks and shop doorways. Reaching the Sheraton, he skirted around the side to the service entrance where Mikhail awaited.

Mikhail was his cousin and worked as a cleaner in the hotel. Following Max's call late that afternoon, Borzov had enlisted his help. He needed to get into the hotel, he'd explained, but without passing through the security checks and cameras at the entrance. Mikhail was family, he could be relied on. Without any questions, he'd agreed to meet Borzov just before midnight.

The two of them slipped through the service entrance into a poorly-lit, dark green corridor.

"Staff elevator's on the left at the end," Mikhail explained, handing Borzov an envelope. "Key card's inside."

"Thanks. I owe you one."

As his cousin disappeared, Borzov continued along the corridor, deserted at this hour. Slipping into the changing rooms, he switched into a staff uniform, then headed towards the lift. A row of laundry baskets on one side of the corridor awaited collection. At the end of the corridor, a dying strip light flicked on and off, and the air filled with the sour scent of cooking oil floating from some distant kitchen. A cleaning trolley stood against the wall. Pulling back the metal-grille door, Borzov wheeled it into the lift and pressed the button for the top floor. As it started to climb, he leant against the side and inhaled deeply.

It wouldn't be long now.

Chapter Fifty-Six

Ashgabat, Turkmenistan

Logged onto the Schultzefinanze Bank's website, Orazov scrolled through the investments in his portfolio. The last twenty-four hours had been good: the markets had performed well. Defensives, as his Swiss investment manager described them, particularly tobaccos and oils, had gained a full percentage point. Things seemed to be looking up in emerging markets too: the currency crisis appeared to have run its course, and the BRICs were back on track.

Still no news from Gutov, though. As he scrolled down to the total portfolio value at the bottom of the page, it brought home to him how much was at stake. Not bad given that he'd started with zilch. Frankly, even this was just chicken feed compared with his potential rewards from the pipeline deal, if it went ahead. Nobody was going to put this at risk, let alone this man, Leksin. His jaw jutted with both determination and disapproval as he realised he'd have to sort out this problem himself. Gutov clearly wasn't up to it.

His phone rang. Max. Orazov winced: Max was never easy to deal with, and he'd wanted to avoid contact with him until the Leksin situation was resolved.

"Still no news," Orazov told him. "I'm taking charge of the search myself."

"Don't screw this up, Ali," Max warned in a slow monotone. "There's no such thing as a free lunch."

"Our interests are aligned, Max, I'll do my part." He hesitated a moment, then changed tack. "Is there still a problem with your sister?"

"Potentially," Max replied, stretching the syllables. "She tracked down Smolinsky."

"So I understand. What did he tell her?"

"That's something only Vika knows."

"So what next?"

"I can't afford to take chances, that's what next! Smolinsky's no longer an issue, but Vika's always been a problem for me," Max intoned dryly as if he were reading out the football results. " It's time to deal once and for all with the meddling bitch."

Intrigued, Orazov asked: "How?"

"I'll take care of my business, Ali. You make sure you deal with yours."

The line went dead.

Chapter Fifty-Seven

Ashgabat, Turkmenistan

The lift juddered to a halt, and a maid carrying a tray got in. Closing the gate for her, Borzov flashed a smile.

"Thanks," she smiled back. "I haven't seen you before, have I?"

He shook his head. "Temporary staff, brought in to help out during the rally."

She raised her eyebrows disapprovingly. "Rally, what a waste of time! What good's it doing?"

"Well, it's got me this job," Borzov commented. "I've been out of work for months now."

The lift juddered to a halt.

"My floor," the maid said.

Borzov pulled open the gate and watched her hips sway as she walked away, then resumed his climb to the next floor. When the lift stopped, he eased back the metal grille door, and following signs to Suite A, wheeled the cleaning trolley silently along the thick, Bukhara-patterned carpet that ran the full length of the corridor. Wall insets, discreetly lit, displayed framed black and white photographs of Ashgabat before and after the 1948 earthquake. Dimmed overhead lighting cast a viscous orange glow.

Parking the trolley on the wall opposite, he rested his ear against the door of Suite A. Silence. He tapped his fingers on it lightly. No answer. Good, Vika must be asleep. Taking the envelope Mikhail had given him from his pocket, he extracted the key card and swept it through the swipe reader. The door clicked open.

A night light above the door emitted a dim glimmer over the sitting room. A blue and white striped sofa lined one wall. In front of it, a coffee table, on which lay the remnants of room service, and two matching armchairs. A pair of tall French windows opened out onto a balcony. Between them, a flat-screen television rested on a display cabinet.

Quietly Borzov crossed towards the bedroom. At the door he stopped again and listened. Silence. He took a small plastic container from his pocket and extracted a syringe. Gently, he turned the door handle and pushed it open. As his eyes adjusted to the dark, he could just make out the figure of a woman lying under a duvet on the bed.

He crept over, then in a single movement, he yanked back the duvet and sank in the syringe. A hiss of air as the needle punctured the dummy, and the lights flashed on.

Two armed men, their heads muffled in balaclavas, sprang from the bathroom. For an instant Borzov stared at them in dismay, then, as he turned to escape, unseen hands overpowered him from behind. Forcing him to the floor, the three maintained complete silence as they trussed him up, stuffing a gag into his mouth.

The last thing Borzov saw before they placed a hood over his head was the slim figure of the maid with whom he'd shared the lift wheeling in a laundry basket. His groan was inaudible as they dumped him into the basket and wheeled it out.

Chapter Fifty-Eight

Ashgabat, Turkmenistan

The traffic was more than usually dense as the car sped Orazov out of the capital, and he stared impatiently from the window. Passing the new Olympic Centre, they drove along Berzengi, the city's equivalent of The Strip with all its rows of glittering post-modernist hotels. Each funded by different government departments anticipating a tide of Western oilmen vying to do business in the city, they were all virtually empty. At the roundabout, they took the main road east towards Geok-Tepe, then turned off into the desert.

Ten minutes later, a low-slung, circular building, its white walls floodlit above the dunes, appeared a kilometre to their right. This was the KNB monitoring station, the hub of the country's intelligence gathering. As they approached the electric perimeter fence, a Canon D60 zoomed in on the car's number plates, transmitting details to the central computer for real-time identification. A second later, in the guards' hut, a message flashed on a screen to warn that Orazov was approaching. Hurriedly straightening his uniform, the guard ran outside to salute as the solid steel gates swung open.

Captain Gutov was waiting in the entrance lobby. Strutting past, Orazov barged into the surveillance room where the staff manned the banks of monitoring desks. Across the room, a huge interactive wall map of Turkmenistan and its neighbouring countries flickered like an out-of-season Christmas tree. The place always reminded Orazov of the pictures he'd seen of the NASA operations room.

"Show me," Orazov grunted.

An operative at the far end had been tasked with keeping track of Leksin. Gutov nodded to him, and the wall map zoomed in on the Garabil Plateau.

"This is where they were last seen." The operative highlighted the track where Leksin and Talgat had abandoned the Blazer. "They headed onto the plateau, and the two agents followed." He paused. "Since then we've lost contact, I'm afraid. It's tough terrain, though, not easy to make headway, so even if they've evaded the agents, we estimate they couldn't have got further than here." Gutov nodded towards the operative, who lit up an area roughly halfway across the Plateau.

"Where's Garkent?" Orazov snapped.

A light indicated the location of the village on the map.

"So with all this information, why the fuck haven't you found them?"

"Patrols are out looking for them," Captain Gutov replied obliquely. "It'll soon be too dark for the helicopters. We're doing our best."

"Well, it's not bloody good enough, is it?" Orazov yelled, giving full rein to his frustration. His eyes radiated contempt, and his Arab nose turned crimson. "I warned you, Captain."

Turning his back on the officer, Orazov addressed the operative directly. "Where's the army camp?"

A light flicked on the map, just outside Garkent.

"Get the commandant on the phone for me, Captain." Orazov shook his head in indignation. "It's high time for some real action around here.

Chapter Fifty-Nine

Garabil Plateau, Turkmenistan

Two shots shattered the silence, some distance behind. Leksin winced: the soldiers on Talgat's tail finishing the job. They'd take no prisoners this evening, that was certain. *Anything happens to me, head for Garkent on your own,* Talgat had told him. But to what purpose? He brushed his fingers through his hair, inhaling deeply, fighting to retain his composure.

Hauling himself up onto a high outcrop, he looked around to get his bearings, then took out the compass Talgat had given him to mark his course. Best estimate: another eight kilometres to Garkent. Between him and the village, the land rose and fell: wastes of gravelled flatland flecked with volcanic boulders and towering slopes of sheer crags, interspersed with dense thickets of juniper and fir. Difficult to negotiate, and as night fell, even harder.

No patrols in sight, he sped across the flat ground, anxious to put as much distance between him and the men who'd cornered Talgat. He needed to make the most of what light remained, press on before the encroaching darkness inevitably slowed him down.

The land fissured into a broad gully. After their earlier experience, Leksin was keen to steer clear of valleys wherever possible – *too easy to get trapped, as Talgat had concluded* – but as he looked around, it was hard to hit upon an alternative route. If he went around, he'd go way off course, and time was critical. Added to which, the longer his journey took, the greater the odds of the patrols catching up with him. With some trepidation he negotiated the rock-strewn slope to the base of the ravine.

The ancient watercourse snaked smoothly across the plateau sporadically widening and narrowing, its steep sides gloomy with wormwood and sagebrush. Skeletal remains of animals, stripped

185

bare by polecats and vultures, showed white in the last vestiges of sunset. Silence hung heavy over him, his own footfall the only sound in the desolate isolation.

Some time later, he reached the protruding lip of an abandoned mineshaft nestled into the side of the rock face and slowed down. A few rusted buildings, linked by derelict chutes and silver asbestos-lagged pipes, clung to the slopes and, at their base, a rough-cut stone table and bench had somehow survived, weathered but solid.

Leksin perched on the bench and took a swig from his water flask. In the distance he could just hear the faint hum of a helicopter engine. Even in this heavy dusk, he realised, they were still out looking for him. He couldn't afford to rest here for long. He took another compass bearing. How much further? Six kilometres, perhaps. With increasingly rugged ground, unseen patrols, and night descending fast, there was no knowing how long it would take. Exhausted and without food, he knew he was already slowing down. At some point he'd have to stop. But not yet. Breathe deeply, he told himself. Get some air into your lungs. Accept the situation, don't fight it. Keep positive.

A rustle to his right, and his eyes snapped open. Rounding the corner, less than thirty metres away, a bear, the colour of cinnamon, and, worse, two cubs. The muscles in Leksin's neck stiffened as the bear caught his scent. Crouching for cover behind the stone table, he backed away slowly, but as the bear rose on her hind legs, her gaze fixed on him and she advanced. As her growls grew louder, he turned and ran inside the nearest building, groping around in the darkness.

A sudden rush of engine noise and swirling air, and a helicopter swept low into the valley. Leksin's body tensed as the beam from its floodlights swept over his hideout, then, through a shattered window, he watched the helicopter descend and hover just out of the bear's reach. Either they were deliberately baiting her, or he'd been spotted.

Picking his way through the debris of fallen bricks and shattered glass, he ducked under a metal spiral staircase just as the helicopter's searchlight exploded through the derelict roof. Deafened by the engine's reverberations in the confined space, he clamped his hands over his ears and waited anxiously as the beams lasered the ramshackle walls and seemed to linger in the spirals of the staircase. Apparently satisfied, the helicopter moved over the other buildings, and Leksin let out a sigh of relief.

At last, the beat of the engine receded. He waited until it was scarcely vibrating before he emerged. Both helicopter and bears had disappeared. Time to get out of this valley. He clambered up the steep rocky bank past the mine shaft, struggling for purchase as he flailed through the flaky tailings.

Chapter Sixty

Garabil Plateau, Turkmenistan

Grunting with disgust, the commandant pushed aside the tray before him. It was bad enough being banished to this God-awful wasteland without the food always tasting like shit as well. He'd no idea whom he'd upset to get saddled with this posting, but if he ever found out, he'd make the bastard regret it.

He'd been stuck on the plateau for nearly four years now. A key component in Turkmenistan's border control, that was the official job description, but who were they kidding? Until the plant had gone into operation not much more than a year ago, there'd been bugger all to protect. Even now, when they were tasked with its security, they just went through the motions. After all, who was going to disturb them in middle of nowhere? The Ashgabat command centre fully appreciated this, of course; that's why they dumped their incompetents and misfits on him out here.

The commandant had always kept his distance from the men under his command, even more so here where he had nothing in common with the scum. He ate alone, spent most days hunting and fishing, and ruled the camp with a rod of iron. The only battle he fought was against boredom. A couple of weeks ago, though, there'd been a fleeting moment of excitement. Word had come through from Ashgabat that a Russian agent was heading their way. He was to capture the man, he'd been instructed, then find out who'd sent him. For a couple of hours, it had been like old times, back in the Tagtabazar interrogation centre. For the first time in ages, he'd felt the flow of adrenaline.

Tagtabazar, he reflected nostalgically. Those had been good times. He'd felt like a proper soldier then. He reached into the bottom drawer of his desk and, taking out a folder tucked under a pile of others, started to flick through the contents.

His eyes lingered on the photo of an Afghan prisoner, whose elbows were bound tightly behind him and linked to his feet so that his back arched. The commandant could still remember his screams as they'd fitted a rope under his arms, looped it over a beam and left him hanging overnight. In the morning the man had told them everything they'd wanted to know, and more. But when they'd let him down, his limbs had been paralysed. No matter, they'd shot him as soon as they'd dragged him outside.

The commandant's mouth creased into a rotten-toothed smirk as he turned the page. The *parrilla*, one of his favourites. He'd learnt the technique from a Chilean secret service agent he'd met on holiday in Cyprus, he recalled. He peered dispassionately at the image of a naked man strapped tightly on a metal frame. In those days he'd insisted on operating the controls himself, instigating the electric shocks that would make the victim's body convulse in a vain attempt to evade the burning iron bars. The technique never failed. Often, just the sight of the *parrilla* was enough to set the prisoner talking.

From another drawer of his desk, the commandant pulled out a bottle of Arassa, cheap Turkmen vodka. He poured some into a cup, then sipped it slowly as, turning the page, his eyes alighted on the photo of a young boy lying in a shallow grave, his terrified eyes fixed on the face of his father who stood above him. Out of picture, the commandant recalled, the man's wife had been positioned on a flimsy wooden stool, a rope around her neck secured to the branch of a tree. The man had been given a simple choice: bury his son alive, or watch his wife hang. Alternatively, he could talk. That was the course he'd chosen: he'd given the commandant the location of the arms cache. Then he watched helplessly as, first his wife, then his son, had been shot. He'd hanged himself that night, the commandant remembered.

A knock on the door, then a soldier entered.

"There's a phone call for you in the office, sir," he explained. "The caller said his name was Ali Orazov."

The commandant raised an eyebrow as he got to his feet. What could such a senior government official want with him at this time of night?

Chapter Sixty-One

Garabil Plateau, Turkmenistan

The last light was fading as Leksin clambered over the summit out of the valley. To the west he could just discern through the purple gloom the outline of vast canyons trending towards the Kopet Deg mountains. As far as he could see the terrain to the south, more or less in the direction of Garkent, looked broadly flat. Not that simple, though, he'd soon discovered. Coarse bracken now covered the ground, and the bristles ripped his trousers and scratched his legs as he waded through.

As he progressed, the silence was broken by the trickle of water somewhere ahead, subtle at first, then as he drew nearer, free-flowing and gushing. He found himself on the edge of a deep channel, through which a river eddied around misshapen boulders and rounded silt mounds. The dark crisscross of a trestle bridge stretched over the canyon, on the far side of which castellated greyish rock glinted in the moonlight. Leksin approached and tested the bridge warily. It creaked under his weight, and he jumped off immediately. Glancing back, he spotted a line of torch-lit pinpricks fanned out not far behind him. Damn, the helicopter pilot must have spotted him after all and alerted a patrol. The bridge was now his only means of escape. He backed off a few metres to get a running start, then ignoring the knot of anxiety in the pit of his stomach, propelled himself forward.

The bridge swung wildly as he sprinted across, and the wooden struts snapped under the pounding of his feet. As he ate up the distance, one of the supporting trestles gave way, and the bridge tilted on its side. Hanging on for all he was worth, he used hands and legs to yank himself forward, bit by bit, all the time conscious that a single sudden, wayward movement would send him and the bridge crashing into the ravine. Eventually he reached the end, and he threw himself onto firm ground just as the echo of voices on the far side floated across the ravine.

He lay there motionless, catching the drift as his pursuers tried to decide what to do next. Had the scumbag come this way? If so, was this wreck safe to cross? The argument swung to and fro. The sergeant asked for a volunteer to test it out, but none was forthcoming. In the end, the sergeant forced one of the young conscripts at gunpoint to start across the bridge.

Leksin held his breath as the soldier's voice got closer, cursing the sergeant as he nervously edged his way forward. Finally the strain on the remaining trestle supports proved too much: one snapped with a loud crack, and Leksin could feel the vibration as his end of the bridge came away from its fastenings. The bridge swung down, crashing into the jagged face of the ravine, and shattered. From below, a wail of terror came to an abrupt end.

Leksin waited until the rest of them stopped wrangling about who was to blame and moved off before setting out again. Under the circumstances a change of plan seemed in order, so he took the forest route rather than the more direct course over the flatlands. The tightly clustered firs blanked out the moonlight, making the atmosphere at once airless and claustrophobic, but, Leksin reckoned, he was less likely to run into a patrol here than out in the open.

Eventually the forest curved west, and Leksin had no choice but to break cover and take another compass bearing. The three-quarter moon cast a pale light over the scene, but not enough to work out how far he still had to go. Exhaustion was beginning to take its toll: tired and hungry, he felt increasingly pessimistic of the outcome. What would he find in Garkent? No idea. Whatever it was, what could he do about it? No idea, either. Having got so far, though, he had to go on and hope a solution would come to light.

In the distance, directly on the line to Garkent, the moon illuminated the granite surface of a sharp peak, bent like a beckoning finger. The Cat's Claw. Head towards that, keep it in sight, that was his only aim for now.

Wearily he moved forward on autopilot. The faint moonlight seemed to throw back its own reflection in the colourless shadowy boulders and spindly pinnacles. The cool grass underfoot hid small serrated sedimentary rocks, over which he kept stumbling. Long, blue, spiky-edged shadows extended from the sparse trees. A little further, he seemed to enter a long corridor where the ground rippled precariously underfoot as if the land were being squeezed by the steep sides.

Voices in the dark, not far away, just over the incline. Leksin gasped and stopped in his tracks. Crawling as quietly as possible behind a boulder, he edged around its side to take a look. Six soldiers, taking a break from patrol duties, obstructed the way ahead.

Chapter Sixty-Two

Garabil Plateau, Turkmenistan

Hunched on a rock, the corporal drew on his cigarette. Just his lousy luck to be saddled with extra duty on his birthday. Back at the barracks, they'd each stumped up fifty manats for the kitty and were well into their beer when the balloon went up. Every last soldier, even the cook and quartermaster, had been rounded up and ordered to comb the plateau for some big-time drug dealer.

He gritted his teeth, struck by the unfairness of it all. He was under no illusions: this was a dead-end posting where nothing ever happened and from which nobody went anywhere. Being sent here was the end of the line, somewhere to be swept away and forgotten, a place in which to while away the last quota of military service. Life here was dull, uneventful and pointless. Why the hell did this have to change on his birthday of all days?

One of his squad approached, holding out a round sausage and an open penknife. "Cut you a slice, Corp?"

He shook his head and waved the man away. Flicking another cigarette from the packet, he lit it with the butt end, held the smoke in his mouth, deep in thought, then sucked it into his lungs. Who the hell was this guy they were looking for? Dangerous drug dealer, the commandant had briefed them. Suspected of killing the two agents following him. Take no chances, shoot on sight. But what was he doing out here? No one was saying.

Peering through the gloom at the conscripts who made up his squad, he doubted whether they'd prove up to the task. What match would this bunch of ill-trained no-hopers be for a dangerous drug dealer? Twice already they'd fired in panic at animals moving in the dark. But what the hell? The odds against them stumbling into anyone in this wilderness were pretty slim. Almost non-existent.

194

Just a waste of time, and on his birthday too . . .

A rifle shot, and a scream rent the dark. Tossing away his cigarette, the corporal jumped up.

"Who fired that?" he demanded fiercely.

"Over there," a spotty-faced conscript young enough to be his son told him, pointing excitedly into the gloom. "Someone moved."

Raising his arm, the corporal signalled for quiet. In the silence he could just make out a soft moaning some way ahead. Circling his arm, he spread out his men, and they advanced slowly, rifles ready. As they drew closer, the moaning turned into an uneasy rasp.

Almost there, the corporal flashed on his torch. In front of him, a young girl, perhaps ten or twelve years old, lay slumped on the ground. Barely conscious, blood seeped through her blue check dress.

Shit, they were in for it now. Better be somewhere else quick.

Chapter Sixty-Three

Garabil Plateau, Turkmenistan

The voices faded, and Leksin crept forward, guided by laboured breathing a short distance ahead. Switching on his Thuraya, its screen cast a murky light over the slumped outline of a young girl. Her eyes remained closed, but she groaned softly as Leksin held the light to her face before hovering it over her blood-stained dress.

Dampening his handkerchief, he wiped the girl's face. Her eyes flashed open and filled with terror.

"Keep still, sweetie," he whispered reassuringly. "I'm here to help you."

She looked confused. "What happened?" she mouthed.

"You've been shot," he replied softly. Summoning a reassuring smile, he asked: "What's your name?"

"Yana."

"Well, Yana, I need to take a look. May I?"

A weak nod.

Very gently he unbuttoned her dress and slipped off one shoulder. Only a flesh wound, she'd be all right if he could stem the bleeding. Tearing a strip off the bottom of her dress, he folded one section into a makeshift bandage and secured it tightly around the wound with the other.

What now? It was pretty clear the army had been put on full alert: patrols were out in force, trigger-happy and gradually closing the net. The last thing he could afford was a delay, he'd experienced too many near-misses already. Making the most of the dark was his best chance. Once day broke, there'd be nowhere to hide. But, equally, as he looked down at the waif-like figure of Yana, it was clear she was in no condition to be left. Even if the soldiers intended to return with a medic, which he somehow doubted, they'd be too late. The wolves would get her if the bleeding didn't first. No, whatever the consequences, he realised, he had to get the girl to safety. He couldn't just abandon her. Not this child, not any child.

Wiping her forehead again, he asked: "Where do you live?"

"Over the hill."

Her eyes indicated eastwards. Leksin needed south.

"Not far," she added, sensing a moment of indecision.

*

The tapping of Leksin's foot against the door brought a scurry of steps within. It opened a crack, an eye peered out, then it flew apart. A broad, lumbering man grabbed the girl.

"What is it, Batyr?" a fretful voice inside asked. "Is Yana back from Galina's at last?"

"She's been hurt, Tania," he shouted back. Laying her on the table, he threw Leksin an accusing glance. "What the hell happened? You do this?"

"Soldiers," Leksin replied. "They left her for dead."

A woman, younger than her husband and still pretty, rushed out from the back with a first aid kit. Batyr watched anxiously as she slipped off the temporary dressing and examined the wound.

"It's going to be OK, darling," Tania reassured her daughter before throwing a disapproving glance at her husband. "Hot water. Clean cloth too."

Leksin stood there awkwardly as Batyr disappeared. "Is there anything I can do?" he asked.

"No, you've done enough," Tania snapped back ambiguously.

Batyr returned, placed a bowl and clean towel on the sideboard, then sat next to Leksin. "She was a nurse before she was stupid enough to marry me," he told him with a stiff smile. "She'll know what to do."

A moment later, they heard shouting on the hillside. Batyr

peered out of the window. Soldiers, and they were coming their way.

"They looking for you?"

Leksin nodded.

Batyr's eyes darkened as he hovered on the edge of betrayal. He studied Leksin closely before reaching a decision. This man had just saved his daughter's life, he couldn't give him up.

"Under the bed, quick."

Leksin slid under the mattress, and Batyr kicked a line of boxes over the gap just as a fist thumped on the door.

Whispering something to Tania in Turkmen, he opened the door and eyed the young soldier with unconcealed hostility. "You the bastard who shot my daughter? Come to finish her off?"

The soldier pushed him aside, his heavy boots stomping on the stone floor. Looking around the room, his sullen eyes rested on Yana spread out on the table. Her bloodstained dress lay in a heap on the floor.

"We're looking for a man."

"Not a ten-year-old girl then?" Batyr replied with heavy sarcasm. "Going to shoot him too?"

At first the soldier made no reply, not hearing or choosing not to listen, then he spun around angrily. "Drug dealer," he grunted, checking inside the cupboards. "Twenty years for anyone who helps him."

Batyr let out a low whistle. "Twenty years, eh? Well, I'd better keep my eyes peeled."

"Mind you do. We'll be back."

The soldier strode out. Batyr spat on the floor and locked the door behind him.

*

Batyr dumped the bedding in a corner of the barn. "You'll be all right here," he assured Leksin. Clasping one corner of a canvas rug, he held out the other. "Here, help me spread it out."

198

A rustle from one of the stalls, and a horse got up, distracted by this late-night intrusion.

"It's all right, boy," Batyr said softly, going over to rub its nose. "I've brought you a friend to keep you company." He paused before adding: "At least I hope he's a friend."

Turning to face Leksin, his eyes rested intently on his guest. "You a drug dealer like they say?" The term sounded odd in Batyr's dated Russian. It was a language he'd have learnt at school, Leksin guessed, but living out here, not one he spoke often.

Leksin shook his head.

"No, I reckon you're not." Batyr frowned. "You shouldn't be here, though – that much I believe."

Avoiding Batyr's gaze, Leksin made no comment. The candle light flickered off the flint stone walls, and he made a show of examining a pile of dried lambskins, the tight black curls of their pelts sprinkled with white crystals of salt.

"So you going to tell me what you *are* doing?" Batyr persisted.

"I'm heading for a plant on the Afghan border," Leksin replied, realising under the circumstances he had little to lose in telling the truth.

Batyr's hand drifted to the knife at his waist. "You're a *musor*."

Leksin's face creased into a slight smile. "No, not the police."

"Then you connected with the other man?"

The question took Leksin off-guard. "Other man?"

"Yes, last week . . ." Stopping in mid-sentence, his eyes seemed to fix on some distant point. All at once the regret on his face became almost tangible, the image of the stranger begging for shelter refusing to fade. "Soldiers caught him," he said eventually.

So that was it, Leksin realised, piecing together the puzzle. He and the agent had both been following the same trail, but the agent had run into trouble. That was why Moscow had suddenly lost contact. "Yes, I guess I'm connected with him," he told Batyr. "Our objective is the same."

"But not the outcome, I hope," Batyr said thickly. "They blinded him, then burnt him alive."

Chapter Sixty-Four

Garabil Plateau, Turkmenistan

Leksin woke with a start to find Batyr towering over him, and rolled away defensively. Seeing the startled look on Leksin's face, Batyr's eyes narrowed into a genial smile, and he raised both arms at the elbow to show that he came in peace.

"What's the time?" Leksin asked blearily.

"Just gone five. We ought to get going while it's still dark."

Leksin gave him a puzzled look. "We?"

"Well, I can't let the man who saved my Yana walk straight into a patrol, can I?" He picked up Leksin's water flask and headed towards the barn door before Leksin could answer. "I'll put a few things together while you get ready."

*

They edged carefully along a narrow ledge carved by centuries of erosion into the cliff. Below, a river flushed down from the mountains, meandering through the shallow gorge between borders of immense talus deposits. After a while, and much to Leksin's relief, the ledge sloped down to the river bank.

This was Batyr's land, and he'd negotiated the difficult terrain with an agility and speed that Leksin had found impossible to emulate. It would have been easier if they'd kept to the top of the gorge, Batyr had explained, but that's where the patrols would be. Instead, Leksin had scrambled over the rough ground in Batyr's wake, straining every sinew in his body, bruising his ankles and half-pulling his arms from their sockets. It might have been only an hour since they'd set off, but already he was struggling to keep up.

"We'll rest soon," Batyr assured him as they descended to the river bank. "When we reach the fall."

Dawn was beginning to break, and in the half-light the scene had taken on that strange black-and-white quality that precedes the onset of colour. As they followed the river's twisting course, they passed under rock shelves that hung precariously over their heads and climbed over rock falls that obstructed their way forward. Gradually the roar of water increased, becoming almost deafening as they neared a massive waterfall. Glancing up, Leksin realised that he was in fact looking at three separate falls, thick flows of water pouring down from the top two before cascading over the travertine rock and fanning out in a curtain of white water that crashed into a powerful whirlpool below.

Batyr hunkered down and patted the ground next to him. Opening the pouch slung over his shoulder, he passed Leksin a handful of pistachios. "Eat them slowly, they'll give you energy," he shouted over the noise of the water.

"How much further?" Leksin asked, cracking open a nut and tossing the shell into the water.

"Worst's behind us, young 'un. Soon be out of here, then we'll take the track to the plant." He paused. "Mind you, that's where it'll get hairy. They'll be looking to trap you there."

Well, nothing unusual about that, Leksin reflected. One way or another they'd been setting traps for him ever since he set foot in this country.

"What about you?" he asked Batyr, changing the subject. "Ever thought of moving to town where things aren't such a struggle?"

Batyr shook his head. "Perhaps before I married, I don't know. Not now. We can be our own people out here, bring up our daughter how we choose. The city wouldn't let us." Seeing the uncomprehending look on Leksin's face, he continued: "You have to pace yourself here, young 'un. We like to say we make haste slowly. You soon learn to adapt to the conditions – just like him." He gestured toward a solar-powered lizard that scudded past, its striped tail swishing above it.

201

"But it can't be – "

He was interrupted by Batyr yanking at his arm and pointing upwards. A line of several soldiers was proceeding along the ridge on the other side. So far, they hadn't been spotted.

"Come, quick."

Without a backward glance Batyr ran along the bank. Leksin followed closely, balking only when Batyr suddenly disappeared inside the waterfall. Glancing back, the soldiers stood ominously on the skyline, their eyes combing the gorge for him. Nothing for it, he charged through the waterfall, floundered on its glass-smooth surface and sprawled over the floor of the rock shelter within. Unable to hide a smirk, Batyr helped him to his feet.

The roar of water echoing off the sides of hollow cave made words inaudible, and they waited in silence for the soldiers to pass. Fifteen minutes later, Batyr made a sign for Leksin to stay where he was while he went to investigate, then he darted through the water curtain. It seemed like an age before he reappeared and, indicating that the coast was clear, guided Leksin out.

*

By now the sun had risen, though not long enough to dispel the freshness in the air, and the terrain had changed, reminding Leksin of the Kolesnikov landscape hanging in his study back in Moscow. Undulating grasslands, topped with huge clumps of fennel bushes spread out like giant umbrellas, nestled in between mountain foothills either side. Fractured rock jutted up at intervals on the slopes, and a black vulture glided menacingly overhead. Here and there stone huts, much like Batyr's, were tucked neatly into the hillside wherever the contours provided natural shelter.

The track connecting Garkent and the plant had been cut through the bushes, its irregular surface rutted by the passage of lorries bringing supplies. This is the only way in and out, Batyr warned him. Think of it like a bridge that has to be crossed at all costs. Bear that in mind for the way back. Get the hell off the track as quick as you can.

So far as it was possible, they kept under the cover of the bushes. From time to time, the bushes grew too dense and they were forced onto the track to bypass them. Without a word they had fallen into a routine: Batyr would go first, check out the way ahead, then let out a low whistle to tell Leksin it was safe to follow. It was inevitable that their luck eventually ran out. The track sloped upward to a slight crest, and at first glance Batyr failed to spot the soldiers approaching from the opposite direction as he broke cover.

"You there!" a man's voice rang out in the silence. "Come here!"

Surprised, Batyr came to a standstill. Fifty metres ahead, two soldiers blocked the way forward, their rifles trained on him. Raising his hands in surrender, his face creased into a broad grin as he recognised the soldier who had stopped him and Yana a week earlier.

"You know me," he said, putting his hands down and approaching. "Batyr, friend of the commandant."

The soldier looked unconvinced. "What are you doing here?" he demanded suspiciously.

"Me? I often come this way."

For a few seconds their eyes met, then with a shrug, the soldier stood aside to let him pass.

Meanwhile, Leksin had circumvented the bushes and was tracking Batyr's progress, out of sight. He'd held his breath during the exchange with the two soldiers and had been about to move on when he overheard one of the soldiers tell his colleague: "Follow him, don't let him see you. I don't trust that bugger for a second."

Running along the outer rim of the hedgerow, Leksin stopped just ahead of Batyr. Out of earshot of the soldiers, he caught Batyr's eye through a crack in the leaves and warned him that he was being followed.

"I'll take it from here," Leksin told him, giving Batyr no time to protest. "You lead them away from me, OK?"

Batyr gave a slight, reluctant nod.

"Thanks," Leksin said. "Say hi to Yana for me." Then he turned away.

The second Leksin first glimpsed the plant, he was struck by how out of place it seemed. Surrounded by a tall lattice-wire fence topped with three rows of barbed wire, four one-storey, whitewashed buildings were set in a neat row. With no visible windows, their flat roofs were crammed with what looked like complex machinery to control ventilation and exhaust fumes. A bright red three-pronged chimney-stack rose tall in the centre. In one corner a square outbuilding, set away from the others, bore the skull-and-crossbones of an electricity generator. Two jeeps and an orange Kamaz truck were parked near the guardhouse at the gates. A young conscript shuffled around the perimeter, looking sullen and bored.

Crouching down, Leksin began to trace a wide circuit around the compound, looking for a point of access. It wasn't going to be easy, he realised immediately, there'd be only one outcome if he was caught. Somehow, despite the risks, he had to find an entry point, or fail. A helicopter roared over the horizon, and he ducked under a flat-topped pistachio bush for cover. Waiting for it to pass, he fought to dispel his doubts. Reaching into his back pocket, he extracted a crumpled photograph of his sister, Lena. He studied it for a few moments, rubbing his fingers gently over its surface. Then, slipping it back in his pocket, he stood up to check the way was clear.

A voice from a hollow to his left made him duck down again.

"Over here – and don't make so much noise."

He knew the voice and spun around.

Talgat grinned back.

204

PART TWO

Chapter Sixty-Five

Moscow, Russia

Anya Politska typed furiously into her laptop, her handwritten notes spread untidily across her desk in the open-plan office of Novy Novoski, the controversial investigative bi-weekly. Her colleagues milled around her cubicle in small groups, talking in whispers. They were all edgy with the sense of anticipation.

Politska paused to read through what she'd written, pursing her lips with approval. Surely the ex-KGB snoop had gone too far this time? Even Karpev, she reckoned, wouldn't be able to withstand the public outcry that her revelations would provoke.

*

Inured as she was by hard experience, she'd wept when the shock news of the mass murder of children and teachers at School No 86 in Pechatniki had broken two days earlier. She'd covered many atrocities, but the day when a massacre of innocents no longer moved her, she'd give up. As a journalist, she had a part to play. Blinking back the tears, she'd assimilated the scene. The banner hastily erected across the front of the school had registered with her immediately. Islamic Democratic Freedom Movement, it had read. Subsequently she'd listened intently as an FSB spokesman confirmed the IDFM's responsibility.

The IDFM was a Chechen group, and as a journalist during the Chechnya war, Politska had established links with its leader. The group were certainly no saints, but the mass murder of children was not their style either. Something smelt wrong. Using her contacts, Politska had succeeded yesterday in talking to the group's leader, who'd vehemently denied any involvement with the school bombing. *It's all a set-up,* he'd told her, and she believed him.

Her next move had been to arrange a meeting with her FSB informant. A reliable source – at a price – in the past, on this occasion he'd refused point-blank to discuss the subject.

"You're walking on quicksand, Anya," he'd warned. "Let this one drop."

"I can't, you know better than that," she'd replied. She'd experienced more than her fair share of threats and intimidation over the years – beatings, poisoning, electric shocks, days of confinement in a pit, even a mock execution. But these were the occupational hazards of investigative journalism in Karpev's Russia, and if you weren't prepared to risk them, then you needed to change your job.

When she'd got back to the office, though, she'd felt despondent. All she had was the denial of the IDFM's leader, but on its own this meant nothing. No one would believe him without independent evidence supporting his claim, yet she was running out of leads. Then, this morning, everything had changed.

When she'd arrived in the office, she'd found an email sent to her anonymously overnight. Nothing in the body of the text, just an attachment and a heading, Look at the date. Opening the attachment, she'd found a draft press release on FSB-headed paper describing the terrorist attack on the school. As she'd started to read through, she'd felt her professional instincts take hold.

The press release summarised an incident at School No 86 in Pechatniki. It detailed how terrorists had taken over the building during school hours, rigged it with explosives and held children and teachers captive. But in this version there was no actual explosion, no death toll, and the terrorists had escaped. Politska scrolled up and down the text, confused. Suddenly her eyes fixed on the top line - the draft press release was dated the day *before* the actual incident occurred.

She swivelled in her chair to stare out of the window as the implications fell into place. The school bombing, as she'd suspected from the outset, was no straightforward terrorist incident. Now she had solid evidence that the FSB had themselves been responsible. The appalling consequences might not have been their intended outcome, but they had always been a possibility. As her father used to say, if you play with fire, there's always a chance you'll get burned.

Of course, she acknowledged, this was not the first time the FSB had stage-managed terrorist incidents. All the evidence pointed to the apartment bombings in 1999 being perpetrated by the FSB in order to legitimise the subsequent invasion of Chechnya and the assumption of power by one of its own. Almost simultaneously, an unexploded bomb had been found and defused in Ryazan, and subsequent police investigations identified the three men responsible as FSB agents. Even these were not isolated examples: it was now clear that the FSB were complicit in bomb explosions in the marketplace in the southern Russian city of Astrakhan in 2001, at the bus stops in Voronezh in 2004 and on the Moscow-Grozny train in 2005. And, as Politska herself knew well, during the Chechnya conflicts, the FSB organised numerous kidnappings of journalists and foreign NGO workers, pretending to be Chechen terrorists, in order to build up international support for the Russian invasion.

Nonetheless the mass murder of children . . . well, that was in another league altogether. She'd got Karpev now.

*

Her editor was holed up in his corner office, sealed off from the rest of the journalists by glass walls. Catching his eye, Politska indicated that she'd just sent him a draft of her article, then went to the kitchenette in search of coffee. Taking her plastic cup onto the fire escape, she lit a cigarette and let the smoke slowly into her lungs.

Ten minutes later when she returned to her desk, she found her editor waiting for her. He looked visibly shaken.

"Are you sure?" he asked her in a trembling voice

"I've checked the facts."

"I don't mean that, Anya. Are you sure you want to go ahead with this? You know the risk you're running?"

Politska nodded. Being an effective investigative journalist was up there with oil and bank executives in the list of high-risk occupations. In little more than a decade, over 150 Russian journalists had been murdered, almost all of them critical of Karpev and his thugs. Many of these journalists had been her friends and, like them, she wasn't inclined to let the bullies win. With a resolute look in her eyes, she turned back to her computer and typed:

Am I afraid?

I write this article in the full knowledge of the personal risks I face. If anyone thinks they can just ignore Karpev's abuse of power and denial of democracy, then let them do so. It would certainly be easier that way, but it would be a death sentence for our grandchildren.

Printing it off, she handed it to her editor. "Add that as a postscript to the article," she told him. "The people should be left in no doubt."

*

On her way home Politska stopped off at the hospital where her brother was dying of liver cancer. Today he was barely conscious. The end won't be long now, the nurse had told her. She'd held her brother's hand for half-an-hour, fighting to hold back tears, then kissed him and left. Taking the metro to Polyanka, she stopped off at Perekrostok supermarket for some groceries and a bottle of whisky before heading home.

Letting herself through the main entrance of her apartment block, she found an elderly woman slumped in a chair in the hall. Her face was white, and she was breathing heavily.

"Are you OK?" Politska asked, kneeling down to place a hand on the woman's forehead. "Should I call a doctor?"

The woman shook her head. "I'm just having one of my turns, dear, makes me feel dizzy," she replied weakly. "Would you mind helping me to my flat? It's on the second floor."

"Of course. Stay there while I call the lift."

The lift descended, and Politska propped open the door with her shopping bag before assisting the old woman in. Removing her bag, she pressed the lift controls.

A few moments later, the lift juddered to a halt on the second floor. Nadia glanced at Politska's body lying at her feet, blood now seeping from the two small bullet holes in her chest. There was a third bullet hole between the eyes. Slipping the Makarov PMM into her coat pocket, Nadia pressed the button for the top floor, then jumped out of the lift before the doors closed. Hurrying down the stairs, she went out into the busy street.

Chapter Sixty-Six

Moscow, Russia

In the library of his house in central Moscow Max sat in near darkness, staring blankly at the television screen on which the all-night news silently revolved and reshuffled. Bach's Second Brandenburg Concerto wafted from Bose speakers, the relentless ticking of the ormulu clock like a metronome in the background.

Reaching for the Chardonnay, the bottle shook as he attempted to pour, and he grabbed it tightly with both hands. "Come on, Max," he told himself, "calm down." Lighting a Black Russian, he closed his eyes and swilled the smoke thoughtfully around his mouth.

Things had not been going well, there was no denying that. Earlier, he'd phoned Orazov and had a short but not very sweet conversation. Somehow the man had managed to lose Leksin. Max could hardly believe it. For fuck's sake, the country had one of the largest per capita security forces in the world. Surely they could have managed such a simple task?

And what about Vika? He'd done his utmost to stop her meddling in this affair – Central Asia was his area, not hers – but, whatever he did, she kept bouncing back. Smolinsky had been the last straw. Of course, he'd never know what, if anything, Smolinsky had told her, but too much was at stake to take a risk. In the end he'd instructed Borzov to take her out. Hopefully he'd make a better fist of his job than Orazov and his bevy of agents were doing of theirs. The clock struck two, and Max clicked his tongue anxiously. With any luck the matter would be resolved by now. Why hadn't Borzov rung yet to confirm?

Less than four days before the pipeline signing, and Max found himself under pressure from all quarters to fly down to Ashgabat.

It was crucial during this period that all the strands held together, he'd been told, and he should be on the ground himself to ensure this. That was probably right: he was so close, best not to rely on the incompetence of others at this late stage. He planned to take the corporate jet down first thing in the morning.

Pouring himself another glass of wine, he clicked the sound on the TV remote as the screen pictured a bare-chested President Karpev wrestling a rare leopard during his whistle-stop tour through the North Caucasus. The animal wobbled alarmingly, off its head with drugs. Pathetic man, Max reflected, who did he think he was kidding? A pretty boy standing in the background caught his attention, and Max did a double take as he recognised him: Francis from Angel's, his crystal-clear aquamarine eyes locked on the President's half-naked torso. The swimmer girlfriend was nowhere to be seen.

*

Max emerged from the shower, enveloped himself in an enormous white towel and splashed cologne over his face. Staring approvingly at his image in the full-length mirror, he brushed his hair with precise strokes before going through to the bedroom.

His lips tightened at the sight of Pasha's naked body sprawled unconscious on the bed, the bruises livid on his pale skin, his thin wrists rubbed raw by the cord that bound him to the bedstead. The game had run away with him last night – and not for the first time. Sometimes, once he got going, he couldn't stop himself, especially when he was stressed.

He snatched a Black Russian from the packet by the bed. Lighting up, he released the cords, straightened Pasha's arms to lie limply at his sides, and wiped away the blood from the torn lips with a corner of the linen sheet.

Ah well, he sighed, not much he could do for the moment. He had a plane to catch. He ran his fingers softly through the boy's blond hair, twisting it into curls. The usual convoluted apology

214

must wait. If he'd time, he'd pick up some expensive present while he was away. That always seemed to do the trick.

Halfway down the stairs, he stopped and clicked his tongue against the roof of his mouth as if he were trying to remember something. Hell, he supposed he'd better . . .

Leaving his case on the stairs, he returned to the bedroom. At the gilded desk under the window, he scribbled a note and propped it up on the bedside table. Then he leaned over and kissed Pasha gently on the lips.

Chapter Sixty-Seven

Garabil Plateau, Turkmenistan

"I thought – " Leksin stopped in mid-sentence, staring at Talgat in astonishment.

"And so did they," Talgat replied, catching Leksin's train of thought and tapping his blood-stained leg. "They were just rookies, though."

"But I heard two further shots."

"Mine, not theirs, Alex." A slight smile. "By the time I'd sorted them, I reckoned you'd be away, and I couldn't track you in the dark. So I came straight here – figured you'd turn up in due course."

Leksin's face relaxed into a smile. "Which thankfully I did, thanks to Batyr." He gave Talgat a brief rundown on what had transpired since they parted. "What's the story with your leg?" he asked when he'd finished.

Talgat shrugged. "Bullet went clean through, stitched it up as best I could. Morphine's taking care of it for now. One vial left, should be enough to keep me going till we're done here."

"And then?"

"One thing at a time, Alex. For the moment, we have work to do."

*

"On my way here I stopped by the village and nobbled the phone lines," Talgat explained. "There'll be no calls in or out, at least not in the time frame that concerns us."

Leksin clapped his hands in silent applause.

"Got here to the plant just after dawn," Talgat continued. " I've worked out the layout." He extracted a pair of binoculars from his

216

rucksack. "Take these. See those two nissen huts 100 metres from the main compound? Larger one's the dormitory and canteen, smaller's where the boss hangs out. At night, there's just a single guard on duty. Hangs out in the guardhouse. Every forty-five minutes, pretty much on the dot, he patrols the perimeter, keeps just inside the fence. Work starts at nine.

"Shortly before nine this morning, a jeep pulled up. An officer, and a change of guard. The officer checked papers as people arrived for work, then drove off with the night guard." Talgat guided Leksin's arm so that the binoculars focused on the row of four whitewashed buildings nearest them. "Most of the activity, whatever it is, goes on there. One interesting fact: the first to arrive just walked straight in – not locked, so far as I could see. Very lax." Talgat's voice took on a tone of disapproval, the agent in him finding this hard to take. "In fact, altogether security stinks, as if they're just going through the motions. I guess they reckon there's not much to guard against out here. One exception: the underground bunker. You can't see it from here, it's near the guardhouse, between the main gates and the edge of the compound. Entrance sunken into the ground, fucking great metal gates, bolts a metre wide, padlocks the size of my fist, alarm fitted to the hinges." He glanced at Leksin, saw his expression, then shook his head. "Don't even think about it. Alex. No way of getting in there."

Outside the compound a group of men emerged from the canteen and ambled across the open ground. Leksin followed their progress towards the main gate through the binoculars. In jeans and tee-shirts and no hurry, there was nothing to mark them out, he thought as they stopped a moment to chat to the guard before heading off to work.

Talgat winced as he shifted position, letting out a faint groan. Reaching down, he locked his hands around his knee and manually dragged his injured leg into position. "Have a look over there, Alex," he said, continuing his guided tour but breathing harder. "If you look carefully, you can just see a roof sticking up at the back. Seems to be the warehouse. I took a closer look earlier. Bit like a

217

barn, huge doors, but no sign of a lock." He paused and looked towards Leksin. "Questions?"

"Just one: how do we break in?"

"Patience, I'm coming to that," he admonished. "Nothing doing till nightfall. After that, Alex, I reckon you'll be going in solo, I'm afraid. With this leg I'd slow you down or, worse, just get in the way if there's trouble." Seeing the dismay writ on Leksin's face, he continued. "But don't look so worried, Alex. See that clump of tall grass the fence runs through?" He pointed towards a spot in the perimeter fence about fifteen metres from the corner. " You can cut through the wire there. You'll be well shielded, especially in the dark, no problem crawling under."

Talgat pulled an AK47 rifle from the undergrowth. "I'll keep an eye on things from here with this," he told Leksin.

"Where on earth . . . ?"

"Belonged to the soldier who shot me." Settling back in the shadow, he winced and closed his eyes.

Chapter Sixty-Eight

Moscow, Russia

The entrance to Max's house was in Kislovsky Lane, a narrow road that linked the main arteries of Bolshaya Nikitskaya and Vozdvizhenka. The small rear garden, its walls lined with creeping roses and beds of pink azaleas, backed onto the Moscow Conservatory and, on a summer's day, with the windows open, the sound of musicians rehearsing drifted over.

That was of no concern to Major Ilukin as he watched his men deploy around the house. Kid gloves, they'd impressed that on him when he'd been summoned to Lubyanka early that morning. It's crucial we interrogate this man, keep him alive. The orders had come from the very top, there could be no screw-ups. Ilukin waited until everyone was in place before giving the nod.

A man in a DHL uniform walked up to the front door and rang the bell. He whistled a tune while he waited, then rang it again, this time keeping his finger on the button. Still no reply. He lowered his head near his collar.

"No answer."

Two men in belted overalls approached and taped charges to the locks on the front and garden doors. They hugged the walls, the doors sagged quietly off their hinges, and Ilukin herded his men inside. Scattering through every room, they reported in turn.

"Clear One, sir."

"Clear Two, Major."

A young recruit, new to the team, came out of an upstairs room and retched over the landing.

"What's wrong, man?" Ilukin barked.

"In there, Major." The rookie stuttered, pointing behind him.

Ilukin bounded up the stairs, rushed into the room, then

219

stopped dead in his tracks. He swore long and loud.

The body of a young man lay naked on the bed, his limbs smudged with livid bruises and smeared blood. A thin cord circled one wrist and dangled over the side. His lips were swollen, bared over grinning teeth.

A scribbled note lay on the bedside table. Ilukin picked it up.

'Pasha, Sorry – I'll make up for it, I promise, Love, Max'.

Replacing the note, Ilukin stared down at the bed. "That's one promise he's going to keep," he growled to the dead boy.

Chapter Sixty-Nine

Moscow, Russia

In his office at the Department of Overseas Development Nikolai Koriakov stared blankly at the open report on his desk, flicking pages without absorbing them. His mind was elsewhere, too anxious to concentrate. Reaching for the bulldog clip that had once bound the report together, he played with it absently, opening and closing the metal jaw, trapping his fingertips, then releasing them again. Glancing up at the wall clock, he frowned. Nearly eleven, and still no news had come through.

The call from Ashgabat in the middle of the night had confirmed his fears. By going down there, Vika had put herself right in the firing line. His agents had caught Borzov, Chestny Kombinat's head of security, breaking into her suite at the Sheraton. Thank God he'd arranged earlier for her to move into the Nissa. She'd be safe there: booked in under a false name, his people were keeping an eye on her.

They'd dragged Borzov off for interrogation. Everyone breaks in the end, but on this occasion time was critical. Rather than relying on their usual techniques, Nikolai had agreed to offer the man a deal: immunity in return for information. After that, Borzov couldn't stop talking. Max was hiding something – he'd no idea what – but it had to be important, that much Borzov claimed to know. Max would stop at nothing to keep his secret, and had instructed him to eliminate first Smolinsky, then later Vika. Yes, in return for immunity, he'd testify to that effect.

Immediately Nikolai had given the FSB the go-ahead to arrest Max. Be discreet, he'd instructed. Don't harm him, we need to interrogate him. Do it quickly and let me know the second he reaches Lubyanka. Nikolai sighed. The operation should be over by now. Why was there still no update?

His secretary entered. "I thought you'd want to see this straightaway," she said, passing him a note.

Skimming through, he frowned and pressed speed dial.

"They missed him, I'm afraid, Vika," he said once he got through. "The house was empty, no clue where he's gone." He purposely made no mention of her brother's dead boyfriend, that would keep till later. "You need to be ultra-cautious, Vika, he's like a cornered animal now, out of control. Stay in the hotel, I'm on my way down."

Nikolai buzzed through to his secretary and told her to book him on a flight to Ashgabat. That was where the end game would play. Not for the first time, the final outcome would depend on Leksin's success, and time was running out. He'd missed his friend's call earlier and tried several times to call back. No reply. Where the hell was he?

Chapter Seventy

Garabil Plateau, Turkmenistan

Sliding through the gap he'd just cut, Leksin reordered the wire mesh behind him as best he could, then sprinted across the open ground for the cover of the nearest building. Head straight for the far side and work your way back, Talgat had suggested, that way you'll keep getting closer to your escape route if they rumble you. Pausing to catch his breath, he glanced back up the hill towards Talgat's hide. No light, the coast was clear. He darted, building by building, along the row, each time waiting for a sign from Talgat, moving on when none came.

The sign on the door read: Laboratory. More in hope than expectation, Leksin rattled the handle and it opened. Right again, Talgat, security *was* lax.

Closing the door behind him, he switched on the light to reveal a room divided into three sections. Spotlessly clean, each section was delineated by three stainless steel units: on the first, a bank of computers, printers and plotters; the next, a long table-height polypropylene work surface, edged by metal stools and topped with open shelving laden with glass tubing, chemical bottles and tote trays; and finally, a row of sinks and burners, each fitted with chemical hoods above. Overhead, an untidy mesh of exhaust, ventilation and electrical cables crossed the ceiling, and underfoot, a sheet of non-slip, rubber flooring.

Slipping outside, he glanced again in Talgat's direction. Still no light. He headed straight for the next building, where the initials 'GA' had been neatly painted in red on its metal door. Just below, a sign warned of the need to follow the safety rules. Entering, Leksin found himself in a narrow room, dimly illuminated by orange back-up lighting at floor level. A room purge button, designed to switch off all power centrally, was fixed where he would have expected to find the main light switch. To his left, three cylindrical storage tanks were clamped to the wall, each with small circular measurement gauges at eye level. Silver insulated pipes emerged from each of these and ran, about a metre off the ground, into one of three independent, interlinked reactors. Leksin searched for a manufacturer's name, but found no markings of any sort. Odd. At the rear of the last reactor a wider pipe emerged, forking into three smaller pipes about a metre apart, the end of each fitted with a control valve. On the far wall, unlabelled chemical barrels in a neat pile waited to be filled.

Heading for the exit, he pulled the door gently open and stood silhouetted by the orange glow inside. A moment later, a flash of torchlight in the hills, less than a second but enough to warn Leksin the guard was on his rounds. He stepped back, pulling the door behind him, leaving just a slim crack through which to watch for Talgat's signal. Eventually, two crisp flashes of light, five seconds apart. Safe to move on, the soldier was back in the guardhouse.

He dashed over to the next building, where this time the initials 'GD' were marked on the door, the same warning to follow the safety rules fixed below. Trying the handle, he cursed under his breath. Locked. He twisted it again, but it wouldn't budge. Damn, nothing he could do – he'd neither time nor equipment to force an entry – so he moved on.

His luck returned as he turned the handle of the door with 'GB' in red, and it slid noiselessly open. Inside, he fumbled for a light. He was in a process control room no bigger than his spare bedroom at home. Two extensively fitted work stations looked out through a thick, reinforced-glass panel onto the plant on the other side. At first sight, the configuration seemed to him to be broadly similar to that in the other building, but as he compared the processes in his mind, subtle differences began to emerge. The same three storage units, but here they fed directly into a single, much larger reactor, airtight and altogether sturdier, rather than three smaller reactors. The single insulated pipe that emerged at its rear passed through a protective glass wall into an hermetically sealed area in which stood a series of distillation columns of varying heights.

Leksin searched through the control room's drawers and shelves for any indication of the plant's purpose. But there were no clues that he could see. Taking a couple of quick snapshots with his Thuraya, he slipped out.

The next stage, he knew, was the most dangerous. One more building remained – the warehouse. To reach it, Leksin would have to move out of Talgat's field of vision, leaving him without back-up. They'd discussed this at length earlier, but could find no way around it. If he could examine the warehouse contents, he might finally come up with the answer. It was a risk worth taking.

Clinging to the sides of the 'GB' building, Leksin side-stepped to the rear. He listened carefully for any sounds, then hearing none, shot across the open ground. Midway along the wall of the warehouse building, a pair of double gates, wide like barn doors, large enough to drive a vehicle through, was secured by two bolts. Leksin winced at the creak as the bolts slid apart. Opening a crack in the gates, he sneaked through.

The inside of the warehouse had been split into two sections: on the left, barrels of chemicals neatly stored on metal frames; on his right, supplies of equipment and tools. He started with the chemical stock, and as he read the labels, a thin veil of sweat formed on his brow. His knowledge of chemistry might be fairly rudimentary, but he'd read enough for what he found to set off alarm bells in his head. Surely he had to be wrong? It just didn't add up. Quickly he tapped details of the chemicals in greatest supply into his Thuraya notes in the hope that Talgat could help make sense of it all. About to cross the warehouse to inspect the equipment, he spotted, half-concealed in the shadows, an area at the back separated off by floor-to-ceiling railings, like a prison. Behind these were two separate stockpiles of chemicals, one in each corner, and in the gloom he could just make out the markings on the barrels: *methylphosphonyl difluoride* and *isopropyl alcohol &*

isopropylamine compound. He could feel his heart beginning to pound. Shit, there could be little doubt now.

On the other side of the warehouse, two stainless steel racks ran in parallel: one containing a miscellany of tools, nuts, bolts, screws, rubber seals and the like, the other stacks of laboratory equipment. Tubes of nickel alloy piping the length of the wall lay on the ground, clasped together by a metal band. On its surface at three metre intervals were stamped the words 'Hastelloy C-276'. Down the centre of the room, between the racks and the piping, various items of equipment were stored on raised aluminium pallets. Leksin's ran his eyes over them, but the only items he recognised were the carbon-activated filtration systems and scrubbers. The rest meant nothing to him.

Never mind, he'd seen enough. Time to get the hell out of here before he lucked out. Turning to leave, though, he found he'd left it too late. The guard had crept up behind him and now stood only a metre away, his pistol aimed directly at Leksin's chest.

"Stay right where you are!" he ordered

Before the man could blink, Leksin's left foot flashed out and knocked the weapon from his hand. It was a standard move he'd practiced many times at the FSB's Sokolniki training centre. Never hesitate, the instructor had repeatedly drummed into him, strike the second you see the gun, or you've had it.

In an instant of disbelief, the guard's eyes followed the pistol as it crashed across the warehouse floor, then he quickly regained his composure. A sturdy, barrel-chested man, neck muscles taut under short-cropped hair, he grabbed a length of metal piping from the rack and approached Leksin. As he launched a series of vicious blows, Leksin backed away, ducking from side to side, edging around the man, forcing him to turn first one way, then the other, awaiting a moment of carelessness. But the man kept coming forward, relentlessly forcing Leksin deeper into the warehouse. The further back he went, the more cluttered with equipment it became, and the less room Leksin had in which to manoeuvre. Eventually, he realised, he'd be cornered, and one of the blows would find its target. He had to act fast.

As if to catch his breath, the guard paused for a moment and stood upright. "You bastard, I'll get you," he hissed through clenched teeth. Then he lunged forward again.

Shifting his weight, Leksin's arms snapped out to grab the guard's wrist as it came within reach, then using the man's own momentum, he yanked him past, simultaneously wrenching his arm backwards and upwards. There was an audible crack as it parted with its socket.

The man opened his mouth to howl, but Leksin was already moving again. His clenched fist connected with the guard's temple, and he slumped deadweight to the floor.

Retrieving the guard's pistol, Leksin secured it under his trouser belt behind his back before making a run for it.

Chapter Seventy-One

Garabil Plateau, Turkmenistan

Leksin glanced time and again over his shoulder as he scrabbled up the hill. Reaching the summit, he threw himself down, out of breath. Rolling over to face Talgat, he frowned with confusion when he found him bound on the ground. His eyes searched Talgat's face for an explanation. then followed the direction of his stare. A uniformed officer crouched behind a bush, his gun trained on Leksin.

"Good evening, Mr Leksin," he said, smooth and self-confident. "I'm the local army commandant. I've been expecting you."

Leksin threw a questioning glance at Talgat, who shrugged as much as he could.

"Your colleague was too busy looking out for you down below to notice me as I came up behind him." The commandant gave a small grunt of satisfaction before continuing his explanation. "I'd been warned you were on your way, so thought it best to spend the night in the guardhouse myself. I spotted someone up here signalling to you."

He waited for a reaction from Leksin and, when there was none, brushed a hand towards Talgat. "Join your colleague, please," he ordered. "And put these on." He tossed over a pair of metal handcuffs, raising his gun to forestall any argument.

Scuffling over to sit next to Talgat, Leksin cuffed himself and stared back defiantly as the commandant rose to his feet and approached. Broad-shouldered, receding hair and a determined jaw, his flesh looked pasty in the moonlight. He inspected the two men through heavy-lidded eyes, and sneered.

"I told my patrols they were looking for a drug dealer," he explained to Leksin. "But *I* know you're a spy."

Leksin stared back blankly.

"Just like the other one," the commandant continued with a tight-lipped smile. "I took care of him too."

"So I gather," Leksin blurted out, and immediately regretted it.

"You do, do you? Who told you, I wonder?" The commandant shrugged before answering his own question. "Batyr, I assume. I saw him at the window sneaking a look, thought it might serve as a warning to keep his mouth shut. No matter, I'll deal with him later."

He paused to remove a baton from his belt. "And now, Mr Leksin, I need to know who sent you."

As Leksin glared back silently, the commandant craned his neck as if he were struggling to hear. "You will tell me," he stated coolly, holding out the baton for Leksin to see more clearly. "Have you come across these before?" he asked, then continued without waiting for an answer. "It works on the same principle as a cattle prod. Look, there are two thin, protruding metal electrodes at the end. All I have to do is, touch it somewhere on your body and depress the switch in the handle – see, just here. This will send an electric current that contracts your muscles, the pain is intense, I assure you."

Without warning he stepped to Leksin's side and prodded his shoulder with the baton. As he depressed the switch, Leksin's face contorted in agony as his muscles tightened.

"There, see what I mean?" the commandant asked rhetorically. His voice lowered to a whisper. "Mr Leksin, I'm very good at my job. You will break. It would be much easier for both of us if you just tell me who sent you."

When there was no reply, he placed the baton on Leksin's hip and counted slowly to three as the current ripped into him. As soon as he removed it, Leksin's body flopped back onto the ground. The commandant waited patiently as he lay there for several seconds, a dazed look on his face. As Leksin slowly pushed himself up, he twisted his body to face the commandant. It was at that moment that Talgat spotted the pistol in the belt behind his back.

"Tell him, Alex," Talgat said. "It's not worth all the pain. Let's get this over with, he's not going to allow you to *come back*."

"Like hell, I will," Leksin replied, using his feet to shuffle his body a little closer to Talgat.

The commandant seemed amused as his face screwed into a little twisted smile. "You should listen to your colleague," he advised softly.

"You may be right," Leksin answered, edging himself back.

"Indeed, I am," the commandant assured him. Tightening his lips, he shook his head to show he was losing patience. "You're running out of time, Mr Leksin. The next shock will ensure that you never have children." Leksin retreated another fraction as the commandant motioned the baton towards his groin. "You have been warned. This is your last chance."

With a sudden surge as the commandant approached, Leksin projected himself back onto Talgat. For a moment the commandant hesitated. It was all the time that Talgat needed. Grabbing the pistol from Leksin's belt with both hands, he swung it up and shot the man in the neck.

"Bastard," Leksin hissed, as the commandant collapsed to the ground, his face suffused with confused horror.

Chapter Seventy-Two

Garabil Plateau, Turkmenistan

"So what did you find?" Talgat asked, as Leksin uncuffed his hands.

Pouring some water into his palm, Leksin splashed it over his cheeks while he determined where to start.

"The four buildings in the front row," he began at last. "One's a lab, two are chemical plants, the third was locked and I couldn't get in." He described the plant layouts, answering Talgat's technical questions as best he could, showing him the photos he'd taken. "It wasn't till I entered the warehouse that things began to fall into place."

Talgat angled his head enquiringly. "Tell me."

"I jotted down the chemicals stored there. Have a look."

Talgat took the phone and scrolled down the list, squinting at the complicated terms. *Dimethylamide . . . phosphoryl oxychloride . . . sodium chloride . . . pinacolyl alcohol . . . phosphorous trichloride . . . isopropyl alcohol . . . hydrogen fluoride . . . methylphosphonyl difluoride . . . tributylamine . . . diisopropyl carbonate . . .* As Talgat read, his face clouded over. If he was drawing the right conclusion, then this had never even figured on his radar screen of possibilities. For a moment, his body froze, and he was so astonished that he could think of nothing to say. Exchanging glances with Leksin, he eventually mouthed an expletive.

*

Leksin circled the compound, keeping to the cover of the bushes on the surrounding banks, until he was on a line with the smaller of the two nissen huts set outside the main entrance, the plant boss's quarters by Talgat's reckoning. Sprinting down the incline, he flattened his body against the wall as he caught his breath, then edged around to the door on the far side. Very slowly he tried its handle, and the door opened.

From somewhere inside, he could hear the sound of gentle snoring. Turning on the torch, Leksin inspected the layout. The front door opened directly into a living area, sparsely furnished with a wooden armchair and a battered formica table. An old cooker stood in one corner, next to a stainless-steel sink. Across the room was a single door, presumably the bedroom and the source of the snoring. Leksin tiptoed over, slipped the door quietly open, and crossed to the bed without disturbing its occupant.

Placing one hand over the man's mouth, Leksin twisted his head towards him with the other. The man's eyes flashed open, and he stared back in anger and surprise. He struggled to move away, but Leksin's grip held firm.

"A few questions," Leksin announced crisply. "Understand?"

A tentative nod.

"If you try to call for help when I release my hand, you won't get out of here alive. Understand?"

Another nod.

Sliding his hand to the side of the man's mouth, Leksin pulled the cattle prod from his belt, held it in front of the plant boss's face, so that he could see it clearly, then positioned it against the man's shoulder.

"A gift from your Commandant," Leksin told him, his voice crisp with assumed confidence. This method of interrogation was not something with which he was comfortable, but under the circumstances he had little choice. "So let's start with an easy one, what's your name?"

"Omer." the man replied, not unwillingly.

"So, Omer, I've already gathered that this plant makes chemical weapons. That's right, isn't it?"

The man hesitated for a minute, then nodded.

"Nerve agents." Leksin paused, waited for contradiction, gave a little nudge with the cattle prod when there was none. "Anything else?"

Omer shook his head. "Just nerve agents," he murmured.

"And how are they stored?" Leksin posed the question bluntly, then clarified the background as he saw Omer's confusion. "We couldn't get into the underground bunker."

Omer opened his mouth to speak, then stopped. His mistake – there wasn't time to play around. Sparks flew from the end of the cattle prod, and Leksin himself flinched as Omer convulsed. He waited for the man's body to settle before he resumed.

"You were telling me how they were stored, Omer," Leksin reminded him.

"Mostly in canisters and shells," Omer rushed to reply. "All except the sarin. For the moment that's kept in binary form, but it'll be inserted in special two-part shells shortly before delivery."

That made sense: it accounted for the separate stockpiles he'd found behind bars. *Methylphosphonyl difluoride* and *siopropyl alcohol & isopropylamine compound.* These guys weren't mucking about, that he knew for sure. But what was their end objective? That's what he needed to find out.

"Who are the weapons for?" he continued, keeping his voice even.

Omer gave a little shrug. "We were just told to get on with the manufacture. There was no further explanation."

"And they never told you who they were for?"

"No."

Wrong answer. Sparks flew against Omer's shoulder, and his body spasmed again.

"I guess it's possible, Omer, the other scientists are here just for the money and haven't a clue about the end user. But someone here – and that someone is, almost certainly, you –has to know in order to keep the operation on track." Leksin paused before repeating his question. "Who are the weapons for?"

A moment's hesitation, a further nudge with the prod, and he had him. Omer's resistance fragmented. "Afghanistan," he capitulated. "They told me they'd reached a deal with the Afghans.

In return for the chemical weapons, they'd guarantee the safety of a pipeline they want to run across the country."

Leksin let out a low whistle. Were there no limits on the measures these people would take to secure their project? It appeared not. He had just one more question to complete the picture.

"Tell me, what are the delivery plans?"

"Transport's due here next week to take the products across the border," Omer replied. Raising a trembling hand, he pointed towards a cupboard on the far wall. "There's a map in there showing the exact location."

On reflex, Leksin turned his head to look. As Omer's hand slid unobtrusively under the mattress, Leksin caught the glint of steel as the man pulled out a knife and made for him. With lightening speed, Leksin swivelled away, grabbed Omer's arm and snatched it upwards. Omer opened his mouth to howl, and Leksin had no choice but to silence him. The edge of his hand sliced into Omer's throat at a precise angle that fractured his trachea. For a few moments Omer struggled for breath, his eyes dark with the terror of impending death. Then, with a last gurgle, he lay still.

Chapter Seventy-Three

Garabil Plateau, Turkmenistan

They'd travelled non-stop through the night and at last stopped for a break. Leksin studied Talgat, his eyes drifting up his body to his face, drawn and ghostlike in the moonlight. Now that the morphine had worn off, the man had really struggled over the rugged ground.

Seated on a rock, Talgat stretched down to grasp his injured leg. Manipulating his fingers around his thigh, he squeezed and prodded as if he was checking it still hurt.

"Tell me," Leksin began, seeking to distract him. "Is it easy to set up a chemical weapons plant?"

Talgat screwed up his face thoughtfully. "Depends on the level of sophistication. You can't quite do it in your garden shed, but a cheap and cheerful chemical process doesn't require much." He paused. "Not the case here, though. Nothing amateur about these operations. Outside two or three countries – Russia, America, possibly Britain – most countries manufacturing CWs fall into two traps. First, it's bloody difficult to make it pure. You tend to end up with a cocktail of nerve agent and acids, which leads them to degrade pretty rapidly. Particularly sarin. As a result, they're forced to make it on demand, rather than stockpiling it, and even then the lack of purity reduces effectiveness by up to 50%. That was the problem in Syria."

Leksin gave him a sideways look. 'Problem' hardly seemed the correct word in this context. If 50% less people died in Damascus thanks to manufacturing deficiencies, then this was surely good news, not a problem. But, given Russia's opposition to regime change, he knew what Talgat meant. "And the second trap?" he asked.

"Even if it's pure, Alex, it still degrades unless it undergoes a very complex, dangerous chemical process."

"Like what?"

"Like being distilled - you remember those distillation columns in the sealed room, you saw? Distil the mixture there, and add in a stabiliser like the *tributylamine* and *diisopropyl carbonate* you found in the warehouse. Bear in mind, by this stage the product's extremely toxic – it's already a CW – so to refine it in this way, you need specialised non-corrosive equipment, like the Hastelloy tubes, and a skilled workforce. Doesn't exist in most countries, but apparently available here. Whoever's behind this has to be in a position to access tightly-controlled secret processes."

Leksin frowned. "There's one thing I don't understand," he declared eventually. "What does the Afghan government think the West will do when it discovers they've got their hands on chemical weapons?"

Talgat gave a little shrug. "Nothing, I guess – and they'd almost certainly be right. What can they do? They were the ones who installed this regime in the first place. The last thing they want is the Taliban returning to power. Of course, there'll be a great deal of sulking, probably some empty threats, even possibly some half-hearted sanctions – but fuck-all action."

Leksin scratched the back of his head reflectively. Talgat's view was probably accurate. The present so-called democratic government in Afghanistan was the West's proud boast, something its leaders put forward to justify the war there. Now they had nowhere else to go. Even if there was a viable alternative – other than the Taliban – the decision to prosecute two useless and unnecessary wars had blown the West's cover. Most of its voters viewed the wars as some sort of ego trip on the part of Bush and his crony, Blair. Further military action was now no more than an empty threat. Syria and Ukraine were just two examples of this new-found impotence. All that was left now were words, and they were no match for sarin.

"But what about Karpev?" Leksin persisted. "Russia wouldn't

sleep at night knowing some lunatic's armed with chemical weapons on her doorstep."

"My guess, then, is she'll just have to stay awake and keep watch. In any event, Karpev doesn't want the Taliban back in power, either. Who knows, in his realpolitik, he might even welcome the present government strengthening its control over the Taliban in this way?"

Leksin thought back to his meeting with Karpev in the Kremlin. In normal circumstances, perhaps Talgat was right. It was not just to the West that the return of the Taliban would be a nightmare scenario, and Karpev's natural inclination could well be to resort to extreme measures to prevent it. *But these were not normal times,* as Karpev had pointed out. Just at the moment, with the Russian President's focus on the Balkans, he couldn't afford any fallout that would risk bringing the conflagration in the Middle East to Russia's doorstep. He'd brought Leksin in precisely to avoid this.

"Anyway, Alex," Talgat said, struggling to his feet with a knowing smile. "You've distracted me long enough. Time we were off."

*

They'd left the compound as soon as Leksin returned from interrogating the plant boss. Key to their escape had been clearing the track that linked the plant to Garkent. *It's the only way in and out,* Batyr had warned him, *get the hell off it as quick as you can.* As a result, they'd taken the most direct route, straight along its course, no fancy footwork darting in and out of bushes for cover. There simply hadn't been time.

When they'd reached the gorge, it was clear to Leksin that the state of Talgat's leg made the climb down to the river impossible. With no other choice, they followed the gorge's edge as it snaked across the plateau. At one point, they'd heard the sound of a patrol somewhere in the dark, difficult to tell how close, and they'd ducked behind a boulder until the voices disappeared.

On the journey with Batyr – less than twenty-four hours ago, but now seeming a lifetime away – Leksin had made a mental note of landmarks along the way. In the dark, of course, these were no use as a guide, but it was Leksin's hope to stumble across them from time to time to validate his sense of direction. So when eventually they reached a cluster of decrepit stone barns marking the point where Batyr had started their descent into the gorge, Leksin had let out a sigh of relief since this confirmed they were going the right way.

In one sense their luck had held out. The dearth of search activity indicated that the break-in at the compound remained undiscovered. If they'd found the missing guard – or Omer and the commandant, for that matter – the news would have got out and the patrols would have had a better idea where to look for them. Fingers crossed, nothing would be discovered until work began at nine the next morning. That at least would give them a head start.

Set against this had been the obvious deterioration in Talgat's mobility. Although he hadn't complained, just winced silently whenever he thought Leksin wasn't looking, the man was in trouble. Without morphine to ease the pain, every step had required an enormous effort of will, and it had become increasingly clear that he wouldn't be able to keep going much longer. One thing at a time, Talgat had said earlier when Leksin had questioned him about his leg, we'll deal with that problem when we have to. Well, that time had now arrived.

When at last they'd stopped to rest, Leksin had run through the options in his mind. There was just one hope, a slim one. It would be a big ask, but he had no choice but to try.

*

Tania opened the door a crack, and glared at the two men.

"What do you want?" she snapped at Leksin. Her eyes narrowed as she took stock of Talgat and settled on the stranger's bloodstained clothes. "What happened to him?"

238

"Shot by a patrol." Leksin spoke loudly so he could be heard inside. "He's in a bad way."

Her eyes filled with horror, and she shook her head violently. "No, my husband's done enough for you already." Backing off, she slammed the door shut.

Leksin could hear the sound of raised voices, then after a heated exchange the door flung open again. Batyr. His face broke into a craggy smile.

"You made it, young'un." His expression clouded at the sight of Talgat, and he waved them in. "Your friend needs help."

Chapter Seventy-Four

Garabil Plateau, Turkmenistan

Batyr slit the leg of Talgat's trousers and examined the angry-looking wound he uncovered.

"You did this?" he asked, inspecting the rough fish-wire stitching that united the torn flesh.

"Best I could manage," Talgat replied.

Batyr gave a slow, appreciative nod. "Not bad, not bad at all." He turned towards Tania who stood muttering disapproval in the background. "Stop whining, woman, look after this man, I'll fetch water and clean cloths."

A sigh from the corner of the room drew Leksin's attention. Yana had awoken and, recognising Leksin, she struggled to sit up. "You're back," she whispered weakly, glad to see him.

Leksin sat down on the edge of her bed, careful not to jolt her. "How are you?" he asked, running a sympathetic finger gently over her cheek. "Better?"

"A little, thank you." She hesitated, glancing over at Talgat doubtfully. "That man, what's wrong?"

"He was shot."

"The soldiers?"

Leksin nodded.

"Like me?"

"Just like you, yes." He paused, pulled up the bedclothes. "Now rest. Everything's fine."

Yana smiled and lay back. Her eyes closed and she fell instantly asleep as children do.

He went over to rejoin Batyr who was watching intently as Tania washed away the congealed blood from Talgat's leg. Underneath, the skin looked crumpled and discoloured. Catching

Batyr's eye, Leksin nodded towards the door, then went outside where the moonlight had turned the landscape to monochrome and shadows, silent save for one of the animals shifting in the barn. A moment later, Batyr followed.

"Your friend, whoever he is, won't be going anywhere in a hurry," he said gravely.

Leksin nodded.

"He can stay here," Batyr continued.

"Thanks." Leksin put a hand on Batyr's arm, sounding relieved. "It won't be for long, I promise you."

Batyr threw Leksin a sceptical look. "And you?"

"I must get back to Ashgabat, it's urgent."

"No point asking why, I suppose?"

Leksin rested a hand on his arm. "Batyr, it's safer for you and your family not to know."

Batyr nodded. "You're probably right," he agreed reluctantly.

The two men stood in silence for a while, each to his own thoughts, then Batyr turned towards the door.

"Come. You need something to eat."

Inside, Tania had finished dressing Talgat's wound. The two men helped him onto a mattress on the floor, while Tania prepared some food. When it was ready, Batyr placed a steaming earthenware pot on the table, stacking rounds of crisp naan bread beside it.

"Help yourself, young 'un," Batyr urged, ladling soup into a bowl. "I'll take care of your friend."

Kneeling beside Talgat, he raised him up with one arm and smiled. "You're fortunate, I haven't done this since Yana was a baby." The two of them talked in low tones while Batyr helped him eat.

*

"I should be off." Leksin told Tania, getting to his feet. "Thanks for everything. I'm sorry for bringing you trouble again."

Far from gratified, Tania was about to speak when the sudden clip-clop of hooves outside made her look around anxiously. The door flung open, and Batyr strode in. "Come, young 'un. I'll lead you off the plateau."

For an instant Tania seemed rooted to the spot, a startled look on her face, then she marched up to her husband and pinioned him with a red-hot stare. "No, Batyr! I won't have it," she remonstrated, her voice shaking with a mixture of fear and anger. "You can't leave Yana and me alone with the stranger."

"This man saved our Yana's life, remember?" Resting his hands on her shoulders, he bent forward to look her in the eye. "Don't fret, the soldiers don't get where we're going. We'll take the quick way down."

She glared back in silence, then pulled away. She loved her husband, but he was a stubborn man. There was no point arguing further, she knew that. In a tone gritty with resentment and resignation, she muttered: "You'll be wanting some food." She went over to the mesh-fronted cupboard where she kept their few supplies, brought out a square of goat's cheese and began to spread it on wedges of naan bread, which she wrapped in a cloth.

"Make sure you get him safe back to me," she warned Leksin, sullenly handing him the package. Meeting Batyr's eyes, she forced an uneasy smile. "You'd better give him your hat. He'll not stand out so much with it on."

Batyr reached for the black sheepskin hat hanging behind the door, but Leksin was reluctant to take it.

Grabbing the hat, Tania thrust it on his head. "Go on, put it on. Whatever happens, you'll need it in the morning when it gets hot."

"Your husband's a lucky man," Leksin told her, as he straightened it.

*

"We'll stop here for a bit," Batyr said. "Eat something while we work out our next move."

242

They'd ridden throughout what was left of the night. It was not a form of transport Leksin favoured. As a schoolboy, his godmother, who'd lived in the New Forest, had held the firm conviction that all young men should know how to ride, and during the summer holidays she'd forced him to take lessons. Over the years he'd become reasonably proficient, but he hated it. Thankfully on this occasion the horse had proved steady and sure-footed, happy to follow docilely in the direction Batyr led.

It was coming up to ten o'clock when they first caught sight of the desert plain below. The sun was already high in the sky, and the temperature was rising fast. Less than a kilometre ahead traffic streamed along the road that sliced westwards through the sand and scrub towards Ashgabat. Cars, trucks, mule carts, motorbikes, all rumbling forward, slow invaders.

Gradually the full extent of the security presence became clear: armed soldiers posted at fifty-metre intervals, militia trucks intermingled with the traffic, vehicles pulled in for random checks. In the distance, a roadblock had been set up to inspect papers. Leksin's heart sank: it seemed as if he'd walked out of one trap into another.

Chapter Seventy-Five

Garabil Plateau, Turkmenistan

The Karakum desert stretched out before them, swathed by a seamless carpet of saxaul and juzgun. Above, the sun dangled like a brilliant coin, casting an ashen light upon the horizon. Here and there saline beds of ancient rivers, now long dried up, meandered across the black sands and shone like crystal.

Seated on a rock, Leksin scoured the scene below with the binoculars Talgat had passed to him before they'd parted. It was not encouraging. With such a large military presence, it would be close to impossible to slip unnoticed into the crowd pressing on towards the capital in an unbroken line. Even if he could, it would be only a question of time before he fell foul of one of the security checkpoints that now punctured the road.

"With all those eyes on the road, how can they watch the desert?" Batyr asked rhetorically, interrupting his thoughts.

Leksin threw him a puzzled glance.

"I've an idea," Batyr continued. "But, first, we must get across."

Standing up, he moved to Leksin's side. "Put your arms around my shoulder, young 'un. Where's that sheepskin hat Tania gave you? Pull it over your head as far as it'll go, keep your head down and shield your mouth. Just act sick and let me do the talking."

They began their descent from the plateau. As soon as they reached the flat ground, hardened by sun to levelled stone, a conscript spotted them and strode purposefully towards them. He glared at them through dark eyes nearly hidden between high Asiatic cheekbones.

"Papers," the youngster demanded, extending his stringy hand.

Batyr advanced, his forehead pleated in a worried frown, and dipped his head towards Leksin. "I need your help, sir. My friend

244

here has typhoid. Can you find transport? I must get to the hospital urgently. Both of us could be infected."

His head bowed, Leksin aimed a hacking cough at the soldier.

Batyr patted his back. "Quick, let him see your papers."

The soldier backed away. "Get him out of here!" he demanded. "And keep off the road."

Shepherding them across the road, he watched them shuffle into the desert.

*

The man on the caravan's leading camel was resplendent in a white sheepskin hat and crimson robe. As he followed Batyr's approach through beady Arab eyes, his weather-beaten face folded into a broad grin. Dismounting, he rushed towards him with aloft arms.

"You old rascal, where've you been?" he asked, hugging Batyr. "Why haven't I seen you?"

"I'm legal these days, Hassan." Batyr's expression was serious. "Young wife and daughter too."

Hassan regarded him sceptically, nodded towards Leksin. "Who's your friend?"

"This young'un saved my daughter's life. Has to reach Ashgabat, but quietly." Resting his hand on Hassan's shoulder, he added confidentially: "He's wanted by the police."

"Police, eh? As legal as that!" With a laugh, Hassan slapped Leksin's arm. "Well, you've come to the right man, whoever you are."

He shouted some orders in an unfamiliar dialect. A young man dismounted, rummaged through his saddlebag, then brought over a knee-length red khalat.

"This is my son, Bulat," Hassan told Leksin. "He'll look after you."

Leksin threw Bulat a grateful look. Dark-skinned and dark-eyed, the young man smiled back as if he meant it.

"Put this on while I sort out transport for you," Bulat said. He disappeared, returning a moment later with a camel. "Have you ridden one before?"

Leksin looked uneasy. "Just once, a few days ago," he replied without enthusiasm.

"Well, hold on tight and let the animal do the rest." Bulat steadied the camel while Leksin mounted.

"You can trust Hassan," Batyr assured him. "He'll look after you. And don't worry about Talgat, we'll take good care of him."

Then slapping Hassan on the shoulder, he angled back to the road without a backward glance.

*

Mingling with the surging crowd, Batyr jostled his way through to the building that served as a café. Little more than a wooden shack, it was set back from the road and nestled into the side of the hill. A long queue snaked in front of it, and he slipped in through the back door.

Inside, a harassed woman was slopping tea into shallow bowls from an enormous orange pot. She glanced up aggressively, then smiled wearily when she saw who it was. "What brings you here, Batyr? Picked a bad day to drop in, I'm afraid, it's a nightmare here with this demonstration."

"I can see." He leant forward and touched her arm sympathetically. "Mind if I use your phone?"

"Help yourself. You know where it is."

Batyr went through to the back where an ancient telephone was fixed to the wall.

It took a few tries to get a line through to Ashgabat, but Batyr was persistent. Eventually a man answered.

"Leksin's heading west back to Ashgabat," Batyr told him. "He's travelling as a nomad trader, wearing a red khalat." He dropped his voice and looked around to check no one was listening. "There's one other thing . . ."

Chapter Seventy-Six

Karakum Desert, Turkmenistan

The camels kept the same steady pace, their splayed flat hoofs splashing up puffs of sand as they moved in near silence across the desert. Leksin by now had grown used to their lurching stride, though he lacked the practised feel of the others for the uneven rhythm. From his vantage point three metres above the ground, his eyes trawled the arid expanse before him to a horizon that seemed never to grow closer. The sunlight dazzled the thin air, and the dunes shimmered as the heat became increasingly intense.

Soon after Batyr had left them, Hassan had led the caravan in a wide arc away from the road along a path he said was centuries old. How he plotted their course in a landscape devoid of landmarks was a mystery, but unerringly they'd headed for a shallow depression marked by a small cairn of stones. Here, the men had dug into a trough in the sand to reach a natural well. The water, carried down from the plateau, seeped into a puddle scarcely a foot deep. Fed by the winter snows, these were the final dregs, Hassan told him. The well would soon be dry until the following spring.

The men had watered the camels, about thirty in all – roughly two for every man – then left them to browse on the scant vegetation. They'd rested throughout the fiercest midday heat, spreading awnings as shelter from the sulphur-yellow sun and sipping the syrupy tea that was to sustain them till evening. It was here that Bulat had introduced Leksin to his friend.

"This is Aziz," he'd told him. "He's the cleverest amongst us. He's like a brother to me."

Perhaps it was Aziz's terse nod in acknowledgement, or the way his narrowed eyes avoided his stare, but Leksin took an immediate dislike to the young man. Watch out for this one, his instincts told him.

When at last they'd set off again, their route slanted back towards the road. Bulat drew up his camel alongside Leksin, and they travelled together. Cresting a low rise, Bulat drew Leksin's attention to the rippling waves in the sands unfolding ahead of them.

"The patterns are caused by the prevailing wind," he explained. "If you know what to look for, you can use them to steer by."

Shielding his eyes with his hands, Leksin gazed ahead, unable to identify a pattern. No matter, Bulat reassured him, the camels never lost their way.

*

As they neared the road, the rumble of traffic in the distance gradually rose above the quiet shuffle of the camels' feet. Shifting in his seat to look in that direction, Leksin spotted a jeep bouncing towards them across the scrub. Attracting Bulat's attention, he threw him a questioning glance. Bulat nodded and reached across to halt his camel.

"Militia," he said calmly, his eyes fixed on the jeep now only a couple of hundred metres away. "Leave this to my father."

The jeep pulled up, and a sergeant jumped out and strutted over. "You seen any strangers?" he asked in Turkmen.

Bulat translated for Leksin under his breath.

Hassan guffawed, and waved his arm expansively towards the hordes on the main road. "How many do you want? Take your pick."

The sergeant scowled to show he was in no mood to be played with. Taking a few steps backwards, he leant back, hands on hips, and surveyed the line of camels. Realising Leksin's size and posture might draw his attention, Hassan eased his camel in between.

"So, who are you after?" he asked with deliberate carelessness.

"Drug dealer. Russian," the sergeant snapped back. "50,000 manats reward."

"50,000 manats," Hassan repeated, sounding impressed. Nearly $10,000. In a country where the average wage was just over $150 per month, it could change your life. He clapped his hands to draw the others' attention. "Keep your eyes peeled for this Russian, we can get rich."

Glancing around, Leksin caught the look on Aziz's face. Something told him that the young man would give him up for much less – and might well do so given half a chance. He needed to keep an eye on him.

For almost a minute, the sergeant stood there in the scorching heat, his eyes scanning back and forth along the line of camels. At last, without a word, he jumped back into his jeep and drove off.

"We'll be watching out," Hassan shouted after him, urging his camel forward.

Chapter Seventy-Seven

Moscow, Russia

Erlan Saidov had lived on his own since his wife had walked out on him in 1991, taking their only daughter to live with her family in Yekaterinburg. Her sudden departure had caught him completely by surprise: it had hurt, though not as much as the loss of his child. He'd made no effort to see either of them since - it was easier on the emotions that way. A few years ago he'd heard his daughter had married a local schoolteacher and was the mother of twin girls. For an instant he'd considered getting in touch, then let it pass. That part of his life was best left dead.

His apartment was in a sprawling pre-Revolutionary block in Romanov Lane, close to the Kremlin. Once an enclave for Soviet apparatchiks, grey plaques on its outer walls paid tribute to the USSR's great and good who'd lived there during that era, survivors like himself. His study, a gloomy retreat in which he now sat, was as big as a ballroom, panelled in mahogany with a moulded ceiling of faded cream plaster. Heavy antique furniture inherited from his father, himself a former apparatchik, cluttered the room. At one end, four dark-brown leather sofas faced each other around a low rosewood table. At the other, his oak-framed desk, and a favoured chesterfield armchair, from which he could just glimpse the red star that topped the Trinity Tower through one of the high velvet-draped windows.

Vremia, the current affairs programme he watched nightly, came to an end. Pouring himself another glass of cognac, he switched channel to the news. He watched with bland disinterest until the newscaster introduced a report of President Karpev's stopover in Crimea en route to Turkmenistan for the pipeline signing. Ever since the flare-up in the Ukraine, Karpev had paid regular visits to the region, ostensibly to thank its inhabitants for their support of Russia in the rigged referendum. Of course, there was more behind it than that: it was a statement that Crimea was back in Russia, where it belonged – and where it would stay, notwithstanding all the West's bellyaching.

Saidov's rugged, deeply-lined face broke into a cynical smile as, even here, Karpev couldn't resist the temptation to put on a show. Christ, he exclaimed audibly at the sight of the tall, wet-suited figure of Karpev emerging from the sea, hauling a harpooned barracuda behind him. Whatever next? Does the man have no shame? Someone should have warned him there aren't any barracuda in the Black Sea? What a prat!

He was still chuckling to himself as Karpev posed for reporters on the beach, his wetsuit clinging to his honed torso, his blond hair glistening in the sun, the barracuda hanging from a set of scales beside him. Slowly the camera panned the scene, taking in the upright figure of General Kutchinsky, head of the FSB, deep in conversation with the recently-appointed governor of Crimea, then lingering for a moment on the bored but decorative figure of Karpev's swimmer girlfriend. A few paces behind her, a young man stood transfixed, his eyes glued on his hero below. A moment later when Karpev waved in their direction, Saidov couldn't resist wondering whether he was waving towards the girl or the boy.

The President's personal assistant appeared at his side, proffering a phone. At first Karpev brushed him away, but when the aide got close enough to whisper something in his ear, he grabbed the phone and drew away from the reporters. He was clearly not a happy man, whatever the message. Usually almost frigid in his lack of emotion, he was rattled on this occasion, his body swaying with agitation as his arms gesticulated frantically. Prodding the phone to finish the call, Karpev immediately instigated another. Covering his mouth as he spoke, his hazel eyes flared with anger.

Saidov felt a wrench of panic as he realised something was very wrong. What the hell was up? He pressed speed dial and, a moment later, the aide answered.

"I've just been watching the report on the Crimea visit on the news," he said. "Your boss didn't look very happy after that call. What's up?"

He listened in silence to the explanation, then put down the phone. Leaning back in the Chesterfield, his face distorted as if someone had just punched him in the stomach. Reaching for the bottle of cognac, his hand shook as he poured.

Chapter Seventy-Eight

Tashkent, Uzbekistan

The old woman scanned the heaving departure lounge at Tashkent airport and grunted with disgust. Chaos, bloody chaos, she muttered, dragging her rickety trolley behind her as she shuffled forward in search of a seat. Catching sight of her reflection in a pillar's stainless-steel cladding, she adjusted her patterned scarf and patted down her well-worn cotton dress. Turning her head slightly to one side, she inspected her face. The scar on her cheek was barely visible under her wrinkled and blotched skin, and she pursed her lips in approval at her handiwork.

A young American businessman from the IFC tapped her on the shoulder, and she spun around. Her suspicious eyes bored through him as he proffered his seat. Pushing him aside, she took it without a word of thanks and extracted that morning's edition of *Norodnoye Slovo* from her trolley. Hidden behind the page, she read until a current affairs programme on television fixed to the pillar in front of her caught her attention, and her eyes moved to the screen. She listened as the presenter examined the timetable and implications of the Russian President's impending visit to Central Asia. Tomorrow, Turkmenistan to sign the pipeline agreement; the next day, Tashkent to see the Uzbek President; finally, Astana to see the Kazakh President. Things never change whatever the appearance, she reflected. All former Soviet apparatchiks, all dictators in so-called democracies, all skimming off the cream for their personal gain.

At last her flight was called, and she trundled to the gate. As she boarded the plane, a steward offered to place her trolley in the hold, but she snatched it from him and continued along the aisle. Reaching her assigned row, she stood still and waited as passengers concertinaed behind her. A stewardess weaved her way over.

"Is anything wrong, dear?" she asked.

"I can't reach the locker for my bag."

"Which is your seat?"

The old woman brandished her boarding pass.

"Well, sit down there, dear," the stewardess said, pointing towards the window seat. "I'll put your bag in the locker."

The old woman sat down and waited for the other passengers to find their places. Once the plane was fully boarded, a porter wheeled a cage carrying two young goats into the aisle. A moment later, the engines started.

*

It had been that afternoon when the mobile Nadia reserved solely for business vibrated to alert her to an incoming call. She'd recognised the voice immediately. Her client – or was he her boss? She was never sure which was the correct epithet, it was a complex relationship.

"Get to Ashgabat immediately," the caller had demanded, without introduction. "The target's there."

Reaching for a pad, she jotted down the details as he gave them. They were somewhat scant, and she'd told him as much.

"If it was easy, I'd do it myself," he'd snapped back.

Caught off-guard, Nadia had let slip a sigh, annoyed by the caller's unexpected petulance. It seemed so out of character.

"Timescale?" she probed quickly.

"There isn't one," the man fired back. "It has to be done before the scheduled pipeline signing tomorrow."

The line went dead. The order had been given and received. There was no room for debate.

*

As the plane took off, the old woman looked out the window, settling her head against the frame. Below her, startlingly green in the evening sun, the basin of the Ferghana Valley stretched in the distance. The snow-tipped peaks of the Tian Shan and Alay mountains enclosed it on three sides, locking in the fertile soil of the richest oasis in all of Central Asia and sourcing the broad expanse of land with vital water. Once part of Tamerlane's empire, the Valley had bred the legendary blood-sweating horses which had blasted open the East-West trade route for China. The Silk Road passed through the valley, which for hundreds of years linked China to the Middle East and Europe. These days, the valley was still crucial, providing both food and water for the region's inhabitants.

As the seat belt sign was extinguished, the pilot's voice announced there would be an unscheduled stopover on their way to Ashgabat in Turkmenabat, a city on the Turkmen-Uzbek border. The old woman groaned and closed her eyes. It was going to be a long flight.

Chapter Seventy-Nine

Karakum Desert, Turkmenistan

The caravan travelled without further incident until dusk. Stopping to make camp, the first priority was to feed the camels and hobble them for the night. Only then did they make their own preparations, setting out rugs and awnings over the sand.

Hassan asked Leksin to join him for something to eat. The two men sat cross-legged, a little way from the others, eating dried meat and drinking camel's milk. Hassan talked of the life of a caravan, how they lived, where they were heading. A note of pride entered his voice as he referred to his two sons: Bulat, the eldest whom Leksin had met, and Khan, his younger son. He's studying at university in Ashgabat, Hassan had proclaimed proudly.

It was only after they'd eaten that Hassan's joviality seemed to evaporate, and his face darkened. Leksin guessed immediately what was coming.

"You're no drug dealer . . ." Hassan asked, clearing his throat. It was left hanging, neither a question nor a statement.

Leksin shook his head.

"No, I reckon not," Hassan continued. "There're aren't many things Batyr wouldn't do for a quick buck, but not drugs. He'd draw the line at that." He paused as if he was waiting for Leksin to say something, continued when he didn't. "But 50,000 manats!" He whistled his respect. "What could possibly make you worth that much?"

With a little shrug, Leksin quickly changed the subject. "How long have you known Batyr?"

"That old rogue? When have I not known him?" He reached for a fistful of dried fruit and chewed it slowly. "During the war these southern passes were the main gateway into Afghanistan. Fucking

256

Russians everywhere. Their officers, the bastards, thought nothing of selling arms to the Afghans as a sideline, didn't give a toss they'd be used the next day on their own troops. I teamed up with Batyr – we acted as their link, smuggled the stuff over the border and took a cut." The shift on Leksin's face made him pause, then he added by way of excuse: "The Russians had stolen our birthright. What did I care? They got what they deserved."

He lapsed into his own thoughts, sensing Leksin's silent disapproval. With eyes fixed on the ground, he ran his fingers through his beard, tweaking it between thumb and forefinger, straightening it, curling it again. After a while, his lined face wrinkled into a conciliatory grin. "So now he's found himself a young wife, you tell me?"

"And a daughter." Leksin explained how he'd found Yana injured by the soldiers.

"Bastards." Hassan spat on the ground. "We were naive enough to think life would improve once the Russians left."

*

Leksin stretched out next to Bulat on a rug spread across the sands. Pillowing his head on his sheepskin hat, he was soon asleep.

Some time later, he couldn't tell how long, he was awoken by a high-pitched rustling that lapped him on all sides. His eyes snapped open, and sitting up with a jerk, he found the moon glistening off the shadows, a sheen of oil on the desert floor. He stretched over to shake Bulat.

"Hey, can you hear that?"

Bulat dragged himself reluctantly up and listened. "Oh that? They're nothing to worry about."

"They?" Leksin exclaimed, unable to hide his alarm.

"Tenebrionids." Reaching over, Bulat scooped up a fistful of black beetles, crusty and wriggling, then spilled them onto the rug.

Leksin recoiled, shifting his weight on the rug. "For Christ's sake, what the hell are they?"

"Desert beetles, they come out in this part of the desert as soon as things cool. They're everywhere by now, clear off again at sunrise." He patted Leksin's arm. "Forget about them, Alex, they're harmless. Go back to sleep."

Leksin lay back, now wide awake. No way could he fall asleep surrounded by these creatures, he was in for a long night. Next to him, Bulat resumed his gentle snore.

Chapter Eighty

Karakum Desert, Turkmenistan

Leaning up on his elbow, Leksin stared blankly at the glow of slowly moving headlights stretching out into the distance. Even at this hour the steady stream of traffic heading towards Ashgabat echoed across the desert. He'd given up trying to get to sleep. Nothing worked.

Spotting a slight movement near the camels, Leksin angled his head in their direction. Something shimmered in the moonlight, and he squinted to focus as a man's silhouette emerged into the open and stole off towards the road. Leksin frowned, realising that, for one of them at least, the 50,000 manats reward had proved too great a temptation. Time to go. Before that, though, he'd better stop this man reaching the police, otherwise Hassan and the whole caravan would be in jeopardy.

Jumping up, he ignored the crunching of beetles under his feet as he set off in pursuit. The man seemed unaware he was being followed, and with his long stride, Leksin made up ground fast. He was nearly on top of him when the man suddenly sensed his presence. As he spun around, Leksin launched himself through the air, sinking his foot into the man's stomach, crashing him winded onto the ground. Raising his arm to finish him off, Leksin wasn't too surprised when he recognised Aziz's face in the moonlight.

"You?" he accused, holding off. This man was Bulat's best friend, he was one of Hassan's tribe and subject to Hassan's law. It was not appropriate for Leksin himself to act as judge and executioner.

Aziz stared back defiantly, his eyes challenging Leksin to take him out. Grabbing Aziz's arm, Leksin forced him onto his stomach. Stripping off the man's cotton belt, he tore it in two and secured both arms and feet. Almost certainly, Leksin guessed,

259

when they found Aziz missing in the morning, they'd come in search and administer their own form of justice. If not, then even if the police later stumbled across him, Leksin would be long gone.

*

Leksin had no difficulty in the dark blending into the stream of people on the road. In his Arab dress, the weary soldiers stationed at intervals didn't even give him a second glance. In the distance he could see a pool of yellow light which, as he approached, clarified into a line of petrol pumps and, judging from the smoke and faint aroma, temporary shashlyk stands. Coming up close, he caught sight of his image on posters plastered on every available surface. 50,000 manats reward, the heading read. Dangerous drug dealer, it stated underneath. He cursed silently.

From the shadows Leksin took in the scene. On the far side, beyond the pumps, rows of lorries, drawn up in tight lines, walled off the desert. In front of him, cars, carts and any other form of transport that could be found were parked haphazardly around makeshift benches and collapsible plastic tables encircling the shashlyk stands. At one of the tables a band of hefty lorry drivers held forth, surrounded by vodka bottles. Studying them for a minute or two, Leksin decided they were too drunk, and too self-absorbed, to present a danger. He moved casually forward and tried the door handles of the cars parked nearby.

"Hey there, Arab!" one of the lorry drivers shouted. "Look at that bugger, he's trying to steal a ride. Let's get him."

A scuffle of chairs, then they lurched towards him, too many for Leksin to take on alone. As they closed in, he made a run for the lorry park, weaving between the massive vehicles in an effort to shake them off. Just when he thought he'd made it, a giant figure, built much like a Kamaz truck, loomed up ahead of him. In the faint light, Leksin caught a glimpse of the bottle twinkling in his huge paw. Smashing it against a bumper, the man lumbered towards him, viciously swinging its jagged edge. Planting his feet,

Leksin prepared himself to take him on, but at that moment he heard the drunken slurs of the others as they rounded the corner and closed in behind him. Slipping under a lorry, he crawled across to the other side, but they ducked through the gaps between the containers and charged after him. Searching frantically for somewhere to hide, Leksin jinked through open spaces when they came, but still his pursuers kept on coming. There wasn't much further until he'd reach the road, he realised, and then it would only be a matter of minutes before the police were attracted by the disturbance.

A voice snapped at him out of the chasm between two huge vehicles. "Leksin, over here! Quick!"

Spinning around, he saw a torch blinking from an open tailgate. With footsteps pounding ever nearer, he launched himself into the gaping black hole, and the man hauled the truck's tailgate shut behind him. Lying prone on the floor, Leksin waited for the mob outside to move on before rolling over to inspect his unknown rescuer.

"Mr Leksin, we've been looking for you," the man said calmly. "My name's Timor. I work for Nikolai Koriakov. My instructions are to escort you to Ashgabat."

Chapter Eighty-One

Ashgabat, Turkmenistan

The militia had imposed a ban on all private traffic in Ashgabat's city centre. Only the army, the police and senior government officials were exempt. The opposition rally, which had been due to start at midday in the Azadi Square, had finally got underway just after one o'clock, and the roar as the opposition leaders mounted the podium had rattled windows throughout the city. Crowds were still streaming in like an unending column of ants intent on their mission: whole families, men and women, young and old. Many wore the traditional dress of their tribes as a badge of national pride, each distinguished by its own unique patterns and jewellery design.

As their truck reached a road block by Ashgabat station, Leksin and Timor jumped out. Still dressed in Hassan's red robe, Leksin fitted easily into the crowd, and the two men joined the masses heading for the rally. Everywhere the military presence was pervasive: soldiers stationed along the streets at regular intervals, their heads twitching as they looked for signs of trouble. Occasionally, whether out of boredom or necessity, one would step forward, randomly stop a passerby, inspect his papers, then wave him on. It was a routine, one designed not to provoke but to demonstrate who was in charge.

No one, though, was looking for trouble. In fact, the scene struck Leksin as more like spectators making for their favourite football stadium on a Saturday afternoon than a disgruntled populace marching towards a make-or-break demonstration. With Rashid's steel grip over the country, Leksin reckoned, this rally was unlikely to have much long-term impact. The army and secret service were both loyal and brutal, and years of subjugation had made the population malleable and weak. Let them have their day of protest, that would have been the order of the day, then herd them back to their regions and stamp down hard.

Here and there, their hair shorter and their clothes newer than those around them, young men interspersed the crowd as it surged forward, their suspicious eyes on constant lookout. Plain clothes KNB looking for trouble, Leksin guessed. One regarded him with close application, then smiled encouragement.

"We'll show them today, eh?" he said, inciting a reaction.

Leksin smiled back thinly, then looking away, dropped back a little.

When the road branched off towards the Nissa Hotel, they forced their way towards the pavement and ducked out of the crowd. Reaching the bus shelter opposite the hotel entrance, they sat down on a low wall in the shade. A poster offering a reward for Leksin's capture stared back at them from the shelter's Perspex frame. Pushing his sheepskin hat down as low as it would go, he bowed his head and shielded his face with his hands. Stay there till you're contacted, that had been Timor's orders; whatever happened, Leksin was not to go inside the hotel.

A mounted policeman rode towards them. Leksin's heart stopped as he pulled up, surveyed them for some seconds, then demanded their papers. Make a run for it, he suggested under his breath. But Timor put a restraining hand on his shoulder and got to his feet.

"Papers," the policeman repeated, his hand moving to his holster. "Now!"

As Timor reached into his pocket – Leksin had no idea for what – a young woman ran towards them, missed her footing on the edge of the pavement, and fell just in front of them. Clutching her leg, she screamed in agony. Rushing to help, Leksin drew a sharp breath when he realised the woman was Tamara, who ran the local orphanage. She turned her head towards him and winked.

"Are you all right?" he asked, making a pretence at inspecting her leg.

"I think I've broken it," she wailed plaintively. "Help me home, please – I live just over there." She nodded away from the road. "I need to call the doctor."

The policeman had more important things on his agenda. With a nod, he gave Leksin permission and waved him away. As he rode off, Leksin and Timor helped the young woman up and, with a shoulder under each arm, assisted her towards the orphanage.

"OK, that'll do," she said, shoving them away when they were out of sight. "I'd expected you earlier, Alex. I've been keeping an eye out for you."

For an instant Leksin was so astonished that for once he couldn't think what to say.

"Don't look so surprised," she continued with an engaging smile. "A man came to the orphanage this morning, told me you were in trouble and asked for my help. He donated $500 to the orphanage, which was very generous. Mind, I'd have done it for nothing after you were so kind to us a few days ago."

Leksin blinked while he worked this one out. How typical of Nikolai, ever resourceful. He couldn't recall telling him about the orphanage, he must have mentioned it during one of his updates.

So what now? He looked towards Tamara for guidance.

"I'm to take you to Lenin Park," she recited. "It's not far."

*

Walking against the flow of the crowd, they made their way towards Lenin Park. Tamara was clearly enjoying the role of tour guide as they progressed. At the State University they jostled their way through the morass of students who milled around its entrance, seething with talk and excitement about the demonstration. Crossing the road, they passed through the War Memorial gardens before turning right by the extravagant new Drama Centre.

The park was quiet, just a few children on the swings under the watchful eyes of their babushkas, a couple of mongrels chasing each other in frantic spirals around the palm trees, and geometric flower beds. From opposite entrances, paths converged on the centre where the upright figure of Lenin stood raised on a tiered plinth. The last statue of Lenin in the city, Tamara explained, the others were all pulled down on independence. This one, though, decorated in the Islamic style, continued to dominate the park, one arm stretched out towards the horizon.

"Your friend's waiting for you behind the statue," Tamara told Leksin. She put a hand on his shoulder and kissed him, a brief touch, no more. "Look after yourself, Alex, be careful."

As she turned to walk away, Leksin called after her: "Thanks, Tamara, I'll be in touch."

She waved at him without turning around. Leksin kept his eyes on her until she left the park, then headed with Timor towards the statue of Lenin in the centre. As they circled around it, the figure of a woman seated on a bench came into view. Leksin back stiffened as soon as he recognised her. He'd walked into a trap.

Chapter Eighty-Two

Ashgabat, Turkmenistan

"He's here," Vika whispered into her iPhone. Adjusting her sun glasses, she stood to face Leksin.

Leksin glared back in silence, all of a sudden remembering it was Vika, not Nikolai, that he'd told about his visit to the local orphanage. How clever of Vika to lay the snare, reckoning correctly that he'd trust Tamara and follow where she led. Unwittingly she'd led him straight into it. He threw a glance at Timor – was he part of the plot too? Turning to make a run for it, Leksin found men blocking every exit.

Vika's face displayed a victor's smile, clearly enjoying his discomfort, then slowly she shook her head in disbelief.

"You don't really think I'm the enemy, surely?" She stepped forward to rest a hand on Leksin's arm, but he backed away. "Come on, Alex, you know me too well for that."

"I thought I did," he snapped back, unconvinced.

"Oh for heaven's sake, Alex," Vika retorted impatiently. "Don't be such a fool. Did it never occur to you that you've been working for me all along?"

The statement completely staggered Leksin, and he allowed himself a few seconds for her words to make sense. But, however he cut it, they didn't. There'd been too many lies and half-truths that countered Vika's claim. They flashed through his mind: Max looks after the operations in Central Asia, she'd told him, the pipeline's nothing to do with me . . . but then she'd turned up for no reason at the Ashgabat head office . . . and denied all knowledge of Smolinsky . . . All these facts pointed to her complicity, not her innocence.

"I can guess what you're thinking, Alex. So let me explain." She sat down on the bench and patted the space next to her. With some reluctance Leksin joined her.

"Nearly three weeks ago," she began, "I received an email from Smolinsky, the general director of our operations in Turkmenistan, the gist of it said that certain aspects of the pipeline project alarmed him – "

"But you denied you knew him," Leksin interrupted, playing his trump card.

"Not true, Alex," she corrected him. "What I actually said was, I couldn't help you find him. Not that it matters. Look, Alex, I knew what you'd be like. The man was frightened enough as it was, you'd just scare him away – I found out later that's exactly what you'd already done and you were setting a test for me. Of course, at the time I wasn't aware of that – I just wanted to get to him myself before you did." She paused, then ignoring the scepticism on Leksin's face, went on. "To some extent, Smolinsky was shooting at shadows. He wasn't entirely clear what was going on behind the scenes, but he had his suspicions. He'd contacted me direct because he was pretty certain Max was involved. For me, as you can guess, that was no great surprise, given Max's propensity for courting trouble – but this time all I could see ahead was a nightmare scenario. The pipeline was more than just great business for the Kombinat – above all, the deal had massive political implications. If Smolinsky's suspicions proved founded in fact, then the fallout would be catastrophic. I confided in Nikolai, who in his turn raised the matter within the Kremlin itself. The decision was taken to plant an FSB agent in our Ashgabat office to investigate from the inside. His initial report led us to believe he was onto something, but then out of the blue he vanished. That's when I suggested bringing you in on the case."

"*You* got me on the case?" Leksin repeated sceptically.

Vika nodded corroboration. "But I suspected, given our past history, you'd turn me down flat if I put it to you myself. So Nikolai and I agreed between ourselves it should be presented as a government commission."

Leksin's mouth dropped open, speechless. Staring back at her, he angled his head to one side as he gradually came to terms with this revelation. "Then the texts?" He opened his hands, seeking an answer.

"From me," Vika confirmed. "I may not have thought it wise that you knew of my involvement, but I was determined to help out if I had the means. I followed my own leads, tipped you off whenever I got a result."

"That bit about your father?"

"I went to see Olga Chernikova, my father's ex-mistress. She explained that, given the way Karpev had been capitalising on the slightest irregularities to pick off my father's oligarch associates, Lev had wanted to be absolutely certain no aspect of the proposed pipeline project could cause damage later. So, he'd set an independent corporate investigator to look at the deal and had been pretty much devastated by his report. His first reaction, she told me, had been to withdraw from the project altogether. On reflection, realising the consequences in terms of political fallout would be enormous, he'd decided to see if there was any way of reinventing the deal rather than take the drastic step of pulling out. Then, of course, he died so suddenly, he couldn't put his plans into action." She stopped for a moment.

"And the location, Garkent?"

"Smolinsky," Vika admitted. "He'd taken all his files to do with the pipeline home as insurance after my brother fired him. He showed me a memo that indicated some link with Garkent which no one would explain to him."

As Leksin parted his lips to speak, the familiar figure of Nikolai Koriakov rounded the statue.

"Love the gear, old boy," Nikolai complimented him in English, grasping his hand. Then reverting to Russian he asked Vika: "Have you updated Alex?"

She nodded.

"Good." Looking Leksin full in the face, he said matter-of-fact: "So it's chemical weapons for the Afghan government."

Leksin gaped back. This seemed to be a day full of surprises. "You know already?" he exclaimed.

"Your friend, Batyr. How do you think we got the information to post Timor on lookout for you on the road back from Garkent?" He paused. "Talgat gave Batyr a message to pass on to us."

Leksin frowned. "Talgat told him about the chemical weapons?"

"Not quite, that would have been somewhat indiscreet, I agree," Nikolai replied. "The message was a set of initials: *'GAGBGD'*. Batyr of course had no idea what they meant, he just repeated them parrot-fashion, but the boys in Lubyanka realised immediately."

Leksin looked puzzled. These six letters were the same as those painted red on the doors at the plant, but until now he'd never attached any particular significance to them. Nikolai helped him out.

"GA – Tabun, GB – Sarin, GD – Soman."

Leksin gasped, struck by Talgat's resourcefulness. "Does Karpev know?" he demanded.

"Yes, as soon as we understood the implications, I got through to him. He was on a goodwill visit to Crimea at the time and scheduled to fly to Ashgabat the next day for the signing ceremony. He should be landing pretty much as we speak." Glancing at his watch, he corrected himself: "In fact, he should have landed by now."

"His reaction?"

"As you'd expect. He's looking for scalps and determined to get them."

"But the pipeline?"

"The deal's dead. Clearly Karpev can't accept trading chemical weapons for pipeline security. Even he has limits." Correctly interpreting the wry expression on Leksin's face, Nikolai paused. His cheek flickered before he continued: "He and Saidov are scheduled to meet Rashid, the Turkmen President, this afternoon for the official signing ceremony. That's when he plans to announce Russia's withdrawal from the deal."

Leksin's mouth dipped to one side, a sign of reservation. "But surely he could simply withdraw. He doesn't have to force a public showdown."

"It's not as simple as you suggest, Alex. For one thing, the weapons and the plant have to be destroyed. We've a task force just across the border waiting to spring into action as soon as Karpev clears the way with Rashid. For another – "

He was interrupted by one of his agents shouting his name across the park. Nikolai waited for him to run over, saw the shock on the man's face. Covering his mouth with his hand, the agent whispered his message into Nikolai's ear. Nikolai stiffened, eyes widening, and Vika noticed his hands clench as the agent retreated.

"What's wrong?" she asked.

Nikolai opened his mouth to reply, but for an instant seemed incapable of speech. His face reddened, and thick beads of sweat gathered on his forehead. He blinked and cleared his throat. "Karpev, he's been assassinated."

They stared at him uncomprehending, then stuttered the first questions.

"What?"

"Where? When?"

"The President's convoy coming in from the airport was ambushed on the way to the palace as they turned onto Berzengi. Around twenty terrorists concealed in buildings either side of the road. They caught the cars in their crossfire. A professional job – there are no survivors."

Leksin remained seated as he struggled to come to terms with the news. Vika stood up and, as she went over to Nikolai, Leksin noticed how stress or heat had made her limp more marked since their last meeting. He watched as, putting her arms around Nikolai's shoulders, she hugged him tight. "I'm so sorry," she murmured.

For a long moment no one spoke. Huddled around the statue of Lenin, they stood rooted to the spot completely thrown by the catastrophic turn of events. It was Nikolai who eventually broke the stunned silence.

"I'd better go straight to the palace," he said, slipping gently out of Vika's clasp. His voice hardened with anger and determination. "Saidov's due to join the President there any moment now. I must explain what we've uncovered before he signs anything."

He glanced from Vika to Leksin, then back at Vika once more, and frowned. "You need to keep a low profile for the next couple of hours. You know too much, they'll be looking for you now. Whatever happens, don't go near the hotel."

"What about the safe house?" Leksin suggested. "I know where it is, I checked it out just in case. Vika, it's twenty minutes walk from here. Could you manage?"

Vika put on a brave smile. "You try and stop me," she retorted.

"Then safe house it is," Nikolai agreed. He beckoned Timor over to him. "I need you to do something for me," he told him. "I'm relying on you."

A moment later, Vika touched Nikolai's shoulder. "Be careful," she instructed. Turning away, she took hold of the red-robed arm beside her. "OK, it's your job to keep me on the straight and narrow," she joked as she limped off, clinging to her support.

Chapter Eighty-Three

Ashgabat, Turkmenistan

A little way along Sewcenko Street they came to the crumbling grey-brick edifice that sheltered Ashgabat's elderly. Shaded under a canopy outside, the inmates, confined in their wheelchairs, sat in a line under a nurse's supervision. By now the temperature had soared to over 45°C, and Vika's leg was giving her hell. Each step became more painful, and she grimaced each time she put down her foot. The nurse looked over and called out to ask if she was OK. Forcing a smile, Vika nodded.

They entered a street of upmarket shops. All were now boarded up, their owners taking no chances in the present unrest. Almost imperceptibly the street narrowed into a lane, at the end of which they found themselves in an elegant residential square where patterned brickwork houses lined all four sides. A gravel drive ran around a central garden, where a manicured lawn was incised with beds of phlox and zinnia. A large fountain of pseudo-classical design wasted precious water at the centre.

In the far corner of the square, they passed through an arch into an alley where the former stables now housed the service staff. Beyond them, a sign told them they were entering Kompot.

"Clearly the part of Ashgabat Rashid doesn't want you to see," Vika observed, taking in the maze of rutted and dusty tracks that branched off at tangents.

As they proceeded over the increasingly rough and stony surface, Vika's stump constantly jarred. The rows of dilapidated shacks seemed unending, each marooned in a clutter of old tyres and rusting junk. Piles of rubbish lay rotting and rat-infested at each corner, emitting a stench so pungent it made Vika's eyes water.

As they emerged from Kompot and entered Kulieva Street, she was, she thought to herself, literally on her last legs. Across the road, she saw the stuttering blue flash of the Jennet Cafe's neon sign.

"Can we stop there a moment?" she asked.

They crossed over. "Why don't you order a couple of beers while I take care of my leg?"

Disappearing around the back, she locked herself in cafe's basic, but thankfully clean, facilities, and brought out the emergency supplies she always kept with her. Applying some bacitracin cream and a new liner, the stump felt a little better though still red-raw. It would have to do.

As she went back into the cafe, she spotted the crimson robe and sheepskin hat of the figure at a table outside. Sitting down opposite, she asked: "How much further?"

"Nearly there, Vika," he reassured her. "Just a street or two away."

*

They reached the corner of Gorogly Lane, the quiet lane in which the safe house was situated. Edging forward, they surveyed the scene.

Halfway along the road, more or less opposite the safe house, two cars were pulled up on the kerb. As far as Vika could make out, the first looked empty. There was someone in the passenger seat of the second, reading a newspaper. Further along the pavement, on the same side, a group of men had gathered around a game of draughts. Studying them carefully, she noted the way their eyes seemed to wander up and down the lane rather than concentrate on the board.

The other side of the crossroads, about 100 metres from where they stood, a solitary police car was parked outside a cluster of private houses. Telling Vika to stay put, he drifted over to take a look. The car was empty, but the keys were in the ignition. The driver wouldn't be far away, he guessed, and he made his way back.

"I think we should check this out first," he told Vika. "Do you have anything in your bag I could use to write a note?"

Vika nodded.

He jotted down a few words, folded the paper, then a minute or two later when a young cyclist, perhaps eighteen years old, rode toward them, stepped out to flag him down. $10 to drop a note through the letterbox of No. 68, the deal was quickly struck.

From the street corner they watched as the young man rode up to the house, rested his bike against the kerb and walked up to the letter box. Immediately the men across the road sprang into action. Pistols ready, they charged over to surround the terrified youth.

They'd seen enough. "Quickly!" he urged Vika, almost dragging her towards the parked police car. Running ahead of her, he jumped in and started the engine while he waited for her to catch up. Then the car bolted off, just as the men waiting in ambush, realising their mistake, rounded the corner after them.

Chapter Eighty-Four

Ashgabat, Turkmenistan Orazov sat puffed up on a cushion behind the huge desk in his office. Across the room, his assistant had wheeled in a gigantic plasma-screen television that now blared out live coverage of the demonstration in Azadi Square, just around the corner.

Next to him, already on the second bottle of Chardonnay, was Max Usenko. He was balanced precariously on a narrow high-backed chair, his legs neatly crossed, his interlinked fingers clasped around the glass resting on his lap. Dressed in a light blazer over an embroidered shirt open at the neck, his eyes had that faded, distant gaze that accompanies an excess of alcohol.

In the other corner, his rounded shoulders moulded into an auburn leather sofa, sat Saidov. By contrast, his almond-shaped eyes were firmly concentrated on the televised events. An assortment of snacks were spread out on a low table before him: red and black caviar on miniature blinis, tiny stuffed pirozhki, and thinly sliced beef wrapped around baby asparagus. All were untouched.

The tall French windows shook as, on screen, the opposition leaders called for support, and over 100,000 demonstrators roared in unison. Without looking up, Saidov asked: "Ali, do you really think you can control this?"

"The KNB have their number," Orazov replied confidently. "We'll let them let off steam today, then crack down the lid again tomorrow." He paused before adding ominously: "The people are rudderless. Without the men on the podium there is no opposition, and they won't be around for much longer."

Saidov raised his eyebrows, his approval equivocal. What Orazov proposed was a very Soviet solution, and the so-called Tulip revolution in Kyrgyzstan a few years ago demonstrated that nowadays these tactics could backfire. On screen the speeches continued with all the old clichés. Abuse of human rights . .

. downtrodden poor . . . rich oligarchs . . . police state . . . false imprisonment . . . The sound bites were the same the world over, Saidov reflected, as each elicited its statutory cheer from the crowd. Perhaps Orazov was right, after all.

The screen suddenly went blank. A few seconds later, the picture changed to the studio where a flustered newscaster rushed out from behind a screen and took her seat. Her hair and makeup were less than perfect, as if she'd been caught unprepared. There was no sound when she started to speak, and a technician rushed forward to adjust her microphone. She started again.

"News has just come in of a terrorist attack on the Presidential cavalcade bringing the Russian President from the airport to meet President Rashid at the palace. We understand that an attack took place en route involving at least twenty terrorists and that there are no survivors." A picture of cars and corpses on a still highway flashed on screen. "We will bring you more details as they emerge."

Saidov caught Orazov's eye. They'd both known this news was coming, but it took the announcement on television to drive home its full impact. Ever since the President's aide had explained the cause of Karpev's reaction to the phone call in Crimea, they'd had no choice and this outcome had been inevitable. The President himself had made no effort to give Saidov the heads up on his intentions. But Saidov *knew*, and given Karpev's love of the theatrical, it was inevitable that he would await until the signing ceremony itself to announce his surprise decision to pull out from the pipeline project.

Saidov himself had no problem making hard decisions, and he'd quickly brought the others around to his way of thinking. They were far too close to abandon the deal now, they all personally stood to make a mint from it, and they had the means to nullify the President's planned intervention. Admittedly assassination was an extreme solution – there'd be repercussions and subsequent investigations that would require careful handling – but under the circumstances it was the only answer. Whatever it took, Karpev had to be removed from the equation before the scheduled signing ceremony.

In the event, he'd left the arrangements to Orazov, who'd also undertaken to deal with loose ends. For this purpose, arrangements had been made for the so-called terrorists carrying out the attack to reassemble for their payoff later this afternoon in an empty warehouse in the outskirts of Ashgabat. The place was already wired, and none would survive the explosion. Later, they'd blame the attack, as usual, on the Islamic Fundamentalists or something similar.

"Can you let President Rashid know we'll be at the palace within two hours to proceed with the signing ceremony?" Saidov asked Orazov. "Please explain that I need to take the necessary steps to assume temporary power and prepare a broadcast for the Russian people later this evening."

Orazov nodded. "I'm sure he'll understand in the circumstances . . ."

His phone rang and, snatching it up, he clasped it to his ear, shaking his head in exasperation at what he heard.

"Where are they now?" he growled. A pause while he listened, then: "Go straight there, Gutov. Max Usenko will meet you at the entrance. You're to do as he says." He threw the phone down as if it was burning his hand.

Until now a silent witness, Max reached for a Black Russian: "So what's happened?" he asked, struggling to clear his head.

"It's your sister. My agents spotted her near the safe house the FSB use with a man disguised as an Arab – "

"That'll be Leksin," Max interrupted tetchily. "Where are they now?"

Orazov grimaced. "The idiots let them escape."

"Shit."

"It gets worse. They stole a police car." Orazov grunted in disgust. "Thankfully we were able to track its position. They headed to the new bazaar. I've told the KBN Captain, Gutov, you'll meet him there."

Saidov frowned. Easing himself off the sofa, he went over to the

French windows and stared down at the street, deep in thought. Then, turning sharply, he gave Max a hard look.

"This time there can be no mistakes. You must eliminate them both," he said coldly. "They're all that stand in our way now."

Chapter Eighty-Five

Ashgabat, Turkmenistan

You earned them, strokes of luck. You just had to be there, know your background if the foreground didn't help. One moment in a blind alley, then something happens and there's a way forward. Just like today.

Nadia had finally landed at Ashgabat after the unscheduled four hour stopover at Turkmenabat where, along with the caged goats, they'd been shepherded into a poorly lit, sweltering terminal and left without explanation or refreshment. By the time they finally reached their destination, the sun had already risen. Anxious not to draw attention to herself, she'd avoided the fast-track service, choosing instead to wait in line for over an hour at the general passport and customs control while bored officials laboriously carried out their routines.

Once through, she'd made straight for the short-term car park and found the space marked H314. Sure enough, there she'd found a dark blue Daewoo bearing South Korean embassy number plates. The key rested on the rear wheel, hidden by mud flaps. Clicking the doors open, she'd eased her shopping trolley on the rear seat and climbed in after it.

It had taken her a few seconds to find the tiny, concealed switch at the side of the front passenger seat. Immediately she'd depressed it, the panel at the back of the seat had sprung loose, and she'd pulled it down to reveal a hidden compartment fitted with the tools of her trade. Methodically she'd checked them off against the mental list of things she'd ordered. Satisfied, she'd placed what she needed in the false bottom of her shopping trolley, pulling her spare clothes over it, then fitting the panel back in position, she'd tossed her trolley in the car's boot.

With the crowds, the drive into Ashgabat had been slow. Police blockades set up at each artery into the city were stopping cars and forcing them to turn around, but seeing her diplomatic number plates, they'd waved her through. Nonetheless it had been late morning by the time she'd turned into a quiet street a stone's throw from Azadi Square, removed the bollards placed by the side of the road to reserve her a space, and parked the car.

She'd spent a while reconnoitring the area, just an elderly woman wheeling her trolley, all the time making a mental note of potential hiding places and escape routes – just in case they proved to be needed. The layout firmly fixed in her mind, she'd bought a local newspaper and settled down in the street cafe opposite an official-looking building, where she now sat. All the time her eyes had kept watch on the building's entrance.

A moment ago, a government car had screeched to a halt outside the entrance. A second later, the man for whom Nadia was looking emerged from the building and jumped in. A break, at last. Her eyes remained fixed on the car as it sped off. At the end of the road it ground to a halt, caught up in the stragglers on their way to the rally. It was all the time she needed to make it to her car. Switching on the Daewoo's ignition, she started to follow.

Chapter Eighty-Six

Ashgabat, Turkmenistan

In the Altyn Asyr bazaar in the desert outskirts of Ashgabat, business continued, despite the protests, in a centuries' old tradition that stretched back in an unbroken line to the legendary silk-road traders. Big as several football stadiums put together, an elliptical roof stretched overhead, below which cramped stalls were set out in numbered rows. In the vast central open space, a random mixture of Turkmen rugs, sheep and camels was displayed for sale beneath an incongruous white-marble clock tower.

From the comparative quiet of a cafe set into its walls, Vika's eyes drifted amongst the traders haggling over local handicrafts as porters powered by with their overladen trolleys. In the distance, a braying camel hung in midair suspended by a crane. The scene was chaos, but, Vika reflected, just the right sort of chaos in which to hide in plain sight.

She watched as her companion weaved his way between tables and handed her a can. "No glasses, I'm afraid," he apologised.

Vika took a swig and sighed her approval. "That's good, thanks," she said. "I was parched."

They sat in silence while they finished their drinks. In one corner a ruddy-faced woman stood behind a huge metal disc of simmering plov, ladling it onto plates for the constant queue that never seemed to get shorter. Vika could smell the steaming rice with its sharp spices as it wafted across their table, and felt suddenly hungry.

The sight of ordinary people going about their everyday lives seemed incongruous under the circumstances. Clearly news of the assassination had not yet spread here. The location's very remoteness made her feel somewhat safer. The KNB couldn't be everywhere, especially today when their resources were already stretched to the limit, and there was no earthly reason why they should look for her here in the bazaar. It was an unlikely hiding place, which in her book made it an inspired choice. As she turned her head to say so, though, she noticed the worried expression on her companion's face.

"What's wrong?" she asked uneasily.

He shook his head. "Nothing really." He hesitated. "How's your leg."

She pursed her lips. "Pretty bloody in this heat," she admitted.

*

The flashing blue lights swooped through the mammoth marble and gilt arch leading into the bazaar complex, and the car pulled up in front of the main gates. As Max jumped out, Captain Gutov came forward to meet him. Huddled behind him were the men who'd been staking out the safe house.

A terse nod of the head replaced the normal handshake.

"You know what you're looking for?" Max asked, cold but steady. Without waiting for an answer, he surveyed Gutov's team and glowered with disapproval.

"This all you could muster?" he asked derisively.

"You may not have noticed, Mr Usenko, but there are other events taking place in Ashgabat today," Gutov replied sarcastically.

Casting a look of sovereign contempt, Max grunted and clenched his fists. He'd have a word with Orazov about this insolent bastard once it was all over. For now, though, he needed the man's cooperation.

"Well, Captain, if I might make so bold," he retorted with heavy irony, "spread your thin resource out and get looking for my sister and her ex-fiancé." He paused to let Gutov dish out instructions, then added: "If anyone finds them, they're not to be touched, understand? Just let me know immediately."

*

From their vantage point in the cafe, their eyes moved in a constant scan along the rows of stalls, looking for anything that shouldn't be there. In this blistering afternoon heat, the market heaved with people in slow procession along the aisles in search of a bargain. For traders and customers alike, the opposition rally was, at best, an irrelevance.

Vika's glance lingered on the sea of colour spanning the local farmers' area. It was quieter there, and the farmer's bored Mongol faces peered out over mounds of oranges, pomegranates, watermelons, peppers and dried apricots. Just to her right, a fight broke out between two traders, and her head snapped around to watch. Upending a stall selling rolls of silk, the two men scrapped on the ground. The crowd parted to let them get on with it, forming a circular audience. Eventually one of the combatants got the upper hand and, sitting across the other's chest, pummelled the man's face with his fists until he was dragged off.

A little while later, two trolleys collided in the main aisle, just in front of where they sat. One of the trolleys toppled over, spilling its contents across the ground. Again, Vika studied the scene, anxious lest their pursuers might have contrived it as a diversion, relieved when it proved to be a genuine mishap. An elderly passerby stooped to help reload the trolley, but the second he touched one of the boxes, it was snatched from him and tossed back on the trolley.

"Don't you dare steal that!" a wiry porter snarled.

Raising his hands in mock surrender, the old man gave a little shrug and walked away.

Vika couldn't resist a smile. "It never pays to be a volunteer, my father used to say."

In that instant, her eyes met those of a man standing about twenty-five metres away, looking towards them. Something about his demeanour warned Vika he might be KNB. Her suspicions were confirmed as the man spoke into a walkie-talkie.

"We need to move," Vika said urgently.

*

Max and Gutov were searching for their prey in the shops inset to the bazaar's external walls when Gutov heard his call sign and, removing his walkie-talkie from his belt, acknowledged his presence.

"I've found them, sir," the voice announced. "They were in a cafe on the west wall. They spotted me, I'm afraid, and are heading towards the rugs. I have them covered."

"Good work," Gutov replied. "We're on our way."

"Lead on," Max ordered. "Look sharpish, man."

As they fought their way through the crowd, neither of them paid any attention to the elderly woman who followed, dragging her shopping trolley behind her.

*

The carpet section, they reckoned, would provide the best cover. While many of the larger rugs were spread out for display over the sand, the majority hung in long lines over collapsible aluminium banisters. It was a tourist Mecca, and the ad hoc carpet corridors teemed with people. With any luck, they'd be able to shake off their tail amongst them.

Vika's leg was now so sore she could barely use it. With a shoulder under her arm for support, they'd edged forward as if in a three-legged race, their progress dangerously slow. If the net grew tighter, she realised, she'd have no hope of making a run for it.

As they shuffled between the vivid red rugs, Vika felt a shiver up her spine as a walkie-talkie crackled into action the other side of the them. She looked at her companion in alarm and saw the anxiety on his face. Yanking her towards the open ground at the end of the row, he glanced around when they reached the last carpet on display, and his grip around her tightened.

"What is it?" she asked, looking over her shoulder. "Oh shit," she exclaimed, spotting Max and a KNB officer barging their way forward. "What the hell's he doing here?"

She already knew the answer. With her gaze still fixed on her brother, she backed out of the row straight into the path of a heavy wood and metal trolley, which sent her crashing to the floor. Her arms clutched her leg protectively as tears of pain and frustration welled in her eyes.

He looked down on her, then glanced at the rapidly approaching figures of Max and Gutov. In desperation he scooped her into his arms and ran towards the bazaar's far wall.

*

Gutov put out his arm to hold Max back until all his agents were in place. There was no need to take any chances. Their prey was trapped, isolated under a shallow vault some fifty metres away. They were going nowhere.

He watched with a predator's concentration as his agents closed in on all sides, surrounding Vika and the man in the red khalat with her, cutting off any escape route. The shoppers nearby sensed something was happening. Shifting aside to let the agents pass, they stopped what they were doing and turned to watch them as they took up their positions. Only an old woman examining a pair of second-hand shoes at the end of the aisle remained oblivious.

At last, satisfied that everything was in place, Gutov and Max stepped forward.

As they came closer, Vika spotted the sullen, dark-faced expression on her brother's face, the arch of his mouth drawn down just as in childhood when denied something he wanted. He had bullied her in those days, but, by God, she wouldn't let him now. Hauling herself to her feet, she stood to confront him.

*

285

With Gutov at his side, Max advanced towards Vika, stopping in his tracks five metres away. Staring at the figure of the Arab at her side, his lips opened as he realised that this was not Leksin. Puzzled, his eyes moved up and down Timor's body, trying to place him. With another step forward, he focused like a cat on Vika.

"Where's Leksin?" he snapped.

"Damn you, Max!" she replied, her tone icy with contempt.

Max's hand whipped out to slash across her face, and she reeled against the wall. "You should have learnt from what happened to Lev, it doesn't pay to cross me."

Amidst the murmur of disapproval among the crowd, Timor came forward to help her up, but she shrugged him off. Limping towards Max, she stabbed her finger into his chest.

"You bastard, you're telling me you murdered my father?" she hissed incredulously. Taking a step back, her voice trembled with rage. "From now on, you're dead as far as I'm concerned."

"Fuck you, Vika!" Max shouted, shoving her away. The hate he'd stored up for her all his life exploded out of control. On reflex, he snatched the pistol from Gutov's holster.

"If only you'd died in that crash – *as I'd intended*." Released from its usual monotone, his screech enhanced the impact of his words.

Vika stared back stunned, ashen-faced. She felt again that moment of impact, the nightmare that had never left her since. *Oh no, Max, you couldn't have done that to me.*

"I won't make any mistake this time," Max went on, raising the pistol towards her.

Vika closed her eyes, waiting for the finish. As Timor lunged forward to push her out of the way, a gunshot rang out. The source, though, didn't sound close, and Vika's eyes snapped open to find Timor standing next to Gutov. Both men were gazing down at her brother, who had collapsed to his knees, blood seeping from a neat hole punched through his left temple. His eyes were empty as, slumping onto his side, his body twitched on the compacted dirt and grit for a few seconds, then lay still.

Gutov knelt down on one knee. Mechanically he felt for a

pulse, though he knew there'd be none. "Who the hell fired that?" he growled, his eyes moving from one agent to the other.

They shrugged back.

The crowd's clamour broke out, bursting the hush. Vika's eyes came to rest on the old woman on her knees at the end of the row, her hand covering her mouth as she stared in horror at Max's body. For a second, she met Vika's gaze, her green eyes cold and determined, the one slip in her careful disguise. Vika arched one eyebrow in silent question, but the woman turned her head away. A moment later, an agent stepped over to give her a hand up, and Vika watched disbelievingly as the woman, all the time mumbling gruffly, slowly hauled her shopping trolley away through the crowd.

Chapter Eighty-Seven

The driver pulled up in the forecourt and rushed around to open the rear doors. Saidov and Orazov got out. A dark-haired, grey-suited man in his mid-thirties rushed forward to greet them.

"Good afternoon, sir," he said to neither of them in particular. "The President is graciously expecting you. If you will follow me, please."

The three men climbed an ornate staircase to the main entrance, where two liveried servants hauled back the weighty double doors. They entered an enormous dome-shaped hall, where tall Grecian pillars of solid marble supported a high ceiling dominated by the largest crystal chandelier Saidov had ever seen.

Crossing the hall, they passed into a wide corridor. Inset in small alcoves along its marble walls were ivory statues of Oriental design highlighted by invisible backlighting. The gilt-panelled ceiling bore paintings of Turkmen landmarks, and the floor was one giant mosaic where a field of rich burgundy guls stretched in perfect symmetry along the length of the corridor like a never-ending Tekke rug.

As the three men silently progressed, Saidov was struck by the fact that here at last he was reaching the end of a long journey. The pipeline deal had been over eighteen months in the making, and it had proved a difficult road. Notwithstanding his well-established contacts in the region, the Turkmen had proved taxing negotiators, and he'd been forced to work hard to bring them around to his viewpoint. After all, he'd needed more than a simple pipeline licence from them for the project to succeed – he'd needed their cooperation in dealing with the Afghan issue.

Of course, it had been his own contacts from his days at Defence in Russia that had found the staff and funds to set up the Garkent plant. In the past, when he'd watched men of science being interviewed on television, he'd often laughed at

288

their pomposity, the self-importance they attached to their work, and the hypocritical way they wrestled with ethical issues versus the long-term good to humanity. But in the end they were just like other people: they had their price. Saidov had experienced little difficulty in finding enough rogue scientists to make the manufacture of illegal chemical weapons a feasible proposition. At a cost, certainly, though peanuts in the overall scheme.

Mind you, the plant could only operate on Turkmen soil with local cooperation. That is where Orazov had come in. Saidov put an arm around the shorter man's shoulder and drew him closer. "Nearly there, Ali," he whispered in his ear.

Reaching the end of the corridor, they entered a great hall, the centre of which was dominated by the giant golden figure of Turkmenbashi, raised on a pedestal. Liveried servants stood at regular intervals along the walls, like life-sized statues. The sun streamed down through glass ceiling panels.

A man wearing a striped shirt and plain blue tie approached and introduced himself as the President's private secretary.

"President Rashid's expecting you, Mr Saidov," he said, shaking his hand. "My colleague will show you in."

As they started forward, the aide caught Orazov's arm. "If you could come with me, sir, there's a detail I need to clarify with you. You can join Mr Saidov later."

Catching Saidov's eye, Orazov gave a helpless little shrug and went off with the aide.

Saidov continued across the hall. When they reached a thick wooden door on the far side, his escort pulled it open, slipped in to announce Saidov's name, then stepped aside to let him pass.

Straightening his tie, Saidov entered a massive marble chamber. Across the room a small group of men stood in a huddle deep in conversation. Standing by the open French windows was the familiar bald, bullet-shaped pate.

With a deep breath and practised smile, Saidov stepped forward to shake hands with Rashid, aka the President of Turkmenistan, Father of all Turkmen and sole living recipient of the Award of the Golden Age.

An instant later, he stopped dead in his tracks, astonished by the tall man who entered through the French windows. Slipping his mobile in his pocket, the man stopped and glared at him. It was President Karpev.

Chapter Eighty-Eight

Ashgabat, Turkmenistan

The old woman hobbled through the stunned crowd towards the exit. Outside the bazaar's walls a cacophony of police and ambulance sirens erupted as they converged on the scene of the incident. People streamed in through the narrow entrance intent on discovering what had taken place.

Hauling her shopping trolley behind her, the old woman fought her way against the contraflow, her shoulders stooped as if she were battling a headwind. She looked weary as she trudged into the car park. As she reached the dark blue Daewoo, her mobile rang, and she fumbled for it in her pockets.

"Yes," she snapped, still in character. Then her expression softened as she listened to her new instructions. Only the slight twitch of her scarred cheek – barely noticeable, there only for the briefest instant – betrayed her surprise.

The call finished, and she checked her watch. It didn't give her much time to get across town. She'd better hurry. Throwing her trolley in the boot, she manoeuvred out of the car park and, a few minutes later, slipped onto the ring road.

She was working on autopilot as she circled the outskirts of the city. Her mind, though, was somewhere else.

*

The starting point had been the aftermath of the assignment in the Arctic wastes of northern Siberia that had gone belly up. Those of her cell who'd survived the fiasco had split up and gone their separate ways. For her part, she'd headed south, her ultimate goal being the isolated dacha she'd bought down in Uzbekistan for just such an eventuality. But crossing the Russian mainland had proved a hard slog, fraught with danger. Each day the news had carried reports of the arrest of another of her cell as the FSB remorselessly tracked them down. In the end she'd been forced to hole up in a grubby apartment in the suburbs of Bratsk in southern Siberia, and wait for things to cool down.

Someone, though, must have ratted on her – she'd no idea who – but one night the security forces had burst into the apartment and hauled her off to the Lubyanka basements. Night and day they'd questioned her. With no sleep and inedible food, they'd used her as a punching bag until she passed out. Each time she'd regained consciousness, she'd found herself lying on the damp floor of her lightless cell, shivering in only vest and pants. Not long after, the process would start all over again.

She'd lost count of the days when, out of the blue, they'd come for her. Dragging her from her cell, they taken her to a bathroom and ordered her to clean up and change clothes. Later, placing a hood over her head, they'd led her down to an awaiting car. It must have been over an hour later when they'd pulled up somewhere in the countryside, and she'd been yanked out. At that moment Nadia had feared she was to be shot. Much to her relief, though, they'd led her inside and plonked her down on a stool.

"Take off the cuffs," a voice across the room had ordered.

She'd felt the click of a key behind her back, then the cuffs being eased off her wrists. A moment later, she could hear the shuffle of people leaving the room.

"You can remove the hood now," the voice had told her.

She'd pulled off the hood, blinked at the sudden light on her eyes, then blinked once more and squinted as her eyes focused on the unmistakable figure of President Karpev looking down on her. Glancing around, she'd found they were alone.

That's when the deal had been struck. Karpev needed someone he could call upon on occasion to take care of people off-book (as he'd phrased it). Reliable, quick, no questions asked. Did she feel she could be that person, he'd asked flatly. If so, then she'd be allowed to escape and he'd call the dogs off (his words again). From time to time, he'd told her, he'd contact her with an assignment. Other than that, whatever she chose to do – so long as it was off Russian soil – would be her business.

She'd stared at him in astonishment without replying. It was only when she'd caught the steel in his eyes that she'd realised he was deadly serious.

*

Nadia slipped off the ring road, then turned into the broad avenue that led up towards the presidential residence. At the checkpoint, about 100 protestors lined the road, their banners waving furiously. An angry-looking security guard stood by the barrier and waved her down. She opened her window as he approached.

"I'm expected," she told him. "You have orders to let me through."

Walking to the front of the car, he checked the number plate. South Korean Embassy, just as he'd been warned. With a nod, he instructed his colleague to let her pass.

Chapter Eighty-Nine

Ashgabat, Turkmenistan

Saidov lifted a hand to shield his eyes against the light streaming through the French windows. President Karpev stared back, his head cocked to one side, his clear, predatory eyes looking for some sign or gesture.

"Yes, Prime Minister?" Karpev said at last, the prompt more like a challenge than a question.

"I thought – " Saidov replied, leaving the sentence unfinished. Quickly regaining his composure, he approached Karpev and clasped his arm. "It's good to see that I was wrong."

"And for that, you must thank General Kutchinsky's foresight." Karpev gestured towards the small huddle of men across the room.

As Saidov turned his head to look, he swallowed hard at the unsmiling figure of Kutchinsky, recently appointed head of the FSB.

"When I explained to the General why it would be impossible to proceed with the pipeline deal," Karpev continued, "he expressed his concerns about my safety. So I accepted his proposal to arrange alternative transport for me from the airport this afternoon."

"We are all very grateful to him," Saidov commented earnestly.

As the others in Kutchinsky's group turned to face him, though, his worst fears were realised. One was Leksin, the other Nikolai at his side.

"Good afternoon, Prime Minister," Leksin greeted him coolly.

"I thought– " Saidov started again.

" – That Max Usenko was sorting me out in the bazaar?" Leksin asked rhetorically, finishing his sentence.

"Then – "

This time it was Karpev who supplied the words. "Leksin

swapped his somewhat original costume with the FSB agent who'd rescued him from the desert." He paused. "Young Usenko unfortunately was not so lucky. Under the circumstances, perhaps it was just as well." He turned to address President Rashid, who'd been watching the proceedings from the side. "I wonder, my friend, if I might have a word with my Prime Minister in private?" he asked, speaking as if this had been rehearsed.

"Of course," Rashid replied. "I look forward to seeing you at the reception in the ceremonial palace this evening."

As he turned to leave, his eyes met Saidov's. Saidov stared back slack-mouthed, searching the Turkmen President's face for some sign or acknowledgement. But, with an almost imperceptible shrug, Rashid left the room.

*

Saidov sat on his own across the table from the President. To Karpev's left, opposite a life-size portrait of President Rashid wearing a lime green suit, sat Leksin and Nikolai, to his right General Kutchinsky.

"We're in your hands, Leksin," Karpev began. "Why don't you give the Prime Minister a brief synopsis of what you've uncovered?"

With a nod, Leksin leant forward and placed both hands upon the table. "As you know," he addressed Saidov, "my assignment was essentially to examine the issue of pipeline security through Afghanistan. A number of people, the President among them, felt this was the project's fatal flaw. The vague assurances to the contrary they'd received had done nothing to alter their view.

"My enquiries took me initially to Chestny Kombinat's headquarters in Moscow and Ashgabat, then later to its Tejen office where the project planning was centred and along the proposed pipeline route itself, at least as far as it was safe to go.

"I was informed of negotiations with the Afghan government, reviewed the detailed plans, budgets and forecasts relating to the bid, and read through the relevant correspondence and minutes.

295

Everything seemed to suggest the work underlying the bid had been very professionally executed. I have to admit, I was impressed."

With a loud sigh, Saidov leant back in his chair and opened his hands as if his case had been proved. "So what's your problem?" he asked, feigning confusion. Catching Karpev's eye, he said: "This is in line with the last conversation we had with Nikolai Koriakov. He told us that Leksin's findings had rung no alarm bells."

Karpev held up a warning hand: there was more to come. "Go on, Leksin," he encouraged.

"I *might* have been tempted to leave it there," Leksin admitted, "if it hadn't been for one other factor."

"Which was?"

"Wherever I went, someone tried to kill me."

Saidov frowned uncomprehendingly. "Enlighten me."

"A painting in my study was booby-trapped, a stage-managed demonstration in Tejen turned violent, zemzens were thrown into my yurt in the desert."

A look of dismay clouded the Prime Minister's face, and for the first time Leksin realised Max had probably organised these events without recourse to Saidov. No doubt, he reflected ironically, if Saidov had been involved himself, they'd have been executed more successfully.

"Nobody's raised these matters with me before," Saidov stated, although it was unclear whether this was a denial of complicity or a simple statement of fact.

"I understand," Leksin replied, and thought he probably meant it. "But what these attempts on my life told me was that, even though I hadn't found it yet, there *was* something to find." He paused before adding: "Then I came across the lead to Garkent."

"How did you come across this lead, as you put it?"

Sitting back in his chair, Leksin noted the fact that Saidov's first reaction hadn't been, as one might have expected, to ask what was Garkent. "Through Vika Usenko," he replied at last.

"Vika Usenko?" The answer took Saidov completely by surprise, and he steadied himself against the edge of the table. "What the hell did she have to do with it?"

"Unknown to Max – " and, if truth be known, to Leksin also, " - the local Turkmen director had alerted Vika to suspected irregularities relating to the pipeline deal."

Karpev raised a hand. "Perhaps I should interject here to say that Miss Usenko informed Nikolai, who in turn informed me. It was the key reason I wanted an investigation."

"You knew?" Saidov exclaimed incredulously.

"I knew there was something wrong, yes. It took Leksin to find out what it was." He nodded towards Leksin, who continued.

"I went to Garkent. I rather suspect, Prime Minister, you know what I found there."

Saidov waved him on.

"A chemical weapons factory. Under some pressure, the plant boss explained a deal had been struck with the Afghans: chemical weapons in return for pipeline security."

Saidov grunted in protest. "I never heard such nonsense in my life."

Until now, Karpev had watched the conversation impassively. All of a sudden, his fury got the better of him. Leaning across the table, he thumped his hand melodramatically down on its surface. "Enough!" he bellowed, his voice trembling with rage. "Do you think we're fools, man?"

Saidov winced under this unexpected assault. Still maintaining his innocence, he asked: "Tell me, how could I know? Garkent's on Turkmen soil, how could I establish a chemical weapons plant there even if I wanted to?"

"I imagine your friend, Orazov, is having a similar conversation with his President right now," Karpev retorted angrily. "Don't waste my time, Erlan! There's a Russian task force crossing the border at this very minute. How long do you think it's going to take the FSB to trace the source of the equipment back to you?"

Saidov shook his head. "But why? What need do I have of chemical weapons?"

"For God's sake," Karpev exploded. "It doesn't take a rocket scientist to work out that, in return for a guarantee of the pipeline's safe passage, you're supplying the Afghan government with chemical weapons to use against the growing Taliban threat."

Saidov opened his mouth to speak, then at the last moment stopped himself. Glancing across at him, Leksin spotted the flash of confusion in Saidov's eyes, the brief telltale moment of hesitancy and indecision. Suddenly Leksin realised that they'd all been drawing the wrong conclusion.

"No, that's not it, is it?" he said, as if he were conceding something.

"What do you mean?" Karpev snapped. "I don't follow you, Leksin."

"It just doesn't make sense to give chemical weapons to the Afghan government," he replied, speaking slower than usual, choosing his words carefully. "Think about it. Even if, by using them, the government keep the Taliban at bay, that's hardly going to put an end to terrorist activity. The Taliban will just take to the hills, as they did before, from where they'll continue to launch attacks on economic targets. What better – or easier, for that matter – that the pipeline, especially as the geography there necessitates large stretches running overground?"

"Then who are the weapons for?" Karpev demanded, unable to hide his frustration.

"They're for the Taliban."

All at once the room fell completely silent as those around the table absorbed the implications of what Leksin was telling them.

"It's only with the Taliban actually in power that the terrorist attacks will stop," Leksin continued. "The Prime Minister and the other parties to the project have been negotiating with them to give them the means to overthrow the present government and take control themselves. In return, they get a guarantee of the security of a pipeline which over its lifetime will make them billions."

All eyes turned on Saidov. With a shake of the head, the man seemed suddenly too weary to argue any more. Sinking into his chair, his shoulders slumped into a loser's pose. Staring down at the table, he avoided his accuser's eyes. "So what now?" he quavered.

"You'll go with General Kutchinsky," Karpev informed him. "He has some questions to ask you."

Saidov threw a sideways glance at Kutchinsky, seated pokerfaced at Karpev's side. He knew about the General's interrogation techniques – they'd yielded quick results with Chechen prisoners. Dampening his lips, he asked: "And then?"

"You go to prison."

"Without a trial?" It was more a statement than a question.

"On the contrary," Karpev replied. "We're not barbarians." With a slow and rotten smile, he added: "For obvious reasons, I'm afraid, the trial can't be in public."

Chapter Ninety

Ashgabat, Turkmenistan

The palace staff had been instructed to form an orderly crowd outside the main entrance and cheer the visiting Russian dignitaries. The word had gone out that this very afternoon, Russia and Turkmenistan were to sign a major commercial agreement that would have profound, beneficial implications for their country's future. This was to be a day of celebration, a triumph for the nation's leaders, and one in the eye for the so-called opposition.

As a result, servants and secretaries, gardeners and administrators, artisans and librarians, all now milled around the forecourt at the bottom of the ornate steps leading up to the palace. Every hand held a miniature Russian flag aloft. Only a couple of young guards stood by to maintain order – these people were all trusted employees, each of them thoroughly vetted, so there was little need for tight security.

An old woman stood in the front row. She was Russian by descent, she'd told the person next to her, her parents had moved to Turkmenistan in the forties. This was a great day, she'd said. But as she passed prayer beads through her fingers, her eyes continuously scanned about her, taking in the lie of the land. The garishly painted pink palace was surrounded by parkland, she noted. In the centre, a path meandered from the forecourt through rows of tall birch to a large temple modelled on the Hera Temple in Paestum. To her left, a nine-hole golf course designed by a former US Open winner stretched out over undulating ground to a private zoo beyond. On the right, down a slight incline, was the visitors' car park surrounded by administrative buildings sunken into the ground to keep them out of sight from the palace.

As a black Mercedes sporting the Russian ensign moved into

position by the front steps, the guards edged back the crowd. A moment later, a ripple of anticipation ran through them as the liveried footmen pulled open the palace's main doors. A hush descended, then a loud cheer and furious flag waving at the emergence of Saidov, closely followed by a uniformed Russian officer.

*

For a few seconds Saidov stood at the top acknowledging the applause, an elder statesman with a practised wave. Then with a quick glance behind him, he noted General Kutchinsky's stern, unsmiling expression and started to descend. This had been a moment he'd dreamt about, but in his dreams he was the victor, not the vanquished. He'd envisaged himself standing on these very steps, clutching in his hands the signed agreement that would bring great riches to his country (and to him). Instead, although the flag-waving crowd didn't realise it, he was a prisoner on his way to a life in obscurity.

As he neared the bottom of the steps, an old woman broke away from the crowd and flung her arms around him in adoration. In the confusion, he barely felt the prick in his neck as she whispered words of worship in his ear. The guards rushed forward to pull her off, and as she moved away, Saidov caught the hard, resolute look in her eyes. His hand reached for his neck as he suddenly realised. Opening his mouth to warn the guards, he felt a massive pain like a power-drill across his chest. Struggling for breath, he collapsed onto the steps.

"Get a doctor," Kutchinsky yelled behind him. "He's had a heart attack. Quick, man!"

Bending down over Saidov's prostrate figure, Kutchinsky undid his tie and loosened his collar. Ordering the crowd to step back and give them space, he studied Saidov's face with blank eyes.

With a low groan, Saidov struggled to focus on Kutchinsky. "Tell Karpev he's a bastard," he whispered before he died.

Chapter Ninety-One

Ashgabat, Turkmenistan

The bar was full. The rally had disbanded about an hour ago, and journalists and tourists alike had returned to the hotel in need of refreshment. It had been a long day, full of hot air both in the atmosphere and on the podium, and everyone was worn out.

"What news of Talgat?" Leksin asked, seated in a corner table.

"Landed in Moscow just before I came here," Nikolai replied. "On his way to the Kremlin hospital as we speak."

"Take care of him, Nikolai. I couldn't have done it without him."

"I know," Nikolai acknowledged, smiling. "Perhaps he should take a cut of your million euro fee?"

Leksin looked indignant. Nikolai was still laughing as he caught the waiter's eye and, circling his fingers, called for another round of drinks. Weaving his way across the room, the waiter brought them two ice-cold beers.

"Odd coincidence Saidov's heart attack this afternoon," Leksin commented with heavy irony, once they were alone again.

"Yes, very," Nikolai replied noncommittally.

"He seemed absolutely fine at the meeting," Leksin commented. "A bit shocked, but who wouldn't be under those circumstances?"

"I know what you mean, Alex. I guess the stress just got to him in the end." Nikolai paused. "It wouldn't have been much of a life in prison. Perhaps it was best for him that way."

"And for everyone else," Leksin suggested.

"That too," Nikolai replied with decisive finality, far too wily to be trapped into an indiscretion, even by his best friend.

With a little shrug, Leksin admitted defeat and changed the subject. "What about the pipeline? Will they approach the Americans now?"

"Not a chance, old boy. That's one thing Saidov got right. Without some extreme incentive like chemical weapons, a pipeline wouldn't stand a cat's chance in hell beyond the Afghan border. The project's dead now."

A young woman flounced into the bar, long wavy blonde hair, her skirt skimping over smooth thighs. Kissing the barman's cheek, she climbed upon a stool and leaned forward, along with her generous cleavage, as he lit her cigarette. She waited for him to pour her a drink before swivelling her stool to survey the room. Spotting the two men on their own at a corner table, she curled her hair around her fingers and pouted. Leksin smiled back and shook his head, and she frowned disappointedly. His eyes, though, remained fixed on her as she went through a similar routine with other men in the room.

Suddenly he spotted Vika in the doorway staring at him, and he felt his cheeks flush. Not your type, she mouthed, shaking her head in mock rebuke.

The two men stood up as Vika crossed the room. Her limp was more pronounced than ever, and someone in the hotel had managed to find her a cane, which she used to ease the pressure as she walked.

"You all right?" Nikolai asked as she sat down between them.

"A bit tired, but fine. Early night, though, I think." Her eyes drifted down to the beer bottles on the table. "I could murder one of those."

Nikolai called over the waiter and ordered another beer. He waited until it arrived before rising to his feet with a reluctant frown. "Now you're here, Vika, I'm afraid I've got to dash to this wretched reception."

"You're not having dinner with us?" She sounded disappointed.

"Wish I could, but there's no getting out of it. I'm taking Saidov's place," He squeezed her arm affectionately. "I'm glad you're safe. Thank God it's over."

*

303

Leksin let himself into his room. A little after ten o'clock, he was not yet ready to sleep. He poured a vodka and tonic from the minibar and sank back into an armchair.

Clicking the remote, he watched with a sense of déjà vu a replay of Rashid's address to the nation earlier that evening.

"It is with great disappointment," the President declaimed, "that I have to tell you tonight that I've learnt that the Minister of Energy has betrayed the people's trust."

The camera flashed momentarily to the Minister of Energy isolated in the front row. With hands rested on his lap, his head was bowed like a child awaiting his parent's decision on a bad school report.

"Ali Orazov and I grew up in the orphanage together," Rashid continued. "I've always regarded him as my closest friend and supporter. We've worked together for over thirty years. Some time ago I appointed him to the crucial role for our economy of Minister of Energy, but now I find he's most seriously abused this position."

With eyes filled with blank detachment, not accusation, Rashid looked down on the Minister seated below him and waved him up. "Ali, you are dismissed from your position. Come forward to admit your guilt and apologise to the people."

Leksin watched with fascination as Orazov flicked the tip of his beard, then climbed onto the podium. As he passed Rashid, the camera caught the look on his face when their eyes met. It did not belong to a minister in disgrace, but to someone who'd kept his end of the bargain but got caught.

Leksin's eyes widened in realisation. Just as Talgat had warned him, nothing happened in this country without the knowledge and consent of the man who lived in the pink palace.

He switched off. Lying on the bed and resting his head on interlocked hands, his mind wandered to dinner that evening with Vika. Seeing her again over the last couple of weeks, he realised, she still aroused feelings within him in a way that no other woman did. Much had happened since the accident and their subsequent break-up, and until now he'd thought he was over it. But, to be honest, he still felt a real connection between them and wondered whether they shouldn't allow themselves another chance. This evening, when they'd finished dinner, he'd been tempted to ask her to come back to his room, but she looked so worn after the day's stresses that he'd held off. Back in Moscow, perhaps.

A knock on the door made Leksin sit up suddenly. Was he wrong – could this be Vika now? Jumping off the bed, he glanced in the mirror and pushed back his hair as he went to open it.

His heart sank to find a porter holding out his computer bag. The KNB was clearly tidying up loose ends.

"This was just delivered for you, sir."

He tipped the porter, and placed the bag on the desk in his room. Unzipping it, he checked that everything was in order. A slow grin swelled over his face at the sight of a small bag of white powder resting on the laptop. Someone had a sense of humour. Inserting a finger, he tasted it. The real stuff.

Spreading a line, he waited for the hit. As he did so, his thoughts strayed to his parting with Tamara that afternoon in Lenin Park. Ten-thirty, she might still be up. He dialled her number.

"Tamara? I know it's a bit late, but any chance of buying you a drink in my hotel bar?" He waited for her reply, strangely anxious. "Great, I'll see you there in ten minutes."

Grabbing his jacket off a chair, he went in search of the lift. All might not be lost, after all.

Chapter Ninety-Two

Ashgabat, Turkmenistan

Vika got back to her room and ran a bath. She'd enjoyed dinner with Leksin, but the stress of the day had caught up with her. Her whole body felt strained as if she'd been through a wringer and, despite the painkillers she'd taken earlier, her leg was still playing up badly.

Sinking into the bath, she let out a deep sigh as the water gushed over her. That's better. As she lay back, only her face out of water, for the first time that evening her thoughts strayed to Max. Her lips tightened with guilt that she felt no remorse for his death. All her life, she'd been forced to tolerate his bullying and cruelty, his fanatical neatness, his obsession with young men, his grating monotone, his lack of scruples . . . The list of his failings was endless. She tried to recall one redeeming feature about her brother, one quality that she'd liked and admired, but she drew a blank. Well, he was dead now, and good riddance. No, she rebuked herself, that was a terrible way to speak of the dead.

Pulling herself out of the bath, she wrapped a large white towel around her body and went through to the bedroom. Sitting on the bed, she examined her leg critically. The stump was blotchy and raw, and the skin was broken in several places. She'd have to see her doctor when she got back to Moscow. In the meantime the bacitracin cream and a fresh liner would have to do.

On the verge of going to bed, there was a soft knock on the door and, picking up her crutches, she made her way over. Her face cracked into a broad smile when she found Nikolai standing in the corridor. Drawing him in, she kissed him passionately.

"I didn't expect to see you again this evening."

"I managed to sneak off as soon as the speeches finished."

"Well, it's a nice surprise. I've just had a bath and I'm ready for bed."

Slithering under the sheets, she propped herself up on one elbow and watched him undress. Suddenly she chuckled and he looked up.

"Something funny?"

"You know, I have a feeling Alex was thinking of making a play for me tonight."

"Really?" asked Nikolai. There was a hint of surprise in his voice, or was it guilt? He slipped in next to her. "Well, we couldn't have done without him, that's certain. You definitely chose the right man."

She laughed and leaned over to kiss him. "Yes, you're right there. On this occasion, I did. Perhaps we should get around to telling Alex about us?"

Her spirits were high – higher than she could remember in quite some time – and the reason made her serious again.

"Do you know, Nikolai, I think it's made me happy to find out how the accident really happened. I'd always blamed myself, and then I laid the pain on Alex. Now it goes back to my brother, where it belongs. And Alex and I can have dinner without a scratch."

Turning off the lights, she edged over and nestled into him.

Epilogue

Moscow, Russia - Two Months Later

The electric gates swung slowly open, and the car edged forward. The driver depressed a switch on the panel, and the rear window rolled down. Holding a Doberman straining on its leash, the security guard stooped to look in.

"Good evening, Mr Leksin, good to see you again," he said, nodding them through.

The car pulled up on the forecourt. Leksin waited for the passenger to get out, and together they walked arm and arm towards the main lobby. Here, his companion took up her position behind him just as Vika opened the door.

He kissed her cheek. "I hope you've got room for one extra," he said with a broad grin, and stepped aside.

Vika's face lit up with surprise and pleasure at the sight of Lena standing behind him, and she rushed forward to hug her tightly.

"Alex, you never told me your sister was back," she rebuked Leksin. Slipping her arm inside Lena's, she guided her into the hall. "It's ages since I last saw you, darling. How are you?"

"Much better, thanks."

Vika shouted for Nikolai who emerged from the kitchen wearing an apron.

"Look who's come to see us," she said.

Nikolai smiled with delight as he recognised her. Wiping his hands on his apron, he placed them on Lena's shoulders and looked her up and down. "You look fantastic," he told her. "All of you, come through. Now we've got two things to celebrate."

The pop of a champagne cork, and Nikolai charged his guests' glasses, then handed one to Vika. Leksin looked fondly at the two of them standing side by side. It had been two months since he'd slipped from his room at the Nissa Hotel to meet Tamara in the bar and spotted Nikolai surreptitiously sneaking into Vika's bedroom. A well kept secret, that's for sure. Well, good on him. Good on both of them. It was hard to think of a nicer couple, they deserved each other.

Tapping his pen against his glass, he proposed a toast. "Lena and I were both delighted to hear the news of your engagement," he told them. "I wish you every happiness in your life together." He raised his glass. "To you both."

As they each took a sip of champagne, Leksin added: "Mind you, Nikolai, if you'd warned me you'd be doing the cooking this evening, I'd have brought a food parcel."

*

After dinner, Leksin caught Lena's eye, and she nodded. He clapped his hands to grab everyone's attention.

"Vika, Nikolai, Lena has a little surprise for you in honour of your engagement."

Their eyes fixed on Lena as she walked over to the piano and sat down. She flashed a nervous smile, then began. Rachmaninov's second piano sonata, Leksin's favourite.

He watched with a mixture of pride and relief as she played with her former panache. Some years ago she'd been among the select few to win a place at the Moscow Conservatory, but ever since the assault had triggered her mental breakdown, she'd steadfastly refused to play. The Swiss clinic had worked wonders. After a slow start, her condition had eventually begun to improve, at first just little by little, then suddenly gathering pace. A few weeks ago, they'd found her seated at the piano in the middle of the night playing as if nothing had ever been wrong. She's nearly ready to leave us, the clinic's administrator had told Leksin earlier this month, let her come and stay with you for a few weeks and see how it goes. And it had gone well. At last, he felt he had his sister back. He'd spoken to the Conservatory, and they'd offered to let her return as soon as she was ready.

Lena finished playing and looked around. "Was that all right?" she asked her brother nervously.

"You were magnificent," Leksin assured her.

"Magnificent," Vika echoed, patting the space next to her on the sofa. "Now come and sit down, I can't get over how good it is to see you."

The phone rang, and Nikolai answered. His body stiffened as he listened intently. Pointing towards the television, he mouthed to Leksin to turn it on.

As the screen clarified into a picture, the camera homed in on a body lying on what the caption said was Azadi Square. "The Turkmen President had just finished opening an exhibition of local handicrafts at the World Trade Congress," the voiceover told them. "As he emerged into the Square, a shot rang out from a building nearby, killing him instantly. Police are looking for an elderly woman seen hurrying away from the scene."

Glancing across at Nikolai, Leksin was struck by the calm expression on his face. This news seemed to be no surprise to him. Their eyes met, and Leksin angled his head enquiringly.

"Karpev doesn't take kindly to anyone trying to assassinate him," Nikolai explained ambiguously.

"Rashid was behind the ambush?" Leksin asked, incredulous.

Nikolai nodded. "Nothing happens in Turkmenistan, old boy, without the blessing of the President."

Sinking back into his chair, Leksin drew a deep breath. He'd heard those words before.

THE END

22265589R00193

Printed in Poland
by Amazon Fulfillment
Poland Sp. z o.o., Wrocław